BRILLIANT

DEVICES

A steampunk adventure novel
Magnificent Devices Book Four

Shelley Adina

Moonshell
Books

Moonshell Books
PO Box 752
Redwood Estates, CA 95044
www.shelleyadina.com

Publisher's Note: This is a work of fiction. Names, characters, places, and incidents are a product of the author's imagination. Locales and public names are sometimes used for atmospheric purposes. Any resemblance to actual people, living or dead, or to businesses, companies, events, institutions, or locales is completely coincidental.

Book Layout ©2013 BookDesignTemplates.com
Art by Claudia McKinney at phatpuppyart.com
Design by Kalen O'Donnell at art.kalenodonnell.com
Author font by Anthony Piraino at OneButtonMouse.com

Brilliant Devices / Shelley Adina — 2nd ed.
ISBN 978-1-939087-04-1

For my readers, with thanks for flying with me on this adventure

And thank you to geologist Jenny Andersen for her research into diamond mines on my behalf

1

The Evening Standard
October 9, 1889

TITANS OF MODERN INDUSTRY DIE
IN TRAIN CATASTROPHE

In a tragedy that strikes at the very foundations of society on two continents, one of London's brightest lights and most brilliant minds, Lord James Selwyn, of Selwyn Park, Shropshire, and the leader of modern railroad invention in the Texican Territories, Mr. Stanford Fremont, have both lost their lives in a train wreck on the plains of the Wild West.
Both men were traveling west on the inaugural journey of the *Silver Queen*, the newest locomotive in a vast railroad empire that stretches from New York in the Fifteen Colonies to San Francisco, the capital of the Royal Kingdom of Spain

and the Californias. Accompanying Lord James was his fiancée, Lady Claire Trevelyan, of London.

The journey was to be a showcase for Lord James's latest invention, the showpiece of the newest exhibition at the Crystal Palace, the Selwyn Kinetick Carbonator. The Carbonator had produced enough coal to power the locomotive and several luxury coaches, as befitted Fremont and his titled guests, with only two stops to take on unprocessed coal during the entire journey across the Wild West.

However, on the second day out of Santa Fe, disaster struck. From what the Texican engineers can piece together from the wreckage, the arid atmosphere of the salt flats caused the coal to ignite prematurely and with such vehemence that it caused the tender and boiler to explode. The locomotive was blown off the tracks, and the passenger coaches jumped the rails, resulting in total loss of life.

Funeral services for Lord James Selwyn will be held at St. Paul's on Friday, the eleventh of October, at eleven o'clock in the morning. His Royal Highness the Prince Consort, patron of the Royal Society of Engineers, is expected to address the mourners. Services for Lady Claire Trevelyan will be held privately at the family estate in Cornwall.

This publication humbly extends its condolences to the Selwyn and Trevelyan families, who have been beset with tragedy in recent months. As our readers know, Vivyan Trevelyan, Viscount St. Ives, was killed in a mishap while cleaning his antique pistols. Old Lord Selwyn himself passed away recently. With the death of Lord James, his only son, the baronetcy now passes to a cousin, Peter Livingston, who recently announced his engagement to Miss Emilie Fragonard, of Cadogan Square.

BRILLIANT DEVICES

Claire Trevelyan smoothed the newspaper on top of the navigation chart. She had been encouraging the Mopsies to read the easier headlines aloud, until they had all stumbled upon this particularly grisly one in the "World" section.

"My poor mother. No sooner does she cancel my first funeral than she must immediately plunge into plans for my second."

Andrew Malvern looked up from the tiller, where he and Jake were jointly calculating how much altitude the airship, the *Stalwart Lass*, would have to gain in the next hundred miles to take them over the aptly if unimaginatively named Rocky Mountains.

"We can send a pigeon as soon as we reach Edmonton. That paper is a week old. The funeral will already have been held, so there is nothing you can do to forestall it."

Maggie laid a hand on Claire's arm. "Yer mum'll be happy to 'ear you ent dead again, Lady. Funeral or no funeral."

"She's going to stop believing in reports of my demise after this, that is certain." Claire angled the paper down so Maggie could see it. "Can you read this line to me?"

"Wiv the death of ... Lord James, 'is only son, the ... Lady, I dunno that one."

"Baronetcy."

"I beg yer pardon, wot's that?"

"It's a title, Maggie. It means that if you met Peter Livingston, whom I once seated next to my friend

Emilie at a dinner party because she was sweet on him, you would call him Lord Selwyn. Once she marries him, Emilie will become Lady Selwyn."

"Instead of you."

"Quite right. Instead of me. I'm sure her mother is delighted that there is no longer any danger of her being left off the guest lists at dinner parties." Claire sighed, gazing out the expanse of glass that formed the upper section of the *Stalwart Lass*'s gondola. "To think that I once worried about such things."

"We've got other things to worry about," Alice Chalmers called, coming along the gangway from the engine at the rear of the gondola. "She's not giving me any lift at all—it's everything I can do to keep her airborne. We can't take a run at those mountains unless Andrew and Tigg can pull a miracle out of their hats."

"Ent got a hat," hollered Tigg from the back. "Alice, come 'ere!"

"Or a miracle." Andrew turned from the tiller and ran a finger down the chart on the table, moving the newspaper they'd picked up in Reno to one side. "If we don't get some lift in the next couple of hours, we're going to run smack into the side of a mountain. Some of these are thousands of feet high."

Claire, whose idea of mountains had been formed while on holiday in the Lake District, could hardly imagine it. "Can we not go around them?"

Andrew shook his head. "Not unless we want to return to Reno, sail east, and turn north on the other side."

"Alice!" shouted Tigg. "We got trouble!"

Alice turned and ran astern, Andrew and Claire hot on her heels. "What's the matter? The ship was flight-worthy when we left Reno," Claire said to Andrew's back.

But that had been two days ago. As she now knew, anything could happen to an airship in two days.

"She may have been, but whatever old wreck of an engine she put in here, it wasn't meant to go much farther."

"It saved your hide, if you recall," Alice snapped, popping into view from behind the engine cowling. "Don't go calling my girl names." Tears flooded her eyes and she blinked them back.

"I apologize," Andrew said at once. "And I hadn't forgotten. I never will, you may be sure of that."

"And mine, too," Claire put in. "Twice. I've never seen anything so beautiful as the *Stalwart Lass* coming through the sky, both times."

"She'll be fallin' out o' the sky if we don't do something," Tigg put in tersely. His round, coffee-colored cheek had a smear of grease across it from chin to temple, and he held a wrench in either hand.

The words were no sooner out of his mouth than something deep in the engine hitched and coughed.

"That's done it." Alice grabbed a safety line and clipped it to a metal loop on her leather belt. "Don't fail me now, girl." She grabbed one of the wrenches and leaped down onto the propeller housing. The wind slapped her pants flat against her legs, and she pulled her goggles over her eyes. One look at the great shafts that powered the propeller must have told its own story. "Who's on the tiller?" she shouted above the sound of both engine and wind. "We're going to go down!"

"Jake!" Claire ran forward. "Alice says we're going down!"

Maggie gasped and clutched her twin, Lizzie, who burst into tears. "I knew it! I knew I should 'ave stayed home and not mucked about in airships."

Claire grasped both their hands and drew them over to the glass, controlling her own panic with a herculean effort. "Look. We're not in the mountains yet." Though they loomed in the near distance, tall and blue and forbidding, rimed with old snow. "Remember what Captain Hollys told us on *Lady Lucy*? Airships don't crash. It's a long, slow glide to a soft landing."

Lizzie did not buy that for a moment. "That were if the gas bags burst, Lady. Wivout an engine? We'll just stay up 'ere floatin' about till we starve to death."

"Naw, we won't." Jake grasped the controls for the elevator vanes with both hands. "One stiff breeze and we'll run into one o' them rocks first. Mr. Andrew, I could use you on the tiller if yer done gawkin' at that chart."

"Quite so." Andrew took the wheel and turned it a few degrees east. "If these charts are up to date, there should be a wide river valley in six or eight miles. Vanes full vertical, Jake, and release some air from the forward gas bags."

Spaniard charts up to date? Claire could only hope. Her brief experience with the Royal Kingdom of

Spain in Reno had left her with no very good opinion of their skills at engineering. How could it be otherwise, when they outlawed airships because—of all things—they contravened the intentions of the Almighty? The *Lass* had been allowed to land in Reno only because Alice was a Texican citizen, and only then just long enough to take on food and water and make a visit to the nearest bank and telegraph office before they were chivvied on their way as though they carried the plague.

No wonder James and Stanford Fremont were to have been received by the Viceroy himself when they and the Carbonator arrived in San Francisco. To the Spaniards, rail technology was the very pinnacle of human achievement. Anything else was practically suspected of witchcraft.

Her stomach lifted in a momentary feeling of weightlessness.

"We're goin' down," Lizzie whimpered, hiding her face in Maggie's shoulder. "I hate airships. It ent gonna be a long, slow glide. We're gonna fall and die and—"

"Shut up, Liz," Jake said through his teeth. "Yer makin' me nervous."

Andrew glanced over his shoulder, in the direction of the stern. "What's happening back there? Claire, perhaps you should check on Alice."

She did not want to check on Alice. She wanted to remain fixed at the window, as if sheer strength of will could bring the ship in for a safe landing.

But that was selfish and pointless. So instead, she ran back to the engine, where an alarming plume of black smoke now trailed in their wake.

"Lady!" Tears were whipped from Tigg's eyes through the open hatch. "I can't hold 'er—she's gonna burn up!"

The ancient engine, which had suffered so many lives, had finally come to its last. "Claire! The kill switch!" Alice shrieked. "Get her stopped!"

Claire reached past Nine, who was standing silently by as if he'd been deactivated, and jerked the engine's emergency ignition lever down. The engine juddered and shuddered, steam hissing out from among the gears and every possible aperture. The smell of burning intensified.

Even the kill switch had died.

She whirled, scanning the engine room for anything she could use.

There!

She snatched up an iron crowbar that had been flung to the floor. There was no hope for the engine, so this would not hurt any more than the utter destruction it was destined for. "Alice, get out of there!" Alice scrambled up onto the gangway and Claire rammed the crowbar into the seam of the red-hot boiler door and pried it open. With a whoosh of surprise, the door blew off, the contents spilled out into the sky—and the engine gasped and gave up the ghost.

The wind whistled through the sudden silence.

And then the earth, spiny and sharp with trees, leaped up to meet them.

2

Claire pulled herself upright with the help of Nine's metal leg. Having magnetic feet, he had merely stuck fast to a structural support during the long slide of their landing and its abrupt halt in a copse of quivering aspens, golden in their autumn foliage. But other than that, he did not appear much damaged. She hoped that was the case for the other members of the crew.

"Mopsies?" she called anxiously, staggering forward into the gondola.

"'Ere." The voice was muffled, and a heap of arms and legs and petticoats resolved itself into two girls. "I fink I'm broken."

Lizzie patted Maggie down, her keen green eyes clouded with worry. "Where does it hurt?"

"In my stomach, where your knee is. Gerroff."

Andrew groaned. He appeared to have gone right over the tiller headfirst, much in the manner of a horseman on an unbroken mount, and had been bent in half with his feet dangling in midair. Claire assisted him to slide off the wheel to the vertical once again.

"Remind me to get some lessons in steering one of these things the next time we meet your friend Captain Hollys," he said. "That was a bruiser of a landing."

"We are bruised, but not dead," Claire pointed out. "Look on the bright side." She adjusted his tawny brocade waistcoat so that it sat upon his shoulders again, more as an excuse to touch him and reassure herself that he was whole and undamaged than because she cared tuppence about how he looked.

"Everyone all right?" Alice came in on wobbly legs, Tigg at her heels. She took in the two of them in one glance and Claire stepped away.

Or tried to. The deck was canted several degrees and her graceful, subtle movement turned into a drunken stumble that fetched her up against the bulkhead. "Yes," she said, trying to recover her dignity. "I feared for us all for a moment."

"You still can," Alice said grimly. Her curly blond hair had been torn from under her airman's cap by the wind, and stuck out in a hundred different directions. "Come on. We need to suss out how bad the gondola and fuselages are damaged."

Getting out of the hatch was not easy—in fact, it was more like climbing out of a window that was tilted toward you. In the end, Andrew and Alice went down on a rope and caught the other four as they slid down one by one.

"It'll right itself once we fill the starboard fuselage again," Tigg said in tones that asked for confirmation. "Port fuselage is topmost. Looks spiff to me."

Alice did not give it. She was already inspecting the double fuselages that contained the gas bags. They hung in the crushed aspens that had stopped their slide, but the trees had bent rather than broken.

"Tigg, Andrew, Lizzie, run round to starboard. Listen for a whistle—that'll be a leak. Claire, Maggie, you're with me on the port side."

Just below the bow on the starboard side, the canvas had been gashed, and air was leaking out with a continuous sigh of hopelessness. If Alice had been brisk before, now she really swung into action. She sent Tigg up into a tree with a bucket and brush and, from the ground, instructed him how to patch it, and when the awful hissing had stopped, she let out a breath as if she'd been holding it the whole time.

"The fuselage is my biggest worry," she confessed to Claire as Andrew and Tigg cleared saplings, aiming to use one of the taller trees as a mooring mast. "The *Lass* can lose a lot and still fly, but she ain't going anywhere without lift."

"We should like to go anywhere as soon as possible," Claire agreed.

"Say, where's the girls?"

Claire looked around her. Aspens, poplars—chunks of tumbled granite—gently blowing grass—and a hundred feet away, the silvery glint of the river that had cut this swath broadly enough for them to land beside it. On a pile of rocks that caused the river to eddy and swing in a new direction, she spotted two little figures, hands shading their eyes as they looked into the distance and turned to cover the points of the compass.

"There. Scouting." She pointed, rather proudly.

"They ought to let us know before they disappear."

"You may certainly suggest it. But they know their duty and it would seem strange to them to warn me they're going to do it."

Alice shook her head and returned to her inspection of the partially buried gondola. "Not like any little girls I ever met. I bet they wouldn't know what to do with a doll if you gave 'em one."

Claire remembered her own nursery and the row of abandoned dolls on the top shelf of the bookcase. "Papa used to give me a doll every year for Christmas." She knelt to inspect a brass plate in the hull, bent nearly double with the force of the landing, but salvageable. "He gave up when I was eight and my nurse reported to Mama that I was disassembling them and making notes on their anatomy. Which, I discovered, bore no resemblance to actual human babies' anatomy at all."

Alice's brow lightened a little and she almost smiled through her worry. "I ain't never had a doll. I wouldn't know what to do with one, either."

"You have the automatons. Theirs may only bear a nodding resemblance to human anatomy, but at least they're useful. Dolls, I'm afraid, are not."

By the time the Mopsies ran up, panting, to report, Alice had finished inspecting as much of the hull as she could see. The rest would have to wait until the gas bags had been inflated once again, and the hull lifted to its normal resting altitude of a few feet.

"You sure picked a good place to crash," Maggie informed Jake and Andrew. "Ent a soul or an 'ouse or so much as an eyelash to be seen for miles an' miles."

"There is a bunch of mucky great creatures on t'other side of the river, though," Lizzie put in. "Horns on 'em as big as Tigg."

"I suspect those might be elk," Andrew said. "They possess antlers, which are solid. Cows have horns, which are hollow."

Lizzie did not look impressed by the distinction. "Solid—hollow—they're pointy, is what I'm sayin'. Big and pointy."

"Duly noted," Claire said. "And no sign of any source of help. Well, on the positive side, neither is there any danger ... of the human sort, at least. We shall only have to worry about bears."

"Bears?" Lizzie's eyes widened. "There's bears 'ere?"

"There was a bear due east of where you found me in the Texican Territory. I have no doubt there are similar creatures here in the Idaho Territory."

"If you folks are done with the nature lesson," Alice put in with barely concealed impatience, "can we get the pump going and get some gas into the bags? That patch oughta be dry enough to hold now."

The pump turned out to be an automaton named Eight, who had hose concealed in his appendages and a small engine as well. Claire watched, hands nervously clasped, as the bags filled, the twin fuselages leveled out, and the *Lass* slowly freed herself from her untidy nest. The trees brushed the lower surfaces of the fuselages as they rose, until finally the airship stalled.

"Gondola's stuck," reported Tigg from the far side. "C'mon, everyone, it'll be like pushin' that barge off into the Thames once we got all the chickens into the garden at 'ome."

Home. The warmth of affection flooded Claire at the thought of the shabby cottage in Vauxhall Gardens—the first place in Tigg's memory where he had an actual pallet to himself and "three squares" a day.

If she had accomplished nothing more on this earth, she had at least done that—given these children their first home.

Maybe some day they would even see it again.

Heaving, pushing, and commanding Nine to help, they dislodged the *Lass* from her clinging prison. With a sucking sound, she lifted a few inches, like a char who remembered better days shaking mud off her shoes. Rosie the chicken, who had been hunting in the fallen leaves as they worked, immediately jumped into the gash in the earth and yanked a fat worm out of it.

"That's it," Alice muttered to the old ship. "Come on, girl. Eight, keep pumping on the starboard side."

The fuselage fattened until it curved like the breast of a healthy hen, lifting the gondola until it bobbed a couple of feet off the ground.

"There." Alice patted a ripped piece of brass, whereupon a number of rivets hit the stones with a *tinktinktink*. "Eight, that'll do." The automaton fell silent and she disconnected the hose.

Then, elbow to elbow with Claire, she studied the hull. "Bow's stove in, but Nine and Andrew can bang it back into shape."

"Tigg and Jake and I can replace rivets."

"The girls can take the ballast out so we can see what's what inside."

Andrew looked from one to the other, then at Tigg. "Aren't we forgetting something?"

"We ain't forgot," Alice said tersely. "We're merely thinking out what we're going to do while we try to figure out what to do about *that*."

"About wot?" Maggie asked.

"About the fact that we have no engine," Claire said gently. "We can bring the ship's body back to life, but if she has no heart, she can't sail."

"We'll figure it out," Tigg said stoutly.

"Yeah?"

Claire wished Alice would not sound so grim in front of the children. Or in front of her, for that matter.

"We got no boiler. Without a boiler, we can't make steam. Without steam, the pistons and props won't turn."

Claire clutched what remained of her chignon with both hands. "Good heavens. I completely forgot! Oh dear. Oh *dear*. I hope no harm has come to it."

She gathered up her skirts and scrambled into the hatch, heedless of the mud that rimmed it. In a moment she reappeared with her valise.

"Going someplace, Lady?" Jake inquired.

"Maybe there's a nice hotel we ent seen yet," Lizzie told her twin in an aside that ought to have been on the vaudeville stage. "Maybe she ordered roast beef an' Yorkshire puddings for all of us."

"Very funny. Andrew, Alice, look." She pulled the valise open to reveal Dr. Craig's power cell nestling like a great bronze cat on her shirtwaists and spare skirt. "Is there any reason we cannot power the *Stalwart Lass* with this?"

Alice handed Andrew Malvern the smaller wrench so he could tighten the bolts on the far side of the hastily fabricated housing for the power cell. The silence as they buttoned up after the flurry of work, while companionable, had gone on long enough. If somebody didn't say something, she was going to leap out of her skin.

"I got to hand it to Claire, she knows how to pull a rabbit out of a hat."

Outside, Claire and the Mopsies were pounding dents out of the brass plates of the gondola with rocks wrapped in spare canvas, which meant she could hardly hear herself speak. She'd heard a wax recording once called the *Anvil Chorus*—if the girls ever wanted careers in music, they could start with that.

"What mystifies me is that she kept it a secret. We've been in flight for days—I would have thought the subject might have come up in that time."

"We didn't need it, Mr. Malvern."

"Alice, we have stared death in the face together more than once. Under the circumstances, I believe it would be quite proper for you to use my given name."

It had been so long since Alice had blushed that it took her a moment to recognize the hot, prickly feeling in her cheeks and forehead.

We, he'd said. *Together.* Dang. In all her daydreams she had never expected to experience the thrill of the plural pronoun in connection with the brilliant mind she had been worshiping from afar—very far—for so long. In the delight of it, she quite lost track of what he was saying.

"—risking my life for the wretched thing, she might have told me she'd liberated it from the wreckage."

In Alice's experience, *liberate* was a word you used when you didn't want to say *steal*. "But doesn't it belong to her?"

"I am not arguing that. Dr. Craig left it as her legacy."

"That mad scientist?" Tigg had told her the whole juicy story. Alice wouldn't have believed a word of it, except that she'd been the one to pull Claire out of the drink half drowned. Anyone who would jump into a flash flood on purpose could break a mad scientist out of Bedlam if she darn well wanted to.

"It is my uneducated opinion that Dr. Craig was not in fact mad. She was being held against her will because she represented a threat to some very wealthy men. But that is beside the point." Andrew heaved on a nut. "The point is that we are both invested in that cell, and she could have told me."

The plural pronoun didn't sound nearly so appealing that time.

Alice stood and dusted off her pants. "Well, in all fairness, we've had our hands full. I got a pile of parts in the hold I've been meaning to make something with, and I haven't given them a single thought, myself. So I can't say as I blame her."

Andrew finished with the last of his bolts and stood as well. He pulled off his gloves and surveyed their work. "You're quite right. Isn't it singular that the four of us—engineers all, and I include Tigg in our number—wound up on this particular ship at this particular time? Without any one of us, we would not have been able to create what I must say must be the first engine of its kind."

Alice couldn't keep her face from breaking out in a smile. "You'd better call her in. After you and her rigged that swinging truss—"

"—and you found that glass for the lightning chamber—I swear it will never cross my lips that it began its career holding a gallon of rotgut whiskey—"

"—and you and Tigg and Jake manhandled poor Four into becoming this housing—"

"—we definitely must all be present when we fire her up for the first time."

Sharing a laugh with him was probably the sweetest moment in Alice's whole life. The part that came after her father had jumped ship, anyway.

A moment later she realized the hammering had stopped, and Claire and the girls appeared in the gangway. "Did we miss the joke?"

"We're just having a moment of celebration," Andrew told her, still smiling.

Claire looked from him to Alice and a shadow passed over her eyes. Was it—could that be hurt?

Well, never mind if it was. Lady Claire Trevelyan had just about everything on earth a girl could want, minus a working airship, but they were about to fix that. If she begrudged Alice a moment of laughter with a certain handsome and brilliant man, well, that was just too bad.

In the next moment, she felt ashamed of herself. Claire wasn't that petty. She probably liked a good laugh as much as anybody, and wanted to be included, that was all. If this worked, they'd have plenty to celebrate.

"Is it done?" Maggie asked, evidently objecting to silences, too.

"It is done. Tigg, are you ready?" Andrew asked.

"I been ready for hours, sir. I don't care if we do have to fly at night, I ent minded to stick around and be dinner for bears."

"I quite agree," Claire said. "Alice, let's see if she'll go, shall we? Girls, is Rosie safely aboard? Yes? Jake, ready tiller."

Jake jogged forward and called, "Ready, Lady."

Who was in command of this tub, anyway? Much as she liked and admired Claire, Alice was the captain and it was her job to give the orders, not someone who was used to ordering maids around and bossing dressmakers and—and whatever else it was fine ladies did in London Town.

"Tigg, stand by engine," she said, moving smoothly but with authority to the stern with him. "Mr. Malvern, take the vanes, please. Full vertical. Passengers, I'd find somewhere to sit. Lift in five, four—"

Claire and the girls scrambled forward and sat wherever they could find a horizontal spot with something to hang onto. Rosie perched above their heads, her feet wrapped around a pipe.

"—three, two, one." She slammed all three levers down, one after the other. "Ignition, Mr. Tigg!"

She half expected to hear the throaty grumble of the poor old Massey. But there was no such sound. Instead, the engine mount seemed to tremble, there was a flash of light that she could see right through the rippled seams of Four's erstwhile chest, and the pistons began to move.

The props turned, slowly at first, then faster and faster. It worked, by golly, it really, truly worked. Alice drew in a breath that was more like a gasp of relief.

"Up ship!"

The Mopsies yanked in the mooring ropes. Andrew threw the levers for the elevation vanes forward and Jake gripped the tiller ...

... and they fell up into the twilight sky with the joy of a lark greeting the morning.

3

Edmonton.

The Northern Light, some called it, the third jewel in the continental crown that included New York and San Francisco, and light it was.

The *Stalwart Lass* circled an airfield big enough to put fifty small towns on, looking for a mooring mast that was free. Through the glass, Claire could see the twinkling lights of the city coming on as darkness fell. It was bigger than Santa Fe, though not nearly as large as London or Paris—but give it time. The lights—not the sallow yellow of electricks, but orange and blue and nearly white, sparkled like the diamonds that gave the city its reason for being.

"Look!" She pointed a little to the west. "Isn't that *Lady Lucy?* Jake, steer that way. Perhaps we can moor close enough to walk over and see the Dunsmuirs."

"Dunno as I want to." Tigg popped out from behind the engine mount and leaned through the gangway door. "Ent they the same ones as left us all behind in Resolution?"

"They didn't intend to leave *us* behind." Lizzie giggled and elbowed Maggie in the ribs.

Maggie, who was holding Rosie and stroking her feathers, nodded. "We left our own selves."

"Be fair." Claire turned from the viewing glass and scratched Rosie's head. The bird, who was getting sleepy with the fading of the light, gave her a polite tap upon the finger with her beak. One did not disturb a lady at her rest. "They believed me to be dead, the two of you in your cabin, and Tigg back with Mr. Yau at the engines. And you know the countess puts Willie's safety before all other considerations."

"Kid's goin' to be spoiled rotten," muttered Jake.

Despite his grumbles, Claire was pleased to see that he had changed their course, and they were now floating nearer to the *Lady Lucy.*

"There's a mast free," Lizzie said suddenly. "Fifty feet off the port side of her."

So there was. Maggie took Rosie to her hatbox in the twins' berth in the starboard-side fuselage while Jake and Alice brought the battered *Lass* in for a smooth landing. One of the ground crew stationed at the field caught the rope and moored them fast, and for the first time since they had left Reno, Claire found herself disembarking like a lady—meaning on her feet, as opposed to climbing out by means of a rope or being hauled about unconscious like a sack of vegetables.

"Cor, it's freezing!" Lizzie bleated as she jumped to the ground from the gondola. She wore her black raiding skirt and striped stockings and boots, but her white blouse was thin voile, much like Claire's own.

"I would wrap you in my coat if I still had one," Andrew told her. "Will my waistcoat do?"

"Here." Alice pulled off her mechanic's jacket and settled it around Lizzie's shoulders. "Air's got a bite to it, that's for sure. It never feels like this in Resolution except in the deeps of winter. But then, we're pretty far north. It's winter here already."

"Let us board the *Lady Lucy*, then," Claire said briskly. "Davina will know where we can buy clothes more suited to this climate." Hopefully sooner rather than later. She herself had two skirts and a waist to her name, and both pairs of stockings had holes in the heels. If she didn't open her mouth to speak, an observer would assume she was a young woman down on her luck—a seamstress, perhaps, or a schoolteacher who had come north to find more opportunity, or a shopgirl.

That was certainly not the case. She had been enormously lucky. Blessed, even. They had simply come to the end of the resources left from the previous stages of their journey. She would visit a bank, and then repair as quickly as possible to the high street to resolve this most immediate problem. Small difficulties like this certainly beat her most recent ones—like having to invent an engine from scratch in the middle of a wilderness.

How she had changed! She recalled clearly the burden that visiting a dressmaker had been even six months ago. But that had been a time when clothes appeared magically in her closets and she never gave a single thought to stockings or coats—or to money, for that matter.

By now darkness had fallen, but the airfield was illuminated by lamps on every mooring mast. The Mopsies and Tigg set off at a determined jog for the warmth of *Lady Lucy*'s salon—where Claire hoped they would be received with open arms and not a lecture upon the evils of abandoning ship. Jake and Andrew followed, and when Claire looked back, she saw Alice lingering at the gondola, pretending to check their repairs to its bow.

"Alice, are you coming?"

"I—well, sure. Maybe later. I just want to make sure things are buttoned up here."

"I'll wait for you, if you like."

Alice hunched her shoulders. "Naw, you should go join your fancy friends. And Mr. Malvern. I'll see what I can rustle up with the ground crew. They're usually good for some news and a laugh."

Claire took in the poor posture, the hands jammed into the pockets of her pants, the scuffed toes of her work boots.

"Alice, you do not need to be ashamed of who you are. John and Davina certainly aren't, and neither am I."

Alice snorted. "An earl, a countess, and a lady. 'Course you're not."

"You are the woman who saved my life," Claire reminded her fiercely. "Who helped us put the cell in the *Lass*, which, as Andrew pointed out, has never been done before. You are the woman who flew across I don't know how many territories to get us here safely, when you didn't have to. You could have gone to Texico City and spent the rest of your life being nice and warm instead of risking your life to stand here in this cold airfield arguing with me."

"That all might be so, but it don't mean I can go shake hands with an earl looking like this."

"He will not hold it against you. Looks are irrelevant, Alice, and I should know. The earl is a man of perspicacity. He will see a lady of resources and bravery when he looks at you."

"Is that what Mr. Malvern sees when he looks at you?" Alice lifted her gaze to meet Claire's. "Now, don't go all huffy on me. I've seen him."

"I hope he does," Claire said a little stiffly. Really, Andrew's looks or lack of them were none of her business. "And I am *not* huffy."

Another snort. Really, it was a most unattractive sound.

"Do you—" Alice swallowed. "Do you think he sees those things when he looks at me?"

"Who, Andrew? Of course. He owes you as much as I do."

"Not because he owes me. He don't. But because—because—"

"Claire! Alice!" came a distant shout from the object of their discussion. "Are you coming?"

Claire grabbed Alice's hand and dragged her along the hard-packed ground, the fuselage of a neighboring airship forming a darker shadow above their heads against the starry sky.

Perhaps it was just as well that Alice had not finished that sentence.

The only reason the Mopsies did not get a stern lecture on the subject of what happened to little girls who abandoned ship was because the countess fainted dead away at the sight of all of them.

In the ensuing ruckus, Maggie and Lizzie made themselves helpful, snatching the towels from around the wine cooling in silver buckets and applying them to her ladyship's pale cheeks while Claire cleared the nearest sofa of its embroidered pillows and instructed her frantic husband to lay her upon it.

By the time Davina had come to herself, sat up, and tossed back a tiny glass of brandy supplied by Andrew, the opportunity for lectures had passed in the general joy of being reunited again.

"And you are all alive, and well, and oh Claire, I am so sorry we fell for the stories those rascals in

Santa Fe told us," Davina said breathlessly. "Mr. Malvern, I am very glad to see you—we feared you would be in gaol for months."

Claire made a movement as if to stop him from telling her the truth, then thought better of it. Davina may look as though a gust of wind might blow her away, but under the tightly laced corset was a spine of steel. "He was not in gaol, my dear friend," she explained gently. "They imprisoned him on top of one of those stone pinnacles and left him to die. If not for Alice here coming to the rescue with the Mo—with the girls, his remains would be up there still."

"No!" Davina laid a hand on her pristine Flanders cutwork blouse. "Shocking—distressing—how could they? And … Alice? Which of your party is she?"

Out of the corner of her eye, Claire saw Jake give Alice a shove in the small of her back. She stumbled out of her hiding place behind Andrew.

"Pleased to meet you, ma'am. Sir. Lordships. I'm Alice Chalmers."

Davina rose and shook her hand, followed by the earl. "You must call us Davina and John. We're among family here. We are so grateful. How did you accomplish such a daring rescue?"

Alice hunched her shoulders, as though Davina's wide eyes and guileless smile were a plague she might somehow catch. "I just flew the *Lass* overhead and we winched him up."

"It weren't quite so easy as that," Lizzie interrupted, ever factual. "They was firing cannon at us and those poor Cantons got blown up and that mucky great engine were flingin' railway coaches at the pinnacle to try and break it in pieces and—"

"Great Caesar's ghost!" the earl exclaimed. "Can this be true?"

"It's quite true, sir," Andrew replied, backing Lizzie up before she did something foolish, like kick his lordship in the shin for implying she was telling a tall tale. "It takes a cool mind and a steady hand on both tiller and weapons to pull off a rescue like that. I owe Alice and these girls my life." He smiled at the Mopsies, and at Alice, who flushed all the way to the edges of her cap.

"But wait, did you say the *Lass*?" Davina asked. "The *Stalwart Lass*, Ned Mose's ship?"

Alice nodded. "Ned Mose is—well, the truth is, he—"

"He was her stepfather," Claire put in smoothly. "They became estranged when Alice took possession of the ship in order to pursue the girls and me to Santa Fe and save our lives."

"Ah," said the earl thoughtfully. "I am astonished that this is the first time we have met."

"Circumstances conspired to keep us apart, but I am glad they have brought us all together again," Davina said. She reached up and hugged Alice. "I for one am delighted."

Alice blushed again, and after a moment, gave her ladyship a squeeze before she stepped back. "I'll get your blouse all dirty, ma'am."

"Nonsense. Rather a dirty waist than no hug, as any mother of a boy will tell you."

There was a pounding in the corridor outside the salon and Willie burst into the room. "Lady!" He dashed over to Claire and flung himself against her skirts. "I knew you'd come back!"

"Yes, I do seem rather like the proverbial penny. I'm very glad to see you, darling."

"Mama and Papa are going into town for dinner. Are you going?"

"I'm afraid I have nothing to eat dinner in, and their company would be scandalized if I turned up in this poor old navy skirt."

"Mama and Papa will send their regrets to the lieutenant-governor," Lord Dunsmuir told his son with a smile. "I can't imagine any society dinner would be more interesting than hearing about your travels, though I must say any dinner with Isobel Churchill at the table will not be dull."

"Isobel Churchill?" Claire let Willie go and he ran to his mother. "She and Peony are still here? Oh, I hope I can send a message to let them know I'm all right—we were to have met some days ago, you know, and they are likely wondering why I did not arrive as planned. There have been some rather, er, alarming reports in the papers lately."

"I should say so," said a voice from the gangway. Captain Hollys stepped into the room and offered Claire his hand, his face alight in a way that would have been most disturbing had Andrew not been standing right behind her. "May I say I am very glad that the reports have been exaggerated?"

"Thank you, Captain. And may I say that the lessons you gave Jake in navigation and aeronautics have more than repaid the time you took to give them. He has been Captain Chalmers' first officer on the *Stalwart Lass* in everything but name."

"Captain Chalmers? The *Stalwart Lass?*" The captain of the *Lady Lucy* looked over the little party, his gaze darkening. "I'd like a word with him, and then perhaps he'd like a quick trip to the local gaol."

"She, sir." Jake gripped Alice's arm and pulled her over much the same way as a tug drags a boat anchor. "An' she ent no pirate. She saved all our lives, one after the other."

Bravely, Alice held out her right hand while attempting to smooth her hair with her left. "Alice Chalmers, sir. I deeply regret my stepfather's treatment of you and your crew."

"You were in Resolution?"

"I was, sir."

"Keeping me and the girls alive," Claire put in.

"And you are not a pirate?"

"No, sir. I operated the locomotive tower, though."

"But that were only cos 'er dad would've shot 'er if she 'adn't." Maggie came to the captain's side and took his other hand. Alice tugged hers free and tried to hush her, but Maggie pushed on. "An' 'e took 'er prisoner and would've shot 'er 'cept Jake set 'er free and they come after us." She gazed up, earnestly. "Don't throw our Alice in gaol, Cap'n. She's in our flock."

Captain Hollys looked bemused. "I would say that no higher character recommendation is necessary, then." Alice straightened. "So young Jake's service has been satisfactory?"

"Quite satisfactory." It appeared that being addressed as an equal by another airman was affecting her spirits positively. "He has a knack for navigation and can read a chart at a glance, even if he has to spell out the names."

Now it was Jake's turn to blush and attempt to hide behind Andrew, who nudged him forward.

"It's the land forms that count."

"You're right, there. How long did it take you to get here from Santa Fe?"

"It would have been three days, but Lord and Lady Dunsmuir took a fancy to a bit of shooting in the Montana Territory. Her ladyship bagged a—"

"Really, Ian, I'm sure our company does not want to hear such things, especially the children," Davina interrupted hastily, covering Willie's ears.

"I do," Lizzie said.

"Me, too," said Maggie and Tigg together.

"Mama, I saw you shoot that big deer," Willie said earnestly. "Mr. Skully and me were looking out the window."

"You were supposed to have been having a nap," his mother said severely. "I shall have a word with Mr. Skully."

"It was a single shot, too," the earl said with proud affection. "Let us have dinner together *en famille*. I confess my appetite is only being whetted more, the longer we remain out here."

When Alice would have melted out the door, both Andrew and Claire took her by either arm and marched her down the corridor to Claire's former cabin, which was possessed of a sink and mirror.

With some water and a comb, Claire decided, she would work a minor miracle on her friend. A little attention from Captain Hollys instead of Andrew would, she was quite sure, go a long way.

4

Alice figured the meal that evening in the dining saloon could have rivaled anything the railroad barons might put on in their fancy New York mansions. The rolling plains of the Canadas produced an enormous shaggy creature that tasted much like beef, much to the delight of the Mopsies, and she was introduced to the finer points of Yorkshire pudding, which in their minds was the epitome of heaven.

The puffy puddings were pretty darned good, she had to admit, though it was hard to beat one of her own biscuits. But what felt even better was a full stomach, for the first time in days. Flight rations consisting of dried fruit and jerky were easy to carry and did very well in a pinch, but they got old fast.

The little boy had been bundled off to bed after insisting on kissing Claire good-night, and the Mopsies had settled without protest in their old cabin, when her ladyship ran into a snag in her assumptions.

"But Claire, I insist that you and the girls stay here with us." She leaned over from her seat on the sofa and clasped Claire's hands. "Our original plan was for you to sail with us to the Canadas and back, and to share our adventures together. I admit that since we made the acquaintance of Ned Mose and his crew, we have not achieved that goal, but we must make a fresh start."

Alice was staying out of this one. Why should she care whether Claire and the girls stayed here or went back to the Spartan comfort of their temporary berths on the *Lass*? In fact, she'd prefer it if they did stay on this luxurious boat. Then if Alice decided to pull up ropes and head off to see where the sun went every day, she could, and it would be nobody's nevermind but her own.

A quiet nevermind, it was true, but there was nothing wrong with the sound of the wind in the guy wires. It would make a nice change. Maybe she'd even start on Ten, and figure out how to get an automaton to talk.

"But then Alice would be alone," Claire replied, pulling one hand from Davina's gentle grip and giving Alice's shoulder a shake. "I wouldn't want her to get itchy feet and leave us just when we're all getting to know each other."

What was she, a clairvoyant? "I wouldn't do that," Alice lied through her teeth, doing her best to look innocent. "What do you take me for?"

"What are your plans, Alice?" the countess asked, her fine dark eyes sparkling with interest, and a flush on her tanned cheek.

Until this moment, Alice hadn't given it a single thought. Just flying here had been enough to knock the stuffing out of anybody, without worrying about what came after. "I—I'm not sure. I hadn't really thought much past getting Claire and Mr. Malvern here in one piece."

Davina actually clapped. On anyone else it would have seemed silly and childish, but Alice had heard the pride in her husband's voice when he'd told them that she'd dropped that elk with a single shot. This woman was the furthest thing from silly.

"Why, then, you must stay and enjoy the delights of the Northern Light with us. The lieutenant-governor's dinner was bound to be stodgy—oh, he's a gentleman, to be sure, but my goodness, one can only talk about mineral rights for so long—but there is a ball the day after tomorrow at Government House, and two shooting parties for grouse, and I can't tell you how many card parties and visits to the theatre. We have missed Madame Tetrazzini, apparently, but Mr. Caruso is expected on the next airship from San Francisco. Our time here will rival anything you've experienced in London, I can assure you."

"Sounds lovely," Alice said faintly. It sounded like purgatory. Like torture. Like an unrelenting exercise in embarrassment and humiliation for one Alice Benton Chalmers.

If this was to be her fate, she was pulling up ropes tonight, no matter how exhausted and full of good food and wine she was.

"I know what you're thinking," Davina said knowingly. "Both of you."

"That we have nothing to wear but what's on our backs?" Claire asked.

Ha! That was the least of it.

"Exactly. But we will remedy that tomorrow. There are Canton tailors here that can construct everything from a riding habit to a ball gown overnight— and with the latest designs from Paris, too. None of this nonsense that the New York ladies adhere to about leaving a dress in its box for a year or two before wearing it, so one doesn't look *nouveau*. Oh, no. If one cannot have Mr. Worth create a gown in Paris, one simply chooses fabric and a fashion plate from Fourth Street, *et voila.*"

She looked so pleased that Alice almost didn't have the heart to disappoint her.

"I'm sorry to disappoint you, your ladyship—"

"Davina."

"Davina, but I ain't got the ready money for this kind of exercise—clothes and balls and whatnot. I have to figure out how to power the *Lass* without Claire's energy cell, and that'll probably mean hiring on as ground crew for a while, till I get an engine in her.

And you're not going to want to take a grease monkey along on all these fancy excursions. Especially one who can't dance and wouldn't know a dessert fork from a carving knife."

"I'll bet you're quite proficient with knives."

"But you see what I'm saying."

"I see what you're *not* saying. Do you think that Claire and I have not been in your position—untried and ignorant of society?"

"When you were little Willie's age, maybe. I bet you learned all that stuff in school. Or from your governess or whatever."

Davina leaned forward, a fierce, predatory look on her delicate features. "Where do you think I am from, Alice?"

Well, that was a poser. How should she know? "Um. England?"

One eyebrow rose. "Try again."

"New York?"

"Farther west."

"Here?"

"Farther still."

What was out there, farther still, on the edge of the world? "Victoria?"

"Close. Picture an island off the coast, peopled by a tribe of what you might think of as wild Injuns. I am a Nan'uk princess. My father is chief of a tribe that populates most of the islands and inlets around Victoria and north along the entire coast to the borders of the Russian Orthodox Empire. Our nation has intimate ties with the Esquimaux and the Athabasca, making ours the largest united peoples in the Canadas.

"I met his lordship when I was a guide on a hunting trip. I taught him how to handle the new Sharps lever-action repeating rifle." Her eyes took on a focus and intensity that were rather like those of an eagle stooping upon its prey, and Alice found herself pushing up against the back of the chair. "I did not grow up in the ballrooms of London, Alice Chalmers. I learned to take my place there, and if you are afraid to do what I have done, then I am ashamed of you."

Alice glanced at Claire, whose jaw hung open as far as her own.

"But—but your speech," Claire stammered. "Your accent—it's Belgravia to the last vowel."

"I have a good ear and am an excellent mimic. You ought to hear my northern loon."

"I knew there was more to you than met the eye!" Claire was beginning to recover from her astonishment. "A woman could not be so good at weaponry and be so comfortable in the wilderness who had grown up in the drawing rooms of London."

Davina smiled and turned back to Alice. "There are those in said drawing rooms who made an attempt to turn a cold shoulder to me because of my birth. They soon learned it is not safe to offend my husband—or Her Majesty, who recognizes a princess whether she is arrayed in diamonds or deerskin. I can assure you, Alice, my dear, that if you accept my guidance and his protection, there will be no opportunity for the embarrassment you fear."

Alice felt a little winded. "Another blasted clairvoyant. Between the two of you, I ain't got a chance."

Claire smiled, a hint of wickedness in the corners. "Among the three of us, neither does Edmonton."

Claire and Andrew walked back to the *Lass* with Alice, since Claire could not be permitted to cross the airfield alone on the return walk. Such silliness, really, but the fact remained that, if she was to submit herself to the chaperonage of the Dunsmuirs, she would have to re-accustom herself to old-fashioned ways of thinking. The Mopsies, dead to the world in one bunk in their shifts, would stay, so Davina felt her battle half won. If she had it her way, Andrew would stay on the *Lass* and the two young ladies on the larger ship, as was proper, but Claire doubted very much that Alice would be talked into leaving her vessel. In any case, Claire needed to return for her much-abused valise.

Alice ducked past a set of mooring ropes and emerged into the lamplight again, shaking her head. The French braid that Claire had fashioned in her hair was beginning to come apart at the end where she had lost the ribbon. It seemed that Alice's hair would be more of a challenge than she had first supposed.

"How about that Davina?" Alice said, apropos of nothing. "A Na'nuk princess. Who'd have thought?"

"Even more astonishing is how little it is talked of in London. Her Majesty and the earl between them must have been quite … firm."

"I doubt Her Majesty'll be giving me the same backup."

"The earl will," Andrew said. "And that counts for quite a lot."

Alice stopped walking. "Claire, Mr. Malvern, it's no use. I got something I have to do here tonight, and once that's done, I'm going to lift and head north, to the mines. And maybe after that I'll head out west and get a gander at this ocean you and Davina were talking about."

Two thoughts combusted simultaneously in Claire's mind. The first was that Alice intended to search for her father, all alone. And the second was that no woman who would set off into the sky all by herself to undertake a journey of at least a thousand miles nurtured any hopes whatsoever of catching the eye of a certain engineer.

Claire did not want her to catch his eye. She liked his eyes trained in the direction they were presently, thank you. But neither did she want her friend, to whom she owed so much, to head out into the unknown, unprotected and alone.

"Please don't go." She put a hand on Alice's arm, and to her relief, was not shaken off. "I am as much a stranger to Edmonton society as you. We must stay together."

"Why?" Now Alice did pull away. They had reached the *Lass*, and as Claire and Andrew followed her through the hatch, she said, "I can see why you'd like it. Balls and theatre and such, they're what you're used to. Heck, you probably know half the people here, not to mention that Churchill girl you were talking about. But I don't." They emerged into the gondola, which was silent and dim and smelled faintly of axle grease and canvas paste. "I don't know a soul but those on the *Lady Lucy*. I don't know how to go about in society. I don't know nothing because it's nothing to do with me. And I'm going to keep it that way."

As if this were the last word on the subject, she shook up a moonglobe or two and placed them in a net dangling from the ceiling, where they cast a soft white glow.

"But Alice, in the salon with Davina, you seemed perfectly willing to go shopping with us tomorrow, and join us for all the rest of it."

"Where I come from, that's called being polite."

"Then let me tell you what I did not say back there. I have been to exactly one ball in my life."

"Two," Andrew corrected her, "if you count dancing with the Prince Consort at the Crystal Palace a ball."

"Now, see?" Alice lifted her hands in a gesture of despair, and they fell to the idle tiller as if by habit … or an unconscious reach for something that was safe and known. "You danced with a prince and it's an afterthought. This is exactly what I'm talking about. I wouldn't know a prince from a pirate if he popped me on the nose."

"You'd know Prince Albert," Andrew told her. "His likeness is on the coinage here."

"My point is, my dad could be up in this territory somewhere, and I aim to find him, not go gallivanting about doing frivolous things in clothes I'll never wear again in this lifetime."

"Then let us help you," Claire said at once. "Is that what you were going to do tonight? Begin your inquiries in the—the honkytonks the airmen frequent?"

"Yes," Alice said reluctantly. "But I won't get much out of them with you along."

"Why not?" Andrew asked. "With three, it will go thrice as fast."

"With Claire in her nice white blouse and you in your brocade waistcoat, everyone will just think you're slumming. Airmen are a chummy bunch. They'll close ranks on you."

"Give me a moment to change," Claire said, "and we'll see about that."

In her raiding rig, with the lightning rifle in its holster on her back, it would be a rare man indeed who would mistake her for a fine lady.

Something else she must make sure never got back to Mama.

5

Andrew kept glancing at her sideways as they made their way to the Crown and Compass, the honkytonk that the ground crew around the *Lass* insisted was the place to begin inquiries about anyone. Finally, as if his curiosity could not be contained, he said, "You brought fancy dress all this way?"

Claire thought back to what must be the only occasion he had ever seen her in her rig—the costume ball she had attended with James at the Wellesleys', when James had upbraided her for showing her legs in their striped stockings in public. "It isn't fancy dress," she said briskly. "It is a very practical rig, and the corselet provides a foundation for the rifle's holster."

"Which you do not intend to fire, I hope."

"Certainly not. Unless we find ourselves in some danger."

"If we do, I will handle it and you ladies will seek safety."

Claire and Alice exchanged a glance of amusement. "That is very gallant of you, Andrew, but you must know by now that Alice and I are quite capable of protecting ourselves."

Andrew cleared his throat and held the Crown's door open, nearly shouting over the roar of the crowd and the notes of the pianoforte playing something fast and loose. "When it comes to fisticuffs—if it does—I insist you leave the protecting to me."

Alice leaned close to shout in Claire's ear. "I ain't never had a gentleman offer to protect me before this. Maybe I'll start a fight just to see it."

"You shall not, you rascal. We are here to gather information, not start fights."

Smiling, Alice bellied up to the bar and ordered tawny-colored drinks that came in tiny glasses. Claire would have preferred lemonade, but to order such a thing in here would have negated the effect of her raiding rig and drawn unwelcome attention.

As it was, the rambunctious crowd ignored them. A table full of airmen sang along with the songstress next to the pianoforte. Men at several tables played cards—cowboy poker, if she wasn't mistaken. Ooh, what an excellent opportunity to strike up a conversation—and gain some ready money in the absence of a bank!

"I'm going to join a card table," she told Andrew, and swiped the third drink.

"You're what?"

But she didn't wait to explain—or ask his permission. While Alice dragged him, protesting, toward a crowd of airmen on the far side, she pulled up an empty stool and smiled beguilingly at the dealer. "Deal me in?"

"What's your stake? Here at the Crown we take gold and diamonds, and paper if that's all you got."

"I have none, unless—" She pulled the raja's emerald off the fourth finger of her right hand. "This is gold. Will it do?"

"Close enough." The dealer tossed her legacy from her grandmother into the center of the table and dealt her in.

Within a few minutes, Claire realized that she might be just the tiniest bit out of her league. Of all the variations of cowboy poker that she and the boys in the cottage had fabricated, she had not yet seen this one. She must remember, when things calmed down a little, to diagram it out and send it to Vauxhall Gardens on a pigeon. Snouts and his merry band of gamblers would make a fortune and confound the denizens of Percy Street in one fell swoop.

But she must not think about London. She must concentrate.

Too late, her ring met its doom in the person of a fat man in a tweed suit of a particularly obnoxious pattern. He raked in a pot of at least two hundred dollars—two thousand if you counted the ring and the sprinkle of tiny cut diamonds that glittered on the green felt table covering.

"Ante up," the dealer said. Cash and gold clinked into the pot, the fat man smiled with anticipation, and the dealer looked at her.

"My rifle," she said.

A flick of his gaze took in the lightning rifle from stock to sights. Then he shrugged and dealt her in.

"And the ring. It goes back in the pot."

"You think you can win it back, little lady?" the fat man said, still smiling. He slipped her grandmother's emerald onto his thumb as if to test the size.

"I know I can."

"I don't know ... I kinda like it." His fist closed around the emerald and Claire's temper ignited.

"Are you afraid of my skill?" she asked, her tone so cool and silky it might almost have been rude.

His eyes widened. "What skill? You lost the hand."

"Ah, but I have the measure of my opponents now. If you do not throw the ring back in, I shall know your true measure, too."

His companions snickered, and his cheeks reddened. "You calling me a yellowbelly, missy? You know what happens to people who backtalk Sherwood Leduc?"

"I know what happens to people who walk away from a display of cowardice." She smiled sweetly, as if he were a drawing-room dowager who must be placated and plied with cakes. "I'm sure they return to their ships and talk about it, don't they? Tsk. It's so difficult to stop people talking, particularly on an airfield the size of this one."

He flung the ring so hard it bounced off the table. A cowboy in a brand-new hat caught it one-handed and tossed it back in the pot. "Deal," snarled Sherwood Leduc.

With a sunny smile, Claire accepted her cards and fell to her task. She did not see Andrew and Alice talking with the airmen, or hear Alice's offhand questions. She did not see the cowboy in the new hat swipe her drink and down it himself. Instead, the shape of the table formed in her mind's eye, and mathematical probabilities, and patterns, all shifting and changing as the minutes crept by.

And when the cowboy and two others folded, only she, Leduc, and one of his cronies laid their cards on the table.

Royal flush. She had won!

"Thank you, gentlemen," she said with real gratitude, raking the pile of gold, the half-dozen diamonds, and the bills toward herself. The ring went back on her finger in the twinkling of an eye, and the rest went into the square leather pouch chained to her leather corselet. The rifle had not left its holster—nor would it now, to her great relief.

"Another game," Sherwood Leduc demanded. "I'll have that rifle and the ring both."

"I think not," Claire told him. "I have other business that calls me away. I'm out."

"Who's the yellowbelly now? You haven't heard the last of me, missy," he called as she pushed in the stool with one foot and turned away.

"Neither has the rest of the company here, I'm sure," she said sweetly, and headed for a door with a silhouette of a dancer burned into it.

Once locked in the ladies' retiring room, which consisted of a hole in the floor with a noxious smell emanating from it, and a broken mirror on the wall, she opened the leather pouch. She redistributed her winnings about her person, since only a fool would walk about the field now with a full purse and Sherwood Leduc's threats ringing in her ears. Her skirt had two hidden pockets in the bustle that fastened closed with snaps, so in those she secreted the gold and small stones. The paper she stuffed down the inside of her blouse, to be held in place by the corselet. Last, she removed the ever-present ivory pick in her chignon, threaded the ring on it, and worked the jewel deep into her hair. Even if Leduc made good on his threats and cut the purse from her, all he would find in it was a few silver coins.

Then she sallied forth to rejoin Andrew and Alice.

Who were no longer at the airmen's table.

Well, goodness, this was no time to be left on one's own. She sidled up to the table and propped her hands easily on the chairs of two airmen.

"Excuse me, but do you know where the two mechanics who were just here might have gone?"

The nearest crewman pushed his goggles higher on his cap and looked her over with appreciation. "No, but if you're looking for one, will I do the job?"

His friends laughed, and she smiled into his eyes. "I have no doubt you would, but it's rather urgent I find them." She leaned a little closer, and hoped he didn't hear the crackle of paper under her blouse. "You see, I confess I was rather insulting to Sherwood Leduc over the matter of the pot, and I'm very much afraid he intends to take it back … by force."

"You don't say." The smile went out of the airman's eyes. "What's a little rose like you doing insulting a coyote like him?"

"I did not know he was a coyote," she said. "And he refused to give me the chance to win back my property, as a gentleman might. I rather lost my temper, I'm afraid, and he took offense."

"We ain't all like that, missy," someone else piped up from across the table. "There's plenty here who would hand over a pot for the chance to insult Leduc. George, walk her over to the Tiller to find her friends. And don't try no funny business, neither. It's obvious to a blind man she's a lady, not one of yer prairie partridges."

George the airman straightened and gave his companion a hard look. "What do you take me for? Contrariwise to what some might think, I'm a gentleman."

"Thank you, sir," Claire breathed, with such a gaze of admiration that two others left their drinks to join the little party.

As they stepped out onto the hard-packed gravel of the airfield, Claire's gaze swept from left to right to take in her surroundings—equipment, the gentle, swelling curves of airship fuselages, mooring masts, the occasional crewman tightening ropes and inspecting landing wheels. Nothing out of the ordinary.

But she had not dealt with the dockside bullies who worked for the Cudgel without learning a thing or two.

"Gentlemen, I appreciate your protection," she said softly, which had the effect of making them close up around her in order to hear. "How far is it to the Tiller?"

"Half a mile or so," George said. "Ten minutes if you don't dally. We might catch your friends if we pick up our pace."

Claire obligingly matched his long stride, and the two others hustled to catch up. "So, missy, this here's Elliot and I'm Reuben," one of them told her.

"And you may call me the Lady."

"Lady? You don't got a Christian name?"

"She's from the old country, you dope," George said. "Can't you hear it? That's a title, not a name."

"Oh. A real ladyship? I ain't never met one of those before."

"Title notwithstanding, I am honored to be among your company," Claire said warmly. "But with the likes of Sherwood Leduc about, perhaps it would be best to keep my real name concealed for now."

"Not meaning to alarm you or nothin', Lady, but ain't nobody gets away with insulting Leduc," Reuben said in a low tone. "We got a couple of his brutes on our tail right now, matter of fact."

"I saw them," Claire said. "They are lurking under that enormous fuselage with the Iron Cross upon it, are they not?"

"More fool them," George said with a snort. "Ten to one the count's men bag 'em before we go another hundred yards."

Claire put crest and title together. "That ship belongs to *Count von Zeppelin?*"

"Yep. Never seen him, myself, and his crew don't mix, but that ship arrived two days ago."

"Why would they not mix?" Claire felt a little breathless at the prospect of a chance meeting with the man who had invented the modern airship. What an honor that would be! Not to mention she could ask him some rather troublesome questions about converting a steam engine to one that harnessed lightning.

"You can't understand 'em, for one, hawking and spitting in that Kaiser tongue. And for two, maybe they think they're better'n us."

"I doubt that very much," Claire said, reining in her excitement. "They are likely military men, and hence would put their duty before fraternizing with potential friends such as yourselves."

"How would you know that?" George said curiously.

But before she could answer, a shout came from the direction of the mighty Zeppelin ship, and three shadows detached themselves from the darkness under it, outrunning and losing their pursuers on the far side of a pair of small cargo vessels.

"They've sussed out where we're going and plan to circle around to meet us before we get there," Reuben said in a low voice. "Look clueless—and look sharp."

Sure enough, they could hear music in the distance—a horn of some kind, maybe two. And in the lamplit space at the base of an empty mooring mast, three men jogged into the circle of light between their party and the Tiller.

"Why, those are two of the men gambling with Leduc," Claire said just loud enough to be heard. "Do you suppose they are anxious to retrieve his—and their—property?"

"I suppose any sore loser would try. What's the matter, Paxton?" George called as they emerged on the near side. "Surprised to find the little lady ain't alone?"

"Don't matter if she is or ain't." Paxton cracked his knuckles. "We aim to take back our property. She cheated at cards."

"I did not," Claire said indignantly, and reached behind her to unholster the rifle. "I suggest you use what few brain cells remain to you and leave while you still can."

"Or what?" Paxton laughed, and his companions moved a few steps closer. "These airbrains will slap us with their gloves?"

Elliot growled and Reuben offered a few most uncomplimentary speculations about the man's lineage. Claire pushed the switch forward and the lightning rifle began to hum. Startled, George stepped to one side just as a rock whizzed past his ear from the darkness behind them and clocked one of Paxton's companions on the side of the head.

He howled and George shouted, "Who's that?" All three of Claire's erstwhile protectors whirled, and Paxton saw his moment. He leaped forward, aiming for

Claire, his arms raised as though he intended to bull his way through and grab her.

The rifle hummed happily at the prospect. She raised it to her shoulder, sighted, and fired. Paxton screamed as a bolt of lightning sizzled across the fifteen feet between them and engulfed his fisted right hand. Tendrils of blue light danced down his arm and his coat caught fire. His men tore it off him and stamped it out, but there was nothing they could do about the cauterized remains of the hand that would have beaten her bloody had she allowed it.

"You may take that back to Mr. Leduc as a warning," she said politely as he wept and howled. "I dislike hurting anyone, but if he interferes further with me or mine, I must and will protect myself."

"You'd best listen," came a voice out of the dark behind them. "Tell 'im the Lady of Devices sends 'er regards."

Claire rolled her eyes as the two men still on their feet helped Paxton away. "Jake, there is no need to be theatrical. You sound as though you've been at the flickers."

Jake emerged from under a neighboring fuselage. "Couldn't resist, Lady."

"What on earth are you doing out at this time of night? I thought you were safe in your berth on the *Lady Lucy*."

"Wait—you know this rascal?" George had finally found his voice, although the whites of his eyes still showed as his gaze swung from Jake to Claire.

"Where'd you learn to shoot like that? And what kind of a gun shoots lightning instead of bullets?"

Claire patted the rifle affectionately and holstered it. "Did you think it just for show?"

"I don't make no assumptions about a man's ordnance," George said. "Guess there was a few I shouldn't have made about a woman's, neither." He grasped Jake's shoulder and shook him. "I'd best not find out that rock was meant for me."

"Course not," Jake said. "You stepped practically in its path. I were aimin' at that miscreant, obviously, or I would've 'it you instead of 'im."

"Do unhand my navigator, George," Claire said.

"Navigator?" the man snorted.

"Assumptions, George," she reminded him gently.

"Fine. Fine. You're her navigator and—" He swung to Claire. "—*you* need about as much protection as a wolverine and—" He set off. "—*I'm* going to the Tiller right now and ordering up the biggest whiskey they got."

"I shall stand you all the first round," Claire called after him, and then pointed up ahead. Two people were ducking into a low door in a long building that appeared to be half of a giant pipe embedded in the ground. "Look, isn't that Alice?"

6

The good thing about airmen, in Alice's mind, was that they tended to congregate with their own kind and exchange news, gossip, wind and weather, and general badinage. They rarely fought among themselves—they were a tightly knit breed, looking down in more ways than one on the men who chose a ground-bound career. If a person needed to find information, an airman's honkytonk was the place to do it.

The bad thing about airmen, as Alice had found in the Crown and Compass, was that you couldn't count on them to stay in one place very long. They were forever moving, following the wind. One word of a storm front and the whole flock of them would scatter like so many starlings with a startled cry of "Up ship!", leaving you standing with your mouth full of questions and nothing to show for your pains.

Her father had been a mining engineer, and had been gone most of Alice's life, but she never gave up hope that somewhere there was an airman who remembered him and could point her to him. The fact that she didn't remember him and couldn't say what he looked like other than that one eye was damaged from falling rock didn't stop her inquiring about him of every airman she met.

In Resolution, mind you, most of them were dead by the time she got to their wrecked ships, so up until now she hadn't actually spoken to as many as she would have liked. But that one man in Santa Fe hadn't been quite drunk enough to forget he'd seen a one-eyed man up here in the Canadas.

That was more than enough for her. It was more than she'd heard in years.

If her mother had been a different kind of woman, she would have stayed to keep her company in the afternoons, before business got going at the Resolute Rose. But Ma, having become the hardheaded practical sort out of necessity, was Ned Mose's kind of woman. A girl had to survive in any way she could, and Alice wasn't about to judge the woman who had borne her for the choices she made.

She had to live with them. Alice didn't.

She'd sent a pigeon from Santa Fe letting her know she was riding the winds and probably wouldn't be back. There had been no reply, but Alice expected none.

Expectations were a luxury Alice Chalmers couldn't afford. But hope didn't cost a thing.

There was a commotion near the door and Alice turned to see Claire and Jake and a crowd of the rope monkeys who had been at the Crown all coming in together. Naturally, Andrew took one look and made the wrong assumption.

"Claire? Are you all right? Are these men being troublesome?"

"On the contrary," she said gaily. "They are keeping me out of trouble. Andrew, this is George, Reuben, and Elliot. Gentlemen, this is Andrew Malvern, and the blond young woman at the bar is—"

"Alice Chalmers." George touched two fingers to his brow in acknowledgement. "I see you found the place."

"Your directions were precise." She turned to Claire. "I'm going to make inquiries at the bar. Do you and Andrew and—Jake? What are you doing here?"

"He was filling in for the Mopsies," Claire said. "May he come in?"

"If he stays out of the way," George put in. "And don't throw anything."

Alice let this go as none of her business, though how these two could have a history in the ten minutes since she'd left the Compass was beyond her. Claire and Jake took a table, and the airmen joined them. Andrew stopped to speak with a man heading out the door, and Alice—you'd think she'd know better—felt a glow of warmth that he had got right down to the business of helping her.

But mooning over that wasn't going to help her find her pa. She ordered something mild in the hopes that at some point later this evening, she would not be caught vomiting all over Mr. Malvern the way she had on the occasion of their first meeting. When the barman didn't seem inclined to move away, but stood there drying glasses, his gaze moving from table to table as he kept an eye out for trouble, she cleared her throat.

"Business good?"

"Middling. I was hoping the count's ship'd bring in business, what with the size of the crew it carries, but no such."

"You see a lot of traffic through here. Different crowd from the Compass, I understand."

He nodded, and wiped out another glass. "Compass caters to visitors. We get a different lot here. More flighty, you might say."

"You might have seen a friend of mine, then. Mining engineer, he is. Was. Accident took one eye."

The barman considered, twisting his towel in the glass. "How old?"

"Your age, maybe. Give or take five or ten years."

He snorted. "Ain't seen anyone like that lately."

Lately? "It could've been awhile ago. Years, even."

"Some friend. Close, are you?"

Caught. "It's my pa," she admitted. "I'm trying to get a lead on him, but I haven't seen him since I was knee-high."

Another snort, this time not without sympathy. "Maybe he don't want to be found."

"That might be. I'm prepared for it. But I'd still like to give him the chance to tell me so."

"Sorry. Not ringing a bell. But I can ask around. What ship?"

"*Stalwart Lass*, out of—"

"—Resolution. I've heard of it. I wouldn't be bandying that about, if I were you."

"Oh? Ship got a bad name? I stole her, if that makes a difference."

Slowly, he set down both glass and rag. "You stole the *Stalwart Lass*? Ned Mose's ship?"

They were thousands of miles from Resolution, and she'd walked into the one bar in the one city to strike up a conversation with the one man who could get her clapped in gaol with one word.

Alice resisted the temptation to put her head down on her arms and weep.

"I did. Used to be I called him Pa, but we had a falling out."

"Pa? Your ma Nellie Benton?"

"She is. We're still speaking, at any rate." It was one-sided at the moment, but he didn't need to know the details.

"I remember Nellie Benton fondly," the barman said, picking up another glass and leaving the first one abandoned where it sat. "You're in touch with her, you tell her Mike Embry sends his regards. Tell her I'm a darned fine prospect now, she ever changes her mind."

"I'll do that." Silently, Alice blessed her mother for treating this man kindly. "She ever talk about my pa?"

His face cracked into what might have been the first smile it had worn in a decade. "We didn't converse much about other men, missy."

"Alice. Alice Chalmers."

"That his name? Chalmers?"

"Could've been." Ma wasn't much on accuracy except when it came to the account books at the Resolute Rose. "I'm pretty sure."

Nodding, he said, "I'll see what I can find out. In exchange, you pass that message on to your ma."

"I said I would, Mike. I'll be around for a couple of days."

Too late, she remembered she was supposed to be pulling up ropes as soon as she could dodge Claire and the rest of her party.

"It'll take me that long to put out the word, find out who knows what. Three days, at least."

With a sinking feeling in her middle, Alice knocked back the rest of her drink, laid down a coin, and pushed away from the bar. At least in a fistfight, she knew what to do. In the air or under an engine, she was in command of her element. But now she was stuck with at least three days of shopping and balls and all manner of nonsense, where she knew nothing and commanded less.

If she ever found him, Pa would owe her one for that alone.

BRILLIANT DEVICES

The shop was the size of the *Lass*'s gondola and yet the entire contents of ten ladies' closets seemed to be crammed into its windows and displays, and layered on mannequins that resembled her automatons.

Alice would never put a hardworking, self-respecting automaton in a corset, though.

"I have it on good authority from Lady Arundel, the governor's wife, that this corsetiere is the best in town," said Lady Dunsmuir, clasping her hands in anticipation and practically bouncing on her toes. "If one begins with a good foundation garment, an elegant, correct silhouette will follow."

Alice had never had a correct silhouette in her life— or stopped to consider that there was such a thing. Wasn't whatever a woman possessed correct for her?

She, Claire, and Alice had breakfasted on the *Lady Lucy* with the family. The Mopsies had pitched a fit and flat refused to come along, so they had been stood up near a window, measured with ruthless accuracy by her ladyship, and then both of them sent to join Willie at his morning lessons. Alice had briefly considered trying the same ploy, but before she could open her mouth, had been hustled down the gangway with no opportunity to beg for mercy.

At which point she had come to a dead stop as though she had forgotten how to walk.

There on the gravel stood the most beautiful thing she had ever seen. Gleaming with flawless curves, its brass wings and swooping lines told everyone within a thousand yards that Serious Money was driving past.

"It's a six-piston Bentley," Claire whispered, elbowing her out of the way. "Isn't it lovely? Davina is driving us into town."

"We're going … in that?" Alice couldn't breathe. How could you waste time on something as prosaic as breathing when a lifetime's dream had just come true right in front of you?

"We had it unloaded before breakfast," Davina chirped, brushing past Alice and opening the rear compartment for her.

Tigg was already there. "Hullo, Alice. The Lady's landau is still in the cargo bay cos we weren't sure she would need it. Ent this fine?"

Alice had forgotten Claire also owned a landau. And had flown it across the ocean on the off chance she might have somewhere to go in it. Did all rich people think this way?

"We can run about in this while we're here," her ladyship said. "Tigg, watch closely. The ignition sequence is slightly different from that of the Henley." He leaned over Claire's shoulder and watched Davina flip switches and turn a series of small wheels.

That was like saying you could run about in von Zeppelin's great warship if you wanted to hop over to the coast for lunch. "It's the most beautiful thing I've ever seen," Alice breathed. She touched the door with one finger. Leather upholstery as soft as butter. Brasswork as smooth and glossy as satin.

"I can give you a driving lesson when we come back, if you like," Davina said. "The airfield is perfect for it. It's much easier to manage the gears here, where it's flat."

Alice was smitten silent at the prospect, and now, standing in the corsetiere's emporium, she still hadn't regained her powers of speech. Not when the steam landau sat right outside, gleaming in the autumn sun and accepting the gawking admiration of passers-by as if it were her due.

There were plenty of vehicles about. In Resolution, they used animals to go across country, there being only the promise, not the reality, of roads. The flash floods were hard on anything the territorial authorities tried to lay down—not that Resolution ever got much attention. That was why Ned Mose liked it.

But here in Edmonton, there were not only roads, but great steam-powered bridges that ratcheted up and down to let boats pass on the river. There were steam drays and clockwork buses that ticked along their cog tracks on a schedule so faithful that if you didn't hustle and get on, they would leave without you. Those, the countess had told them, worked in the summer and autumn. In winter and spring, when the roads were impassable with either ice or mud, everyone used the Underground system, which had been modeled after the one in London.

Every street was as straight as a rifle barrel, laid out in a sensible grid so that the cog tracks would work most efficiently. And along the streets, shops and houses and warehouses were packed, bustling with the activity of the biggest city in the Canadas.

How in tarnation was she to find her pa? Outside the city, the plains stretched into the distance, with lakes and rolling hills thrown in for relief, until you reached the mountains on one side or the diamond fields on another. Somewhere in all this busy vastness was her father—and she was one girl searching for one man, like a tiny gear looking in a huge machine for the other little gear that would match it.

"Alice, are you listening?"

She came back to this pretty, fluffy prison with a start. "Sorry, Davina. What?"

Her ladyship held up two corsets. "Do you prefer the pink with the roses, or the burgundy brocade?"

Heaven help me. "Neither. Isn't there something more ... practical?"

"What about this?" Claire held up a plain coutil garment that at least possessed hooks down the front. Alice had tried on her mother's best back-laced corset once as a young girl, and words could not describe the torture of trying to get out of it when Nellie had been called away. She'd screeched so loudly that one of the customers had finally come in to discover what the racket was all about ... which had subsequently caused a ruckus of a different kind when he'd mistaken her for a desert flower.

"Fine."

When Davina went back with the clerk to commandeer a dressing room, Claire rummaged in a wardrobe and pulled out a black brocade number with patent leather grommets. "I'm going to try this one, too. White underthings are so inconvenient when I'm trying to accomplish something at night."

Alice couldn't remember the last time she'd been as shocked as this. She knew Claire led something of a double life, but this? "You tend to flash your underthings when you're out?"

"Not on purpose. But think how useful this would be. I wonder if there is a black lace petticoat to go with it."

"There is." Alice pointed. "Good luck getting them past Davina."

Claire snorted. "She would have a right to speak if it were her money buying them. But it is not. With what I won last night, I can outfit us both and the girls besides, and still have enough for a new pair of boots."

"I'd like to know where you learned to play cowboy poker. Can you teach me?"

Claire's smile lit her eyes. "Of course. Though I suspect it may be a gift. Now, come. This nice, plain coutil should fit you."

Alice was shoved and tugged into the corset, and after that a series of petticoats and walking skirts and a couple of waists of French lawn embroidered within an inch of their lives ("Don't they have anything that's just white?" she said in despair, only to be blithely ignored). Then, just when she thought they might stop for tea or maybe something stronger, Davina halted outside a shop with a gilded sign that read REGINA COUTURE.

"Here we are," she told them. "Ball gowns to order."

"I'll just wait outside with Tigg," Alice said, a little desperately.

"Oh, no, you don't." Davina took her wrist and pulled her in. For such a tiny thing, she had a grip like a bear trap. Something like this dad-blasted corset— Alice could swear her ribs were actually grinding against one another under its merciless compression, never mind her lungs.

The Canton modiste was as delicate as a lily, but there was nothing delicate in the way she moved Alice in one direction then another, the measuring tape hissing this way and that upon her body. Good grief. Why did anyone need to know how big she was around the bum when it all got covered up with fifty yards of material anyway?

"Heavens, Alice, the last vestige of the bustle went out last year," Davina told her briskly. "Now one leads from the bosom, with slender hips and lots and lots of *froufrou* under the skirt from the knees down."

Alice was afraid to ask what *froufrou* was, exactly, in case it was something that hurt.

Silks and organdies and velvets became a blur, and when she couldn't answer or make a decision to save her life, Davina conferred with the modiste and made said decisions herself with the expertise of long practice.

Who knew she spoke Cantonese, too?

The only good part was when Alice's measurements were duplicated on the expandable body of a gleaming bronze automaton, whose arms and legs ratcheted in and out depending on the customer's stature. But even then, she was whisked away for a conference on bodices and forced to choose between puffed sleeves or cap, instead of examining the way they made the automaton duplicate her gait so the skirt would accommodate her stride.

At this very moment her father could be on a train for goodness knows where, and she was required to make a decision about sleeves?

Again she fought the desire to weep.

7

The dresses were delivered the next evening, two hours before they were to depart for the governor's mansion. The Mopsies both came to Davina's stateroom to watch the three of them dress.

"'is poor lordship," Maggie remarked. "Booted out of 'is own room?"

"His lordship has a dressing room of his own and many fewer yards of material to manage," Davina told them. "Make yourselves useful, girls, and help Claire and Alice with those skirts. No, Alice dear, it must go on over your head. Try not to disturb your hair, for we do not have time to put it up again."

"Ain't nothing disturbing this hair," could be heard from the depths of the aquamarine silk. "There's enough pins in my head to melt down for a pistol."

To Claire's relief, Maggie played ladies' maid for her while the countess and Lizzie saw to Alice, snapping snaps and tying tapes and fluffing organdy. This was nothing like the blue gown that Ned Mose had taken from her in Resolution. Her new gown was a deep emerald green that brought out the red lights in her auburn hair. A cluster of yellow velvet roses pulled up a flutter of pale gold organdy on each shoulder— and not much else. Claire had never exposed so much of her arms and bosom before, nor been laced in the new style of corset which actually gave her a bosom, not to mention a very tiny waist. The skirts belled out below, embroidered with yellow roses in a border a foot above the hem.

"Ent you pretty," Maggie said, standing back so Claire could admire the train behind her in the mirror. "You look like a daffodil, Lady."

Claire bent over and kissed her. "And you are kind to say so. Will you wind the pearls about my neck? At least they'll cover some of me."

It was the first time she had had the use of a full-length mirror since the riots in Wilton Crescent, and she almost didn't recognize herself. With her grandmother's ring and the St. Ives pearls, and a yellow velvet rose pinned next to her chignon, Claire had to admit that for the first time in her life, she was almost satisfied with what she saw in the glass.

What a pity Alice could not say the same.

Alice regarded herself with some dismay. The aquamarine blue brought out the vividness of her eyes, and her hair had been curled within an inch of its life and braided into a coronet about her head. Between two panels of cream lace on her bodice, ruched organdy arrowed into a satin belt whose circumference could almost be spanned with two hands. The skirts spilled to the floor in a froth of silk and organdy, but the countess had wisely ordered no train. It took practice to manage one, and Alice had had none.

Alice flicked at the blue feather curling around her ear and held in place with a diamond clip loaned by the countess. "This is gonna drive me batty." She gazed at herself in dismay. "I have no idea who that person is."

"Then you must become acquainted with her." Davina looked like a slender Roman goddess in draped crimson and cream silk. Upon her hair rested a diadem of tawny diamonds. "You must face the unhappy truth, Alice—you clean up very nicely."

"I can't breathe, I'm swimming in all these skirts, and if I shake my head, this stupid feather will make me sneeze."

"Chin up," Claire said. "You'll get used to it. Just remember to lift your hems going down stairs as well as up, and use the loop sewn into the skirt to lift it a little when you dance."

"Claire, nobody is going to dance with me."

"I'll lay you a bet that you're wrong."

"Name it."

"If you are a wallflower, I'll give you my landau."

All the color drained from Alice's face. "Are you crazy? You can't do that."

"Of course I can. I am not a simpleton—I know I cannot lose."

"I say you're going to. But if you win, I'll give you Nine."

Claire opened her mouth to refuse. The last thing she wanted about her was that eerie, eyeless presence, its servomotors whining every time it moved to do its owner's bidding. And then she caught herself. Besides the *Lass*, Nine was the creation Alice valued the most—the way Claire valued her own landau. It was a fair bet.

Fair, but rather like taking candy from a baby.

"Done."

"All right, you two," the countess said. "Find your cloaks and fans and let's be off."

When they entered the main salon, the gentlemen came to their feet. Claire could not tell which was more rewarding—Andrew's gobsmacked face as he realized who the lady in seafoam was, or the warmth in the eyes of Captain Hollys as he bent over her own hand.

"You will outshine every woman there," he murmured. "If you do not save a waltz on your card for me, I shall sign on with a mining crew and never come back."

"I must save you from that fate, then." Claire smiled at his nonsense. "The first waltz—and be forewarned that dancing is not my strong suit."

Andrew was still staring at Alice as if he had never seen her before.

Well, no one had ever seen *this* Alice before, but that was no reason to be rude and to make the color rise in her face.

"Captain Hollys, do rescue Alice. Andrew is making her uncomfortable."

The good captain did just that, and Andrew snapped out of it as Claire stepped into his line of sight. "Claire. You look very pretty. No rifle?"

Pretty. Hmph. So it was the first time he had ever told her she was pretty. But need he sound so— distracted?

"Not tonight. I trust that with Count von Zeppelin and the governor himself there, we will be troubled neither by thieves nor pirates. However, I do have an ivory hair pick if my assumptions prove incorrect."

"I knew I could depend on you."

She narrowed her gaze. "Andrew, do not stare. It is abominably rude."

"But can that really be Alice? I swear I thought her a complete stranger when she walked in."

"She will think *you* completely strange if you do not behave more naturally. I do hope you told her she was … pretty."

"I shall. The moment I secure the first dance."

Which rendered Claire speechless until they were well on their way. Government House lay in several acres of park and gardens that Davina told them duplicated exactly the estates of Sir Geoffrey Arundel, the governor, in Derbyshire, though sadly, the elms and maples of that county had not survived the winters of the Canadas and had been replaced by pine and fir. The gardens still glowed, however, in the middle of October, and—

"My goodness!" Claire exclaimed as the Bentley came to a stop under the portico. "Today is my birthday and I completely forgot until this moment."

"You've chosen a nice way to celebrate." The earl smiled at her and kissed her cheek. "Happy eighteenth, Lady Claire. All Edmonton will be at your feet by midnight, or I'm a sad representative of the species."

All Edmonton, it seemed, was in the ballroom, whirling in the patterns of the dance and chattering with such gusto that Claire could barely hear her own name as the majordomo announced it.

Earl and Countess Dunsmuir, of Hatley House, London, and Craigdarroch Park, Victoria.

Lady Claire Trevelyan, of Gwyn Place, Cornwall.

Miss Alice Chalmers, of the Texican Territory.

Mr. Andrew Malvern, B.S., R.S.E., of London.

Captain Ian Hollys, Baronet, Royal Aeronautic Corps, London.

Baronet? Heavens. What was a baronet doing flying a ship for an earl, companions at arms notwithstanding? She must find out during their waltz.

"So much for keeping a low profile," Alice whispered as they descended the grand staircase. She clutched a great handful of her skirts so hard they would be fearfully crushed. "I should've given an alias."

"I am very glad you did not," Davina said behind her. "I plan to introduce you to everyone, and I should hate to have to remember it."

Alice groaned, and before she could recover, Andrew had stepped up to write his name upon her card and then whirl her off onto the floor.

"Dear me," Davina murmured, watching. "I am afraid our attempts at teaching her a few steps this afternoon were … inadequate."

"Andrew will make sure she comes to no harm." And sure enough, when Alice turned the wrong way, Andrew tightened his hand upon her waist and steered her back into the frothing current of the dancers. "She must learn that the first rule of dancing is to allow the man to lead."

Davina looked amused. "Is this wisdom the product of personal experience?"

"I have not had much personal experience. But that is what the dance mistress at school always told us."

"Claire, you must not stare at them so."

"I am not staring. I am merely following the pattern of the dance and admiring the gowns of the other ladies."

"If you say so, dear. Come. I want John to introduce you to Count von Zeppelin."

With a determined effort, Claire pushed the image of Andrew's gloved hand on Alice's corseted back out of her mind. A dream was about to come true. She must not let that pleasure be muted by … by … well, she must not let it be muted.

She followed Davina and John to a small group standing next to the royal purple drapes that framed the tall windows overlooking the garden. A slender man in his fifties turned with a smile, his moustaches curled at the ends like the feather in Alice's hair. "John, *mein lieber Freund.* We meet again."

The two men embraced in the European fashion and John turned to indicate his wife. Davina smiled her charming smile and extended her hand in its pristine opera glove. "Count, it is lovely to see you again. I trust the Baroness is well? Did she accompany you on this trip?"

Von Zeppelin bent over her hand. "Alas, no. She has just become a grandmother for the third time, so she has stayed at home to assist our daughter."

"I hope you will give our best wishes to the new mother," John told him. "I would like to introduce you to a young lady who admires your work greatly. Count Ferdinand von Girsberg-Zeppelin, allow me to present Lady Claire Trevelyan, a dear friend of the family."

Claire dipped into a curtsey as the count bowed. "I am delighted to make your acquaintance, Lady Claire. Are you familiar with my ships?"

"I am indeed, sir," she said rather breathlessly. How charming he was! And what lively intelligence danced in those eyes, glinting through his formal manners. "In fact, I own stock in your company. I am quite certain that the Atlantic shipping lanes will belong to Zeppelin before many more months pass."

His eyebrows rose, and then he gave a bark of laughter. "She is prudent as well as pretty." He had not released her hand, and now he patted it. "I shall do my utmost not to disappoint you."

"Claire aspires to be an engineer, Ferdinand," John told him as he released her hand at last. "When we return to London, she will be entering the university to study."

"Is it so? What field interests you?"

He had not laughed. He had not even behaved as though this were unusual. What an extraordinary man. Of course, things might be different in Prussia. After all, Madame Bertha Mercedes ran the largest manufactory of steam engines in all of Europe. Perhaps women were accepted to the universities there as a matter of course.

"I hardly know which to choose, sir, so many interest me," she replied. "But since my travels have brought me here, I find my fascination with flight grows daily."

"One can hardly function in this vast land without some way to get about," he said, nodding in agreement. "A landau depends upon the existence of roads. A water vessel upon a river or sea. But an airship..." He gestured into the distance, as if his great ship were moored outside in the park. "An airship can go anywhere and be put to nearly any use in the service of mankind." His gaze returned to her. "I think you would be wise to pursue aeronautics, my dear."

"Thank you, sir. I appreciate your counsel."

"And do not forget the stock market." He laughed at his own joke, clicked his heels and bowed from the waist to her and Davina, and drew John aside.

"Come, Claire," Davina said. "I believe I see someone you know."

"But—"

"We will leave the gentlemen to themselves for a moment."

Claire resigned herself to being social when what she really wanted was to ask the count about his plans for a Zeppelin airfield outside New York, and follow that with her questions about the power cell and its ability to replace a steam engine. "Yes, Davina."

"Claire!" A small commotion seemed to be moving toward them, which resolved into none other than Peony Churchill. She flung herself upon Claire in a huge hug. "Oh, I am so glad to see you—Mama was quite convinced you had decided to stay in London and marry James Selwyn. See what a low opinion she has of you! But I knew differently." The laughter and joy faded from her face. "Claire? Are you quite all right?"

"Peony, did you not hear? James was killed in a train accident nearly two weeks ago."

Wide-eyed, Peony lifted her gloved fingers to her lips. "No, I did not hear. We have been in Esquimaux country, documenting conditions there for a petition to Her Majesty."

"I am very sorry to spring it on you in this fashion."

"Are—are you all right?"

There were a number of ways to answer this, but Davina took the matter out of her hands. "They had not been engaged for some weeks."

"Yes—yes, I know, but—" Peony suddenly seemed to realize to whom she was speaking. "Your ladyship, I do beg your pardon." She sank into a graceful curtsey. "What a pleasure to see you. When I got your note that Claire had arrived, I hardly knew what to think. For all I knew, she was in New York awaiting passage here after her voyage on *Persephone*."

"We must contrive a way to catch you up on my adventures," Claire said. "I need at least two hours, and we will not get that here."

"You certainly will not. I intend to see you dancing before this mazurka ends." Davina sounded very firm. "Come along, you girls. There is Mrs. Abercrombie. She owns the second largest diamond mine in the Canadas, and her unmarried sons dancing attendance upon her stand to inherit the lot."

"Who owns the largest one?" Claire asked.

"Why, John and I do, of course."

Within moments of their introduction, Davina made sure that Claire and Peony were launched onto the ballroom floor in a lively polka with the Abercrombie boys, and Claire had not another moment to think until Captain Hollys appeared at her elbow.

"This one, I think, is mine."

The boy—Conrad? Charles?—relinquished her with a smile, and Claire found herself slowing both steps and heart rate as she relaxed. What a blessing it was to dance with someone familiar.

"Small talk is so exhausting," she said on a long breath.

"I hope that is not meant to discourage me," Captain Hollys said, clearly taken aback.

"Oh, no, I didn't mean you." She smiled up into his eyes. "I merely meant I am glad to dance with someone I know. Remarks upon the weather and the state of the roads have their place, but one can only take them so far. Thank goodness the polka does not require much conversation."

"And were you required to make small talk with Count von Zeppelin? I saw his lordship introduce you."

"Is he not a fascinating man? Imagine being the one to invent something so marvelous as the airship—something we use for such magnificent purposes, and that we cannot imagine living without. I wonder if he realizes what a great thing he has done for mankind."

"If he does, it is likely he gives the credit to his engineering staff. He is not proud or self-involved."

"He advised me to take up aeronautical engineering when I return home."

"And is that your intention? You do not plan to stay here?" He moved her smoothly into a turn that would take them close to the French doors.

"Goodness, no. I was only to come for a few weeks, until—" *Until I turned eighteen and James could not force me to marry him.* No, it would not do to bring up old hurts. "Until John and Davina wished to return to London."

Another turn and he waltzed her out onto the terrace. The night air was cold, but braziers had been set up at intervals along the stone balustrade, so it was not unpleasant.

"Captain Hollys, Davina will be looking for me."

"I think we have been through enough together that you might call me by my Christian name. Ian."

She hardly knew where to look. Part of her wanted to flee to the crowded ballroom and find Peony—find Davina—find Alice and see if she was still dancing with Andrew.

Andrew. She was in love with Andrew, was she not? How did one know? With him, she did not have this fluttery, nervous feeling in her chest. Instead, she felt a sense of safety, of homecoming. To be sure, a Kensington address might elicit the same feeling—so that could not be a symptom of love at all.

And yet ... she had kissed Andrew, and it had been heaven.

She had kissed James, too, and it had been quite the opposite.

But now, here on this lovely terrace in a beautiful dress, she stood with a handsome man whose eyes told her he would very much like to be the third man to kiss her.

If she were in love with Andrew, then why was she filled with such ... anticipation ... at such a wicked prospect?

"Claire? What are you thinking?" He stood only inches from her, as though he might take her in his arms.

"I—I cannot say."

"You can say anything you like to me."

"You would be shocked."

"From the woman who jumped into a flash flood ... who sacrificed herself to save a friend's life ... who managed to find her way across miles of desert practically unaided ... I think not."

"Are you going to kiss me?"

Oh dear.

She had shocked him now.

8

"Should—should you like it if I did?" Captain Hollys was clearly attempting to regain his footing.

"Logically, you know, that question is unanswerable until after the fact."

That surprised a laugh out of him. "You are a minx. But I should have expected nothing less. You are quite right. But logic notwithstanding, perhaps you might tell me something."

It was not quite fair. She stood in the light of the brazier, while his face was shadowed. She stepped to the side so that both of them shared equally in the light. "Certainly."

"How does it stand between you and Andrew Malvern?"

She would give a great deal to know that answer herself. "We are very good friends. We owe each other our lives."

"Owing a life is not quite the same as promising one."

"We are not promised. I have been too recently engaged for that." Belatedly, it occurred to her that her affections were not really any of his business unless he planned to make them so. "What is your purpose in asking, Captain?"

"Ian. I should think that when a man and a woman discuss kissing under the light of the moon, his purpose should be rather obvious. You cannot doubt my feelings for you, Claire."

If her racing heart was any indication, that was a fact.

"But I should very much like to know yours."

"If—if I knew them myself, I might be able to tell you." Oh dear. She sounded like a perfect featherhead. Snouts would be ashamed of her. "But Captain—Ian— there must be many other ladies here tonight with whom you might have this discussion."

"I'm sure there are. But I am having it with you."

"Many others with whom your time would be better spent. Ian, I am not the best prospect in the world. If you knew—there are things that—" She took a frustrated breath at her own inability to speak her mind. For if she did, he would bolt into that ballroom and for the rest of the voyage she would have to endure the loss of his friendship and the pain of his avoiding her.

She rather enjoyed being the Lady of Devices. She suspected, however, that the Lady would not make the best choice of wife.

"If you mean to frighten me off, you will have to do a better job than this." He smiled down at her, and moved a step closer. The tips of his polished boots touched the hem of her gown. "I have nothing but admiration for you. If it is your family's straitened circumstances that you're thinking of, that does not matter to me. I am not without resources."

This reminded her of something she had meant to ask him. "How does a baronet come to be flying a ship for an earl, taking his orders and ferrying him about the world?"

"You did not know I am a baronet?"

"You wear no such insignia on your collar, sir. Merely an airman's wings and an officer's bars."

"And I am proud to wear them. For me, they are the important ones. As for taking the earl's orders, he takes plenty of mine, too. We have seen too much together and had each other's backs too many times to let something as unimportant as rank affect our relationship. I am, in fact, John's cousin."

"Ah." That certainly explained the ease with which he came and went among the members of the family. "But what of your responsibility to the baronetcy? Your home?"

"The estate is a small one, but it is in the capable hands of a steward I trust. And until now, I have not been overly concerned with taking up, as you say, my responsibility. Should I be shot down, the estate will be folded into the Dunsmuir holdings and managed as efficiently as they manage everything."

"I imagine your family would prefer you not be shot down. Though I must say, you came rather close on this voyage."

"My mother would agree. She would like you, I think."

I doubt that very much. My own mother has a difficult time with me.

"Ian, we cannot speak of these things."

"I mentioned that I had not thought much of my responsibility until now. But I could see myself at Hollis Park, settling down, with a gray-eyed girl who makes my heart lift like a ship each time she enters a room."

She must put a stop to this. Could he be about to propose? If so, she could not toy with a good man's affections in this manner.

"Ian, I am … encumbered. I have the girls to think of, and Tigg, and Jake." *And there is Andrew.*

"It is heroic, the way you look after those children. I can be of assistance to them. I believe I have already offered young Tigg a position. Our chief engineer, Mr. Yau, is standing ready to take him on as midshipman, if you and he agree, and Jake has the makings of a fine navigator now that he has decided which side he wants to fight on."

"You may have to fight Alice for him. He got us here, all the way from Reno, when none of us had ever been in these skies before."

"Do not change the subject."

"But I must," she said desperately. "I am so confused. One moment I'm a giddy girl, thinking you might kiss me. The next moment I'm as old and wise as a professor, thinking of my wards and their futures. And then there is my own future. If my application is accepted, I will be going to university when we return. I will not have time for—for courting. And in any case, you will be off to the Antipodes with the Dunsmuirs. It seems a hopeless case."

"Not hopeless," he said softly. "Never hopeless."

And before she could take another breath, he dipped his head and kissed her.

Knots in one's stomach were anatomically impossible. Yet there they were, growing tighter with every moment that Claire and the *Lady Lucy*'s captain did not reappear.

Finally Andrew had had enough.

He smiled at his partner, the daughter of one of the governor's cabinet ministers, bowed over her hand, and made his way through the crowd to the French doors. He stepped through just in time to see Captain Hollys gather Claire into his arms and kiss her.

Just the way he himself had kissed her, that day in the lab when she had been engaged to another.

And she allowed the captain's kiss, just the way she had allowed his.

The breath rushed out of him and he actually flinched, as if someone had delivered a sucker punch to his stomach. Blindly, he turned before they could see him, and stumbled back into the ballroom.

"Mr. Malvern!" Lady Dunsmuir emerged, smiling gaily, from between two large matrons. "Good heavens, sir, you look ill. Are you all right?"

He must pull himself together. He and Claire were not engaged. They were not even a couple. They were … whatever two people were who had shared a kiss and had both acknowledged that it meant something, however wrong it had been at the time. He had never had a chance to speak of what lay on his heart, and she had been too busy looking after the children and flying about the country saving people's lives to remember that she carried it in her hand.

"Mr. Malvern, I am becoming quite concerned."

He focused on Lady Dunsmuir, who was gazing up into his face, two worried lines between her brows. She laid a gentle hand upon the fine wool sleeve of his new dinner jacket. "Is there something outside that upset you?"

The breath he had managed to catch rushed out again. "Claire is kissing Captain Hollys on the terrace," he said dully.

"Ah." She pulled him aside, between the drapes and a huge potted topiary tree shaped like a series of lollipops piled one upon another. "I rather think Captain Hollys is kissing *her*. He has been smitten since the beginning of the voyage."

"The result is the same." He came to himself with the realization that discussing Claire with anyone else was the height of disloyalty.

Not that loyalty was counting for much anywhere he looked at the moment.

"Dance with me," she commanded, and when he obediently whirled her out onto the floor, the action seemed to clear his mind.

"I beg your pardon, Lady Dunsmuir. It is wrong of me to say such things."

"Why? You have her affections, I know. One does not sacrifice oneself to save a man's life if one does not care."

"She risked her life to save James Selwyn, and she did not care for him. It seems to be her way."

"She is brave and impulsive and fiercely loyal. And, I suspect, rather inexperienced when it comes to matters of the heart. You must make allowances, Mr. Malvern. She is only just eighteen."

"I know," he sighed. "I do not know whether to propose or pack her off to university."

"The latter is not within your control, is it?"

"No. Nothing is. I do not even have passage back to England—and if I did, I would not leave her."

"Do not worry on that account. You are most welcome to travel with us. *Lady Lucy* has any number of empty cabins."

"At this rate you will have to open your own shipping company."

She laughed. "I would say we already have one, but in truth, that is under negotiation."

"Oh?"

"I am not supposed to breathe a word, Mr. Malvern. You must not provoke me to be indiscreet."

"Then I shall not."

She allowed him several turns before she spoke again. "We are to tour our mine next week. Isobel Churchill has been agitating up in the north for indigenous control of natural resources, so it is becoming rather urgent that we go."

"Does your mine infringe on that control?" Somehow he had not suspected the Dunsmuirs of the exploitation with which Mrs. Churchill had inflamed the London papers.

"No indeed. Nobody wanted that land until diamonds were discovered—and even afterward, the land could not be bought or sold in any case. Instead, we have a most amicable agreement with the Esquimaux, but there are those who would argue it reaches further than it should." She laughed. "I fear I must remind them that those lands remain under indigenous control—merely in the hands of a member of a different nation."

This was such a mystifying statement that he could not even frame a way to question it. Instead, he changed the subject.

"Are you acquainted with Count von Zeppelin?"

"I am indeed. We have visited Schloss Schwanenburg—his estate in Munich—on a number of occasions. In fact, I believe John is to stand as godfather to the newest grandchild. We will be going to Prussia for the christening before long, I daresay."

"Perhaps you might introduce me? I saw that Claire met him, but I should very much like to as well."

"Of course. I shall have John make the two of you known to one another. I imagine you will have no end of things to talk about."

"Thank you, Lady Dunsmuir."

"Oh, goodness. You must call me Davina. I will not have my friends standing upon ceremony."

"And I am Andrew."

The orchestra swung into the final figure and in moments ended the waltz with a flourish. Andrew could not resist the temptation to scan the crowd once more over the top of Davina's tiara.

There.

Claire stood with Peony Churchill and Alice, laughing over something the latter had said. Peony slipped an arm around both their tightly corseted waists and they moved in the direction of the refreshments. Captain Hollys was nowhere to be seen and Andrew hated himself for even caring.

"You see?" Davina said as he kissed the back of her gloved hand. "She is a girl yet in some ways. She needs those ways, Andrew. Do not rush her." She squeezed his hand. "I will find John and see about that introduction."

And she slipped into the crowd, a small, regal figure whom he had no doubt the leaders of industry obeyed without a moment's hesitation.

Do not rush her.

He did not want to rush Claire in the least. In fact, he wished she would slow down before she left him behind altogether.

9

Claire hardly knew what she was doing or saying—she was only thankful Peony did. She and Alice nodded and smiled at the people to whom they were introduced, allowed gentlemen to claim the dances on their cards, and when those were full, allowed other gentlemen to provide them with ices and sparkling champagne.

"Not too much of that," Peony warned her, "or you'll forget which end is up."

"I have no idea which end is up as it is," Claire said without thinking, and Alice, who was looking much more cheerful now than she had at the beginning of the evening, smiled at her.

"As long as Captain Hollys does," she teased.

"Oh, do give over. Though I am grateful you turned up just then."

"Why, can't the man kiss?" Alice's eyes were big and blue and innocent over the rim of her champagne glass.

"He certainly can. But what does one say afterward? That is where the two of you saved me."

"If you don't know what to say afterward, it means two things." Peony tossed back an iced oyster with the finesse of one who had done this many times. "Either you're overcome with maidenly confusion, or you have no conversation with the gentleman anyway."

"Neither of those things are true in my case, so your theory needs work." Claire considered the oysters and turned away, shuddering. "I have no difficulty discussing any number of subjects with Captain Hollys under normal circumstances, and I am not confused."

"Liar." Peony's eyes sparkled. "If I had to choose between two handsome men possessing both intellect and resources, I would be no end of confused."

"I'd be happy with just one," Alice said to the ice sculpture of a bear in the center of the table.

At which point Claire spotted Davina talking with her husband, Andrew, and Count von Zeppelin. She put down her glass so firmly that the champagne sloshed onto the damask tablecloth, and took two steps over to join them.

And stopped. Of course she should include Alice. She turned back. "Alice, come and be introduced to Count von Zeppelin."

Alice's eyes grew wide in truth this time. "What, me? Why should he want to know me? I'm no one."

"Nonsense." Claire linked her arm in Alice's and pulled her along while Peony turned her attention to some serious flirting with a gentleman who also liked oysters. "I've already won Nine from you. Are you going to make me wager again? Because I will bet Nine back that the count will be delighted to meet you."

"You don't have to do that. You won fair and square."

"Then stop saying such untrue things. Anyone in this room would do the same—and has, if Peony is any judge. She told me while you were in the powder room that you have made quite a number of conquests."

"So have you. I wonder what Captain Hollys and Mr. Malvern think about that?"

But Claire was saved from a reply when Davina turned to them both and introduced Alice to the count without a moment's prompting.

"Alice has a great deal of natural ability as an engineer," Claire told him as he straightened from bowing over her gloved hand. Alice had blushed as red as one of the mesas overlooking Resolution, so to give her a moment to recover, Claire went on, "She has created nine automatons."

"Have you indeed." Von Zeppelin took her in with renewed interest. "I have noticed that automata are much more in demand here on this continent than they are in Europe or England. Can you enlighten me as to why?"

Alice gulped at being asked for an informed opinion by a man she held in such esteem. Claire supposed it would be akin to being asked by Apollo if she could suggest a more efficient way to travel across the sky than by sun chariot.

"I—I suppose it's because there aren't so many people over here to hire on as servants and such," she finally managed. "Folks find it easier to mechanize their help."

"Is it so? Does this theory apply in the larger cities, where there are people looking for employment?"

"It depends on the employment," Alice said, warming to her subject now that he seemed honestly interested and not merely making polite conversation. "There are more people exploring resources than cleaning latrines, and more women interested in engineering and science than being housemaids. Not," she said hastily, "that there is anything dishonorable in being a housemaid. My ma was one, once. But if those tasks are taken care of by an automaton, and her family has the resources, then a girl can look to what interests her. That's what I think, anyway." The tumble of words slowed on the rocks of propriety. "I can't speak for the whole territory."

"I think you have spoken very well," Davina said. "Can every household afford one?"

"It depends. All the rich folks seem to have 'em."

"And what of families that do not have the resources?" Andrew asked. "Are they a status symbol?"

"Maybe," Alice allowed. "But mine are just useful. I build 'em with what I have on hand, so that often determines what they'll be used for."

"Nine, for instance, has magnetic feet for locating items buried underground," Claire put in helpfully.

"Six and Seven work in the engine room, Eight has his hoses, and Four—"

"We used him for an engine housing, I'm afraid," Andrew said with a laugh. "We were stranded in the Idaho Territory and he sacrificed himself to get us back in the air."

The governor appeared behind John's shoulder. "Earl Dunsmuir, Count von Zeppelin, I hate to tear you from your lovely companions, but we are meeting in the library. May I show you the way?"

Claire and Alice smiled at the reluctance with which the count allowed himself to be led away from a discussion that clearly interested him. Claire was rather more interested in what the meeting might be about.

"Men," Davina said. "How can they think about business when the orchestra plays so divinely?"

Andrew gave her an odd look before he said, "Perhaps you would honor me with another dance?"

And then Claire and Alice were claimed, and it was not until the evening ended that they saw the count again. They were putting on their wraps in the great entry hall with its black-and-white marble parquet when he came out of another door swinging his driving coat on.

"Lady Dunsmuir," he said, "might I offer your protegées a ride to the airfield? I am most interested in continuing our discussions about automata. You too, Mr. Malvern. I am a great reader of your monographs and would be honored if you would accompany us."

"You—you drive yourself, sir?" Andrew said.

"Certainly. My captains will follow in their own landau. They think I drive *zu schnell*—how do you say? Too fast."

Claire bit back an eager acceptance, and turned to Davina. "May we?" After all, they had come with the earl's party and were his responsibility.

"You will be careful with them, Ferdinand," Davina said, half teasing, half stern. "They are precious to us."

The count bowed, sweeping his beaver topper from his head. "As my own daughters, my dear lady."

"Then you must enjoy the ride, girls. We will see you later at the *Lady Lucy*."

Andrew handed Alice down the steps and into the rear compartment, and Claire seated herself in the front next to the count.

"This is a *Daimler*," Alice breathed, looking about her as if she were in a palace.

"Eight pistons," the count said proudly, flicking levers and spinning a great wheel next to his knee. "She'll do nearly sixty miles in an hour, if the roads are good."

"Sixty...! Oh sir, when we get to the airfield, may we please look in the engine compartment?" Claire begged, and was thrown back against the seat cushions when the Daimler took off like a horse from the starting gate.

"I will give you a personal tour of it tomorrow," the count assured her. "Now, *Fraulein* Alice, I beg you to tell me more about these automata of yours. You say the one has magnetic feet?"

Claire relaxed in the seat next to him as the count kept one eye on their route over the prairie and the other on Alice as he peppered her with questions. When he had extracted her promise of a demonstration in exchange for a good look at the engine in daylight, he said, "It is my belief that man was not created for drudgery, but for genius, and craft, and good, profitable work. Why should the factories not be run by automata? Why should machines not be operated by machines?"

Claire had never devoted much thought to the subject of mechanized labor, but clearly, the great man had. On the other hand—

"But, Count, machines cannot solve problems, or take a line of action to a logical conclusion. They can only obey."

Andrew chuckled. "I could say the same about many a fellow student in school."

"Yes, but those students are likely not inventing great devices in manufactories."

"God has given us many gifts," the count said, "among them creativity, logic, and consideration for the needs of others. But I am not speaking of these. I am speaking of rote tasks on the manufactory floor.

Why encumber a man with such when he could be in the laboratory, conducting experiments?"

Something about this argument bothered Claire, but she could not put her finger upon it. She gazed into the darkness, thinking, as the landau's lanterns illuminated the road ahead. *Road* was a generous term. The landau took its bumps and potholes in stride, its great wheels floating over them as if they were nothing. The moon had moved across the sky to the point where Claire could tell it was very late. Past midnight, at least. She hoped the Mopsies had not waited up to hear about the ball.

"Count, do you not think that—"

He cursed as a deer or an antelope of some kind bounded into the lamplight and across the road, and hauled back on the bar that controlled the rate of steam. Simultaneously, the sheet of isinglass next to her ear exploded inward, showering her with glittering fragments. She screamed and leaped to her left as the landau swerved and hit the bank on the driver's side. The heavy Daimler's nose lunged at the sky and then dropped them half on top of the bank, the engine laboring at nearly full throttle as its wheels thrust them up and over the other side.

The deer bounded right, then left, and then disappeared into the darkness.

"Count!" Andrew cried. "What are you doing?"

And then Claire saw the blood.

The right side of his head was awash with it, dripping black into his pristine collar and soaking the gray wool of his driving coat.

"Count!" she shrieked. "Andrew, he's hurt!"

Without a second thought, she grabbed the acceleration bar from hands that had convulsed around it. Between her position and her inability to move the unconscious man, it was awkward, but she pulled back on it with all her strength.

The Daimler had been moving at a speed of at least forty miles to the hour. The bar fought her, bucking and shuddering, but she did not release it. Instead, she threw her weight against it, wedging herself against the instrument panel and trying to gain purchase on the floor.

"Claire, the wheel!" Alice shouted. "You must turn the wheel to reduce the steam pressure!"

"I don't have another hand," she managed on a gasp.

Alice flung herself over the back of the seat and, hanging bent in half, feet in their delicate dancing slippers braced against the bench, reached for the wheel and spun it with both hands.

Something groaned deep in the belly of the landau and dual clouds of steam hissed out of both sides of the bonnet.

It seemed like an hour before the great landau came to a reluctant, canted stop against a small rise crowned by a stubby tree that had seen one too many winters. With a sigh, the vehicle settled onto its wheels, as blown as a horse.

Andrew gripped Alice's waist and assisted her to slide back against him, and all three of them pushed open the wings and scrambled outside.

"Alice, grab one of the lanterns," Claire said. "Andrew, help me get the count out where we can see him. Oh, please don't let him be dead!"

Andrew slipped his arms under those of the unconscious man, and they pulled him from the Daimler. Once he was laid out on the long grass of the prairie, Andrew laid an ear upon his chest.

"Alive," he said, and Claire's knees went weak.

Alice bent down with the lantern. "This don't make a lick of sense," she said, "but it looks like he got creased by a bullet."

"A bullet!"

"You're right, that doesn't make any sense," Andrew agreed. "But only because we don't have all the facts. But they must wait for another time. At the moment we must act, and quickly."

"We have to get him back to Government House," Alice told him in a tone that said there was no other option. "It's a good couple of miles, but he needs a doctor, pronto."

"Where are his captains?" Claire said suddenly. "They can help us. They may even have medical training."

"I'll fetch them." Andrew leaped up. "See if you can stop that bleeding."

The sound of his dress shoes thudding on the ground faded into the dark. Claire scrabbled under her skirts. "At last. A sensible use for *froufrou.*" She ripped an entire row of eyelet ruffle from her innermost petticoat and wrapped it carefully around the count's head. "I need something to secure it with. Do you have a pin?"

"Nothing," Alice said in despair, waving her hands at the frothing pool of skirts. "This is the most useless outfit in the world."

"My kingdom for my corselet and all its pouches. Never mind. If you would be so kind as to remove the ivory pick from my hair, I shall thread it through these holes. At least this fine cotton will provide some protection and absorb the blood."

Alice pulled the pick from her chignon and sucked in a horrified breath. "Claire, you're bleeding yourself!"

Claire secured the count's makeshift bandage before she lifted a hand to her cheek and brought it away smeared with blood. "It doesn't hurt, and I am fully conscious," she said in a wondering tone. Would she collapse without warning at any moment? "It must have been the isinglass window. Is it very bad?"

"Head wounds bleed like a son of a gun," Alice said quietly, her fingers gentle as she investigated. "There's a lot of glass in your hair, and a bunch of tiny cuts, but nothing big. The count's in much worse shape. If it was a bullet, and even if it did just graze him, we have to act fast."

"Alice, the ground is freezing. We must get him into the back of the landau and cover him up."

"You're right. Come on. Lucky job he ain't built like that Lord Arundel. We'd never manage it."

Claire dropped the poor man's feet once, but together, with much huffing and a few whispered curse words from Alice, they got Count von Zeppelin into the rear compartment of the landau. Claire activated the storage door in the side, and there, like a miracle, was a heavy traveling blanket and a can of kerosene for the lanterns.

"At least we won't be left in the dark." Alice refilled the Daimler's lantern carefully while Claire tucked the blanket around the count's unresisting form. "Where is Andrew, for gosh sakes? This man doesn't have any time to waste."

They could hear nothing but the sound of the wind, whistling through the dead branches of the tree.

"He should have been back by now." Claire closed the compartment door with a *thunk*.

Alice gazed at her, eyes huge and becoming increasingly frightened in the lamplight. "I didn't hear a shot."

"We didn't before, either. The window simply blew inward with the force of the projectile."

"It would've got you and him both if he hadn't swerved for that antelope."

"Alice?"

"Yes?"

"Perhaps they're still out there. Perhaps you should put out all the lamps. We are not, after all, so far from where it hit us."

"I've got a better idea. Let's go get Andrew and get out of here. Can you pilot this thing?"

If only she'd watched more closely as the count had initiated the ignition sequence! But no, she had been too bothered by the thought of Andrew and Alice alone in the rear compartment to pay much attention.

Of all the silly geese ...

Never mind. She must focus on the task at hand. How different could the Daimler's instrument panel be from that of her own Henley Dart?

"Yes," she said.

"I don't see we have a choice. The count has to get to a doctor, and the longer we wait, the poorer his chances are. If we can't find Andrew, why, we ... we ..." Her voice faded.

The same dreadful thoughts hovered in both their minds. What if he had been shot, too, as he came over the rise? And why had the count's captains not come to their aid as soon as they saw the Daimler go off the road? In Claire's mind, there was only one answer. If Andrew had shared their fate, she did not think she would be able to bear it.

"Come." She shook away the ugly thought before it could root in her mind and terrify her. "You must ride in the rear compartment and hold his head."

Alice climbed in and gingerly took Count von Zeppelin's head into her silken lap, heedless of the blood. "This has to be one of the most valuable heads in all the world," she muttered. "How'd this come about, I'd like to know?"

Claire tried to remember the order in which he had flipped levers and spun the wheel. After a number of false starts, not to mention some suggestions from the back, the mighty boiler rumbled to life and steam began to issue from the pipes extending out the side. She leaned on the acceleration bar and spun the wheel to give it more steam, and they began to roll.

With the other hand, she guided the landau into an arc that took them back the way they had come, and in a moment, they half rolled, half slid onto the road.

She had underestimated the other landau's location, and they were now behind it. But where were—

"There's Andrew," Alice said urgently, craning her neck to be able to see over the padded cushions. "Thank God."

"What is he doing?" Claire murmured, half to herself. For he was not administering aid to anyone. He crouched against the wing of the captains' landau, head down, his body stiff and focused into the distant night. Cold fear cascaded into her stomach.

Claire piloted the landau as close as she dared. "Andrew!" she called through the broken window. "Are you all right? Where are the men? Come quickly—we must get the count—"

Without warning, the rearmost window exploded and Claire distinctly felt something thud into the cushions upon which she sat.

Alice screamed and Andrew jerked upright as though he had been struck by lightning. He flung himself into the front compartment, shouting, "Go! Go!"

"But the captains—"

"Go!"

Claire leaned on the acceleration bar and the engine coughed, like a horse who has been struck with the crop when it expected to stop and nibble the grass. It had gathered a small head of steam while she had paused it and forgotten to release the pressure valve, and with this, they leaped down the road at a head-long pace.

With one hand on the steering wheel and the other on the acceleration bar, Claire peered wildly into the night hoping nothing would smash their one remaining lantern.

"What happened?" she managed between chattering teeth.

"Dead, both of them." Andrew's tone was grim, his face carved in stone at the edge of her vision. "And while I was searching for signs of life, a bullet missed me by half an inch." He raised his arm. "It passed right through my sleeve. The second one went over my head when I ducked behind the landau."

Claire could not look, though she heard Alice gasp. Her gaze was fastened on the ribbon of road ahead and she could not look away.

"But who—how could anyone—"

"I do not know, but I fully intend to find out," Andrew said. "It could only have been someone who knew when our party would leave Government House—and that the count would be piloting. For it must be he who was their target."

"An assassination?" Alice squeaked.

"With a silent weapon." Claire risked a glance at Andrew. "You heard no report, such as gunpowder would make?"

"None. Nothing but the whine of the bullet, and then the impact."

"So no indication of where the gunman stood."

"We must return in the morning to search the area, and notify the authorities."

"We can't go back to Government House," Alice said. "Not now. It's too risky."

"We can only hope there is medical aid on the count's airship." Claire pushed the acceleration bar out as far as it would go, and they flew through the night on the landau's towering wheels as though the hounds of hell were after them.

10

Claire had barely brought the Daimler to a hissing, growling stop—something must have been punctured under the chassis during their plunging flight to the airfield—when it was swarmed by the count's men. In less time than she would ever have thought possible, he had been removed from the rear seat and borne aboard the ship.

She was bundled off to sick bay herself, and a stinging concoction applied to her temple and cheek where the isinglass fragments had struck her.

"You were lucky," the officer murmured, dabbing the excess away and applying sticking plasters. "The hood of your cloak protected your arms and shoulders, and the cuts are not deep."

"I wish I could say the same for the count." Claire's voice wobbled. "Please, can you tell me if he will be all right?"

"It is my first concern, after your welfare," he said gallantly. "Please, rest for a moment and I will find out. In the meanwhile, *mein Herr und Fraulein*, you are certain you are not injured in any way?"

From the white-sheeted bunks next to her own, Alice shook her head and Andrew said, "No, not at all. Lady Claire and the count suffered the brunt of the first attack. When the captains tried to come to his assistance, they were shot. By the time I reached them, it was already too late."

"War das so?" The second officer's gaze hardened. "We will send a detachment. They will bring in our fallen companions and search for the ones who did this."

Claire had a feeling they would find as little evidence of anyone being there as they'd had warning of a shot, but all the same, she was glad that men of competence were swinging into action. This was an international crime, she thought, struggling to keep her mind clear. If the count took a turn for the worse, the consequences could be grave.

There might even be war, if Prussia blamed the government of the Canadas.

She did not want to be in a war. She wanted to go home, to the cottage by the river, to Carrick House, to Gwyn Place …

"Claire! *Herr Doktor*, she is going to faint."

The darkness feinted at the corners of her vision, and no matter what she did, she could not stop its advance.

When she opened her eyes several minutes later, Alice's and Andrew's anxious faces were hovering over her. "Claire? Can you hear me?"

"Yes. I am perfectly well." She struggled to sit up on the pristine white pallet. "I was merely overcome for a moment." Her head still swam a little, but if she said so, they would fuss, and this was no time for fussing. "Have we heard anything of the count's condition?"

The medical officer assisted her to a sitting position, honorably keeping his gaze averted from her ankles until she had settled her velvet skirts over them.

"Our ground captain has sent out men to the site, *Fraulein*. Also, I have a report from my superior that he has examined *der Landgraf*—the count, I should say. You did well to bind up the wound and get him here so quickly. The loss of blood was not as great as we feared, and my superior is stitching him up now. He will have a most interesting scar that will fortunately be healed by the time we all must face the Baroness."

"Is she a woman of character, then?" Alice asked.

"She is, *Fraulein*. Like a lioness in defense of those she loves. It is indeed fortunate she was not in the landau with you, for she would have leaped out and hunted these men herself."

"I think I would like the Baroness," Claire said, and winced when her attempt at a smile pulled at the sticking plaster on one side.

"I see some similarities," the officer allowed.

From the gangway area on the deck below, they heard a commotion, and in a moment, Captain Hollys appeared in the door of sick bay. A soldier panted up behind him. "My apologies, *Herr Doktor*, but he would not wait to be announced."

"Claire!" Ian exclaimed. "What on earth happened? Her ladyship was ready to send out a search party, and when the messenger came from the *Margrethe*, she—"

"Get out o' the way!"

A second commotion could be heard in the hall, and like a pair of jack-in-the-boxes, the Mopsies evaded the grip of someone behind them, popped past Captain Hollys's legs, and flung themselves on Claire. "Lady, we was so worried!" Maggie exclaimed. "Her ladyship's fit to be tied."

Claire gathered them both close. What a gift it was to feel their warm bodies, their coats still bearing the night's chill, but the warmth of love and concern flowing between the three of them acting like a tonic to her spirits. Hot tears welled in her eyes and she buried her face in Maggie's hair as she blinked them back.

Captain Hollys appeared to be restraining himself with some difficulty—but whether it was to castigate the Mopsies or to fling himself to his knees and hug her, she could not tell. Perhaps that was just as well, though it was very dear of him to be concerned.

"Her ladyship will be even more so when she finds you have followed me over here," was the only observation he allowed himself, however.

"O' course we followed you," Lizzie told him. "'Ow else was we to find where the Lady was?"

In the face of such irreproachable logic, he merely said to Claire, "Lord Dunsmuir has sent me to escort you personally back to the *Lady Lucy.*" He glanced at the medical officer. "And we have dispatched a messenger to Government House by air, informing Lord Arundel of this outrage. Be assured that we will not rest until these miscreants are brought to justice."

Ignoring Andrew's protests, Captain Hollys offered Claire his arm and was all solicitude during the measured walk over to the *Lady Lucy.*

"Count von Zeppelin is fortunate that his ship is fitted out so well," Andrew said tightly as its golden fuselage came into view. "That medical bay is the very last word in modern equipment."

"The *Landgrafin Margrethe* is a military flagship," the captain said, not relinquishing Claire's arm in the slightest. "It was named for the count's mother and is the crown jewel of the Prussian fleet."

"Wot's a Prushin?" Lizzie wanted to know.

"Prussia is the European kingdom on the other side of the English Channel, past France," Claire told her. The cold night air was invigorating, and she was feeling much less woozy and sick. "We must add geography to your studies in mathematics, mechanics, and language arts, I see."

"So wot's 'e doin' 'ere, then, this Zeppelin cove, besides getting shot at?"

"The shooting does change the answer to that quite substantially," Andrew mused aloud.

"Perhaps it has something to do with his meeting with Lord Dunsmuir and Lord Arundel at the ball." Claire squeezed Lizzie's fingers to let her know that her questions had not been impertinent. "Lizzie, you have quite the discerning eye for politics."

The eleven-year-old snorted. "'E's a long ways from 'ome, that's all."

"Like we are," Maggie put in. "Oh! Alice!"

Claire turned. "Alice?" But there she was, walking next to them, perfectly safe. "Goodness. Do not frighten me so, Maggie. I have had quite enough excitement for tonight, thank you."

"Sorry, Lady. I only meant that a messenger come for Alice earlier, after supper. Tigg talked to 'im, and 'e said to give you this."

She dug in the pocket of her fashionable short coat with its rounded collar and bows on each pocket. The note was crumpled, but Alice was able to read it in the lamp light from *Lady Lucy*'s mooring mast.

She folded it up. "I have to go, just as soon as I get out of this confounded rig."

And without another word or a good-night or any such civility, she hurried across the field to the *Stalwart Lass,* hauled up her skirts, and leaped aboard without benefit of gangplank.

"Who does she know here who would be sending her notes?" Andrew wondered aloud.

"Perhaps it is someone she met at the ball." Captain Hollys assisted Claire up the gangway into the warm familiarity of the ship. "May I do anything else for you, Lady Claire?"

"You have already done too much." Claire gave him an equally warm smile. "Thank you for coming to our aid."

He flushed, and would have said more, had not Maggie tugged on Claire's cloak. "Best come and see 'er ladyship before she 'as us all skinned alive."

Laughing, Claire allowed herself to be led into the salon, and in explaining the night's misadventures to the Dunsmuirs, and speculating on the possible reasons for them, her questions about the author of Alice's note completely slipped her mind.

Alice let out a sigh of relief as she struggled out of the corset, and resisted the temptation to kick it across the cabin. It had cost too much and was far too beautiful for such treatment. But like many such things, it was hard to live with and belonged in a closet. Besides, where she was going, it would be more of a hindrance to useful movement than anything else.

The note had been brief.

> *Heard a word or two on the subject you're interested in. Come by anytime.*
> *M.E.*

She buttoned her denim pants with a sense of relief at their comfortable familiarity. After she heard what Mike Embry had to say, then maybe she could shake a leg out of this place and find somewhere she didn't have to look at certain people queening it in high society and being handed about by handsome men, in places where certain other people didn't belong and never would.

She shrugged on a flight jacket and rammed her Remington 44-40 into the long inside pocket. She didn't usually go armed, but after tonight, lugging around the extra weight might prove to be worth it. When she jumped down onto the field, she nearly screamed and whipped the blessed thing out when a shadow moved under the *Lass*'s fuselage.

"Who's there?"

Andrew Malvern stepped into the cone of light cast by the lamp on the mooring mast. "I beg your pardon if I startled you."

Alice released her grip on the Remington with a sigh. Her heart rate, however, didn't change one bit.

"I thought you were explaining tonight's goings-on to the countess."

"Claire is quite capable of doing so, and in any case, it's not likely she'll be allowed to set foot on the ground again tonight, if her ladyship has anything to say about it." He matched her long-legged stride even though he couldn't know where she was going. "In fact, if *Lady Lucy* doesn't lift in the morning, I'll be very surprised. Lady Dunsmuir will not allow any danger to young Will, even if it's five miles off."

"And she thinks the diamond mine will be safer?"

"It is theirs. I imagine so."

He paused to turn his head her way, but she kept her gaze resolutely forward. She could hear the plinking of a pianoforte now, so it seemed Mike hadn't closed the Tiller yet.

"May I ask why you're headed to the Tiller, Alice?"

She didn't know what he was up to, traipsing around the airfield with her, and she had no business being glad about it. Maybe it was a thing men did after nearly being shot.

"I have business to take care of."

"Would you allow me to accompany you? It does not seem safe for a young lady to be going about by herself at nearly two in the morning."

For answer, she slid the Remington partway out of her jacket.

"Oh." It took him a moment to recover. "You know how to use that thing?" Then he shook his head. "I'm sorry. That was stupid. Of course you do. You and Claire both know how to take care of yourselves and make yourselves useful, whereas I must be satisfied with getting in the way and being rescued repeatedly."

She slowed under the lamps Mike had burning outside the door of the half-round pipe shape of the honkytonk.

"Of course you're useful." She could hardly credit what she'd heard. "You're one of the most brilliant scientific minds in England—you heard Count von Zeppelin. Even he reads your monographs. Why on earth would you think that? It wasn't your fault some crazypate shot at you."

"Perhaps not." He seemed to find the posts that held up the awning over the door highly interesting. "But the fact remains that my usefulness on this voyage has been limited to partnering ladies in the ballroom and not much else."

"There's men who make an entire career of that," she said dryly. "Stop feeling sorry for yourself, man. If you're coming in, then fine—do me a favor and keep your ears open. There are who knows how many gunmen and only two honkytonks on this quadrant of the field, if you get my meaning."

One eyebrow rose. It was such an appealing sight that she turned away and grasped the door handle.

"You mean that there's a fifty percent chance that whoever shot at us might have come here for a drink to celebrate?"

"See?" She grinned over her shoulder as she pushed the door open. "You're not so useless after all."

He straightened his shoulders and waited outside for a count of ten while she let the door swing shut behind her. When she looked again, he had come in and was making jokes with a group of mechanics.

Her idol thought he was useless. Honestly, it was no wonder she stuck to automatons. People were too hard to understand.

She bellied up to the bar and held up a finger when Mike glanced over. "Mescal?" he asked, setting a glass down in front of her.

"Not a chance. Do you have elderberry cordial?"

He snorted. "Use it for flavoring."

"One, please."

Shaking his head, he unearthed a bottle of cordial from beneath the bar. The smell of it reminded her of the days when she'd been a little girl, curled up in her mother's boudoir while they waited for her pa to get home from the mine. They'd share a glass of cordial and tell silly stories and forever after, she would miss the woman her mother had been. Once her pa had gone for good, Nellie had changed her name back to Benton, found her way to Resolution, grown a carapace over her heart, and taken up the only profession open to her.

Mike filled the glass with purple liquid. "Been talking to some of the fellows hereabouts. It seems a mechanic with one blind eye was working the cargo ships a couple years ago."

"Cargo ships? For the mines?"

Mike nodded. "Not much grows up that way, nor eats what grows neither, except for three months in summer. The cargo ships keep foodstuff and parts coming in, except for when the weather closes everything down from November to April. Seems this man was working the routes keeping the boats in the air."

"Is he still?"

With a shrug, Mike topped up her glass, though she'd only taken a sip or two. "No telling. Other than that, I couldn't dig up a word. Either your pa didn't associate much, or he just ain't been around for folks to notice."

With a nod, she swallowed half the drink. "I appreciate your taking the time."

"You remember what I said."

With a smile, she repeated, "'Tell Nellie Benton Mike Embry sends his regards.' You ought to take a trip to Resolution, Mike, and tell her yourself. She runs the Resolute Rose—you can't miss it. It's the only garden of desert flowers in town."

"I might just do that if I get tired of this place. Cold gets to me in the winter, and it's coming on. Ships'll be clearing out soon."

"Clearing out?"

He stopped wiping glasses and frowned at her. "You mean the port authority didn't tell you? Foreign ships got to lift and be out of here before the snow flies; otherwise, they're grounded until spring."

And the countess wanted to fly even farther north? How come nobody in their party seemed to know this? "Because of the snow?"

"Nope. The ice. Behaves peculiar-like up here. Ships get coated with it and the gas bags contract. If the foreign ships didn't leave, we'd have a field full of ice balloons, until the weight collapsed the fuselages and crushed the gondolas under 'em. And don't get me started on the icicle problem."

Alice did not want to know about the icicle problem. Foreign capital or not, San Francisco was beginning to look mighty good.

"Believe me, a couple of days at the mines and I'll be heading south for warmer winds." She knocked back the last of the cordial, laid down a coin, and pushed away from the bar. "Thanks, Mike. I'll write to my ma before I leave, I promise."

"We're square, then," he said, nodding. "Good hunting."

She worked her way slowly to the back, as though she were looking for someone, keeping her ears wide open to the conversations going on all about her. Most of them were about the cards—the weather—Sherwood Leduc—the latest accident in the mines.

She slowed and bent to adjust a loose bootlace.

"—couldn't save him," a grizzled engineer said into his beer, pushing his goggles further up on his battered hat. "He was a good friend, as miners go. Not a waste of oxygen like some."

"Something's gotta be done," said the man next to him. "Dunsmuir mine's had a good record a long time. Somebody's behind this, you mark my words."

"All we'll be marking is a target on your back, you don't keep your voice down," another man muttered. "I say it's Sherwood Leduc."

The engineer snorted. "He's small fry. A thug. You think he's got the muscle to blow up them big engines? We're talking serious money—and serious engineering skill." He noticed Alice kneeling on the floor between the tables. "You lost something, missy?"

She tugged her bootlaces and stood. "Nope. Just trying to keep from falling on my face. You fellows from the Dunsmuir mine?" No answer, just a lot of black suspicion. "I'm looking for a man with one blind eye, said to work the cargo ships up that direction. Ever seen him?"

"What, did he leave you with a pup?" the man next to him said, laughing.

"Naw, I *am* his pup." She grinned, as if he'd told a good joke. "Got his talent for mechanics and figured I'd try and partner up, make a living maybe."

The engineer snorted. "You'd do better here. Mine's no safe place for a woman."

"A man neither," somebody muttered. "Not lately, anyhow."

"Oh?"

But the conversational stream, such as it was, dried up to nothing, and Alice was forced to take herself off.

Andrew waited outside. "All right, then?"

"I guess. Seems the Dunsmuirs have trouble up at their mine."

"I got that impression as well. Something about an explosion."

"One of the big engines—whatever that means. General feeling is it would take a lot of money and skill to pull off such a thing."

Andrew walked beside her, his back straight, his gaze moving constantly from fuselage to wheels to gangways as they passed them. "I wonder if sabotage is a normal part of mining operations?"

"Doesn't sound like it. They said the Dunsmuirs have a good record."

"Until now. When they happen to be in the country, and Isobel Churchill is agitating the Esquimaux nation for indigenous rights."

"You think them Esquimaux got that kind of money?" In her experience, the Injuns kept themselves to themselves and didn't care much what the Territorial folks did, as long as they left them alone.

"I know nothing about them, Alice. But it might be worth a word in the earl's ear."

"For which he'll tell us to mind our own business. I don't know about you, but I ain't getting mixed up in his affairs. All I want is to find my pa."

"And all I want is to find the miscreants who shot at us. But the tables were silent as the grave on that subject."

"Maybe they're still out on the prairie, hiding."

"Or maybe they're professional marksmen who know how to keep their mouths shut."

"Or maybe they were just hunters after that antelope, we got in the way, and they're afraid to come forward and admit it."

"I think it unlikely, Alice."

"I know," she sighed. "What is Claire thinking, coming to this place, anyway? Seems awful dangerous, for all its balls and fancy dress and money. At least in Resolution, I knew what was what."

"Did you?" Now it was his turn to sigh. "I wish I knew what was what."

"Meaning?"

Silence, during which she did not dare to look at him. It was too dark to see his face, anyway, as they passed into the massive shadow of the *Landgrafin Margrethe*. Fifty yards off, a pair of sentries paced back and forth before the gangway, and another patrolled the bow and mooring mast. The crew was taking no chances with the count's safe recovery, it seemed.

"Alice—"

"Yes?"

"How soon do you plan to leave?"

"Tomorrow, I expect. Other than you nice folks, I got no reason to stay here. And I understand foreigners have to lift before the first snow, anyway, because of the ice problem."

He had stopped, so she stopped with him, his form a darker shadow in the shadow under which they stood.

"Alice, would you object if I—"

What was he trying to get out? Great snakes, if he wanted her to take some lovelorn message to Claire, she was going to give serious consideration to whacking him on the skull with the Remington.

"Oh, dash it all, this is impossible!" he exclaimed.

Then he seized her roughly by her upper arms, and before she could even take a breath, his mouth came down on hers in a bruising kiss.

11

They were interrupted at breakfast by a messenger from the *Landgrafin Margrethe*, who was escorting a rather pale and silent Alice.

"Alice, do sit down and join us," urged the countess, while Tigg jumped up from his seat and pulled her over to the table.

"I don't want to be any trouble," she mumbled. "This gentleman brought me over here all willy-nilly. I didn't mean to interrupt."

"You are welcome at any time of the day or night," Lord Dunsmuir told her. "Come and sit. Sir, you have a message from Count von Zeppelin?"

The officer dragged his gaze away from Rosie the chicken, who was enjoying a biscuit and some berries on a saucer under the sideboard, and straightened as if the count himself had spoken. He clicked his heels together. "*Der Landgraf* has bidden me to convey to you his greetings. He inquires as to whether you are at home to visitors this morning, as he wishes to thank the young ladies and the gentleman in person for their care last evening."

"We are indeed at home. But the count cannot mean to come over here himself when he is injured. The young ladies and Mr. Malvern will wait upon him at his convenience."

But the man shook his head. "My lord is a man of action. If he were to put himself to bed every time he was a target, he would never get up. No, he will attend upon you here as soon as he may."

The earl clearly knew when to back down in the face of a stronger force. "If the count would like to join us for breakfast, we should be very glad to see him."

The officer bowed and vanished down the gangway.

"I adore the informality of this country—this airfield." Davina returned to the table after giving the steward rapid instructions. "A request that would have been shocking in London—for who receives anyone before three in the afternoon, never mind at breakfast?—is utterly normal here."

Claire sipped her tea and marveled at the strength of a man who could be shot in the evening and invite himself to breakfast the next morning. He was a man indeed whom any soldier would be glad to follow. "Society ladies would faint in ranks at the very thought," she agreed.

"I am afraid the count is more likely to faint—from loss of blood," the earl said unhappily. "I do hope he has not been hasty in attempting a visit so soon after his injury."

"If he does faint, you will catch him, Papa," Willie piped from his father's lap, where they had both been engaged in dissecting several walnuts and an orange. "Will he wear his sword?"

"This is not a formal occasion, my boy." The earl opened his mouth so that Willie could feed him a walnut meat. "We shall hold out hope for pistols, however."

To Willie's joy, the count was indeed armed when he arrived, though he divested himself of his twin Ruger pistols immediately upon coming into the countess's presence, and handed guns and belt to one of his officers. When he bent over Davina's hand, Claire saw that the bandage around his head had been replaced by a more discreet sticking plaster, partly covered by his flight cap.

"I am delighted to see you on your feet, my lord." Instead of offering him her hand, Claire astonished herself and the whole company by rising on tiptoe and kissing him on the cheek. "I feared for you, truly."

The count's face reddened and Claire would have given anything to be able to drop through the floor and hide. What on earth had she been thinking?

But then she saw that his heightened color was the result of emotion, not affront.

"My officers have told me that you piloted the Daimler overland to bring me to safety, despite your own injury," he said gruffly, blinking the moisture from his eyes. "Words express my gratitude poorly, I am afraid, but please allow me to thank you."

"I did nothing that any friend would not." Her own face was flaming scarlet by now—probably blotching in a most unappealing way. "Andrew risked his life in an attempt to give chase and to assist your captains, God rest their brave souls. And Alice was the one to ascertain your injuries at first and suggest a course of action."

He pulled Alice and Andrew close and somehow managed to enfold all three of them in a hug that made up in feeling what it lacked in finesse. "I will never forget it." He released them and cleared his throat, seating himself at last in the chair the earl held for him. "You have only to say a word and I will do anything in my power to repay my debt."

Alice shook her head. "There is no debt, sir. Seeing you on your feet is reward enough for me—for us, if I can make so bold as to speak for Claire and—and Mr. Malvern."

Claire could only nod in agreement, and wonder why she did not look at either of them. Both she and Andrew seemed unusually silent this morning. Had some other dreadful thing happened? But how could it? Perhaps there had been more in the note Alice had received last night than she had believed.

They settled around the table. On either side of Claire, the Mopsies seemed torn between choosing a jam for their biscuits and staring at the count. They knew the entire tale, of course, but Claire wondered whether they knew exactly who their guest was. Or perhaps they did not need to know. Perhaps it was enough for them to count him as a friend, with no trappings of rank or strings attached.

Davina passed a tray of eggs on toast to the count, and followed it with another loaded with sausages. "We have just been discussing our plans to lift today, Ferdinand. I must confess to a mother's fears for her child's safety. Balls and visiting and outings to the theatre are all very well, but when laid in the balance next to last night's events, they come up very short indeed."

"You must not blame Edmonton for last night, my dear," the count said, putting three fat sausages on his plate. "I have long since resigned myself to the fact that there are those who do not see progress and achievement in the same light as we."

"Perhaps not, but when they start shooting to prove their point, something must be done."

"Believe me, something will." He glanced at Tigg, who was cutting a sausage for Willie. "But we will not speak of it in front of the children."

"Why not?" Lizzie asked, suddenly as prickly as a cactus at this affront to her capabilities. "The Lady ent afraid to start shooting, nor Alice—and me and Maggie, we're not so shabby with the gaseous capsaicin, neither."

Count von Zeppelin choked on his sausage, and while the earl clapped him on the back, Claire tried heroically not to laugh.

Lizzie seemed rather pleased to have caused such a sensation. Maggie elbowed her and spoke up. "Jake's the Lady's second cos Snouts ent 'ere, so 'e can fire the lightning rifle when 'e's got it. Even our Willie's done his duty as a scout when 'e's 'ad to. None of us is little babies in prams." She considered for a moment, then added, "Sir."

The count drained half his coffee and gave a mighty swallow. "I consider myself corrected, and look forward to discovering exactly what is this gaseous capsaicin, to say nothing of lightning rifles."

"Don't forget the firelamps, Lizzie," Willie said. "I like those the best."

Davina stared at him. "What on earth...?"

"Getting back to our plans," Claire interjected hastily, "I should be glad to go to the mine sooner rather than later. His lordship has been telling us of the great engines in use there to drill down to where the diamonds are embedded. I should like very much to see them."

"From what I hear, sooner is better than later," Alice said, and told them about the danger of the ice. "We'd have to lift and be out of here pretty soon, anyway," she finished, "considering the snow will fly any day now."

"Then let me tell you what my men have discovered," the count said with a long look at the Mopsies, who smiled sunny smiles and addressed themselves at last to the jam pots. "They returned to the scene at first light and were able to discover where the gunmen lay as they fired."

"Were there shell casings?" Alice asked.

"Alas, no. These weapons do not seem to depend on powder or brass, but rather on air pressure. The grass was flattened in a fan shape for ten feet, and there were depressions in the soil as though a large weapon had stood there. And they found one of these buried in the bank opposite the wreckage of my captains' landau." He dug in the pocket of his uniform jacket and held up the strangest projectile Claire had ever seen.

It was shaped like a bullet, but it had a tiny engine and propeller on its stern. Its nose was pushed in, likely from impact with earth instead of flesh. Her mind's eye reconstructed what had happened in a flash. "That's why we heard no report," she exclaimed. "If they are using some kind of air gun, and the projectile's speed is enhanced with an engine, it could do its damage silently."

"And if it hits its target," Andrew said slowly, "death is unavoidable, considering its size. You could conceivably drop a bear in one shot with one of these, could you not?" He took the projectile gingerly, examined it, then handed it to Tigg. "Was there any—Tigg, what are you doing? That is not yours."

For Tigg had picked up his unused butter knife and had begun removing the screws holding the engine in place. His fingers were nimble, his actions precise, and before the count could say yea or nay, the tiny engine had been removed and an even tinier compartment revealed in the body of the projectile.

Yellow liquid drained out, and in less than a second, a slender plume of smoke rose as it ate its way through the bottom half of the casing and into the mahogany dining table. The countess gasped as Tigg pushed away from the table so hard he knocked his chair over. Andrew grabbed the heavy porcelain gravy boat and caught the dribble of acid when it ate its way through to the underside. Sinking into the gravy, the liquid seemed to extinguish itself.

"Mr. Andersen," the countess called in a voice that did not resemble her own, "remove the gravy, if you please, and return with a ceramic container and some gloves."

"Looks like an effective way to get rid of the evidence," Alice said, her gaze locked on the hole in the table. "Can't imagine there'd be many survivors, either, and the body's liquids would neutralize it."

"Fiendish device," the earl snarled. The countess had already hustled Willie over to the window seat, half a sausage still in his chubby hand.

The count snapped something in Prussian to his aides, and when the chief steward returned with a freshly scrubbed thunder mug, they waited until what was left of the projectile had been deposited within, and removed the damaged leaf from the table.

"Tigg, the engine, too," Claire said. "There might be traces of acid left on it."

"There's something here, Lady. Let me get a good squint at it." He carried the engine casing over to the window of the salon.

"Tigg, I must insist—"

He looked up. "Lady, wot's M-A-M-W spell?"

Maggie made a face. "Nuffink."

Lizzie nudged her. "Wot, you know all the words in the world now?"

"No, but I know that ent one, unless you got a mouth full o' toffee."

"Maggie is quite correct," Claire said, cautiously examining the interior of the tiny engine's housing. "It is not a word. These are initials, most likely indicating the maker."

"Perhaps if we discover who made this so small engine," Count von Zeppelin said grimly, "we may discover who tried to assassinate me."

Andrew had never passed a more uncomfortable hour in all his life. It was worse even than sitting the board examinations for the Royal Society of Engineers—at least there, he had been prepared and had a good idea of what to say once he took his seat opposite his examiners.

With women, one never knew what to do—and when one did something, it was inevitably wrong.

He had wanted to apologize profusely last night, there in the *Margrethe*'s huge shadow, for his ungentlemanly conduct. He didn't know what he expected from Alice upon being kissed—a modest shrug, a chummy laugh at his stupidity, a return to their cordiality—but it wasn't what he got.

Alice's lips had parted in surprise, and then she had melted in his arms—for about five seconds. Then she'd come to herself with a shocked noise in her throat, pushed away, and fled into the dark so fast that by the time he'd emerged into the light of the mooring mast, he could no longer see her.

Or apologize.

Or figure out what on earth was the matter with him for treating her in such a fashion.

Because was he not promised to Claire—in his heart at least, if not in words acknowledged on both sides? What madness had seized him and compelled him to kiss a woman whom he respected as a fellow engineer and liked immensely as a person? Because such a stupid move was bound to shatter both respect and liking on her side. If she and Claire should happen to exchange confidences, then the jig was well and truly up, because he would not blame either of them in the least for giving him the air and sending him on his sorry way.

Stop lying to yourself, man. You know why you kissed her.

No. He was not that much of a cad.

You kissed Alice because Ian Hollys kissed Claire.

He hadn't. That was ridiculous.

It was a jealousy kiss. And you used your friend poorly.

Oh, sweet mercy.

If he could have flung himself down the gangway and never come back, he would have. But no. He had to sit at this breakfast table and smile and smile, and be a villain—and see her opposite, pale and having clearly spent a sleepless night on his account.

He could not meet her eyes. The fact that she could not meet his, either, was almost a relief.

Claire handed the projectile's engine casing to the count, who pocketed it. "Here is what I propose," he said. "John, do you and Davina plan to lift this morning, taking Lady Claire and Mr. Malvern along with you to the mine?"

"We do," his lordship said.

"I'm going that way, too," Alice said quietly. "I got a lead on my pa last night from a man who used to know my ma. He says pa might've been working the cargo ships up there, so I'm going to see where that takes me."

"Excellent." Count von Zeppelin nodded briskly. "I will leave an officer and six men here to make inquiries while I go also to the mine. I believe our discussions at Government House may bear fruit, but they need more in the way of tending, do you not agree, John?"

What discussions? Andrew would give a good deal to know what the two nobles had to talk about besides the merits of efficient flight, but that was none of his business.

"So we shall be a flotilla, then?" Claire asked with a smile. "An impressive sight, to be sure. One almost wishes one could watch from the ground."

"I don't." Davina adjusted Willie's sailor collar gently, and touched his cheek. "The sooner we lift, the happier I shall be."

"One thing, though," Alice said diffidently. "I'm going to need a navigator. The automatons are all very well, but they don't read charts."

"I do." Jake lifted his head like a pointer scenting a pheasant. "I'll go wiv you."

"Me too," Tigg said. "You'll need someone in the engine compartment who 'as a foggy clue about 'ow to work the Lady's power cell. And since you ent got a replacement steam engine yet, that would be me."

"Power cell?" The count's hawk-like gaze stooped upon Tigg, who took a breath and bore up bravely under it.

"Aye," he said. "It got kidnapped 'ere by—" Claire cleared her throat and Tigg changed course without missing a beat. "—by mischance and we put it in the *Stalwart Lass* when 'er engine burned up in midair."

It was fortunate the count did not wear a monocle, for it would have fallen out when his eyebrows rose under his cap in astonishment. "*Was sagst du?* How extraordinary. You must tell me this adventure sometime soon. Tonight at dinner, perhaps."

"Dinner in midair?" Maggie asked. "'Ow we gonna get from one ship to another?"

"The Firstwater mine is not far, as the crow flies, Maggie," Davina said with a smile. "If we leave before noon, we shall reach it by sunset, even with the days as short as they are now."

The count glanced over his shoulder, and one of his aides sprang to his side. Andrew didn't know much Prussian, but it seemed he was giving instructions for the dinner party. He suppressed a sigh. Once again, it seemed, he would have to face Alice across a table. He must resolve this, and sooner rather than later.

As soon as he figured out how.

"Master Tigg," Lord Dunsmuir said, "are you prepared to abandon your post so soon?"

"My … post, sir?" Tigg looked from his lordship to Alice in some confusion.

"I believe you were to sign on as midshipman to the *Lady Lucy*, Tigg," Claire said gently. "Have you changed your mind?"

"No, I ent … but Lady, Alice needs me. Four could've 'elped, but 'e 's an engine housing now."

"I would not shanghai you if you have a prior commitment, Tigg," Alice said. "I'll manage with Jake."

Andrew could not imagine her flying the *Lass* with fewer than three in her crew. This was absurd. "I will go as chief engineer," he blurted. "I know that cell as well as Tigg, and you cannot fly with so few. Besides, we have already been attacked once. Each ship should have someone aboard who can fire a gun."

"That would be us," Lizzie announced. "If the Lady makes us some capsaiceous bombs, we can take 'em with us."

Alice had gone as white as the damask tablecloth. "The girls will help me, Mr. Malvern. I won't trouble you."

"Nonsense." The count looked her in the eye, and if it were possible, her skin paled even further. "As a personal favor to me, *Fraulein* Alice, I beg you to accept *Herr* Malvern's assistance. I wish to continue our discussions of automata over dinner this evening, and if something were to prevent it, I should be most distressed."

"Nothing will prevent it, sir," she managed. "But—"

"Good. It is settled, then. Shall we lift at eleven o'clock? I will notify the port authority."

And so it was done.

Andrew would have an entire day within the cramped confines of the *Stalwart Lass* with three children who all had a bad habit of popping up when one least wanted them. The possibility of seeing Alice alone for even a moment to apologize for his behavior seemed more remote than ever. And yet, the prospect of five hundred miles of strained white politeness was unendurable.

Something would have to give.

12

"Claire." Alice put a hand on Claire's sleeve, and even through the fine batiste, her fingers felt chilled. "You have to help me."

"Of course." After transferring Rosie to her left shoulder, Claire tucked Alice's cold hand into the crook of her arm and drew her into her cabin, where her valise sat packed and ready for lift. She had packed it before breakfast, having a feeling that Davina's concern for Willie's safety would carry the day. "What is it?"

"You have to fly with me, and manage the engine. I can't—we have to—" She broke off with a gasp that sounded almost like a sob. "Please."

Was this Alice? Had someone switched her sensible, down-to-earth friend with this pale woman whose hands were now tucked into her armpits as if she had an ague?

"Alice, whatever is the matter? Here, sit by me." Claire put Rosie on the bedside table and sat on the velvet coverlet of her bunk, but Alice did not. Instead, she paced from door to porthole and back again.

Rosie shot her a gimlet glare and proceeded to preen her feathers.

"I can't sit. I feel ready to fly out of my skin. I wish I'd never come here. I wish I'd gone when I wanted to go, and not let hope flamboozle me into staying. Hope will kill you every time, Claire, like a rattler on a rock."

"You are not entirely making sense," she said gently. "Please, dear. What has happened?"

"I can't tell you," Alice moaned. "But you have to come with me. I can't fly all that way with him, whether the girls are aboard or not."

Claire's eyes widened as the real source of her friend's agitation became clear. A strange, chilly feeling settled in her stomach. "You mean ... Mr. Malvern?"

Alice leaned her forehead on the panels of the bed cabinet. "Yes, Mr. Malvern," she said into the glossy wood. "Who else?"

"Did something happen last night? Has there been some other trouble?"

A huff of breath might have passed for a laugh. "Trouble. Yeah. Only I would see it as trouble. Any other woman with a lick of sense might have enjoyed it, but me? I'm a darned fool."

The chilly feeling solidified into certainty. Claire was no mathematician, but she could put two and two together as well as the next person. Speaking aloud the sum of her conclusions was another matter.

"He escorted me over to the Tiller," Alice said, turning to lean a shoulder on the cabinet. "I talked with Mike, and then we came back. And under the *Margrethe*, in the shadow, he—he—"

"He kissed you?" Claire whispered.

"Yes!" Alice wailed, and flung herself down on the bunk, burying her face in Claire's shoulder. "I know it was wrong, but I liked it! Until I thought about him, and you, and what a mess it all is, and so I—I ran away." She sighed, and sat up, swiping the flat of her hand over her cheek.

Claire's face felt stiff. But this was ridiculous. She herself had been kissed by another man last evening, and had been just as confused as Alice was now. Was she such a dog in the manger that she could begrudge Andrew's giving a kiss when she had been guilty of accepting one with every appearance of enjoying it?

She could not say such things. Better to let her friend talk away her burden, and keep her own secrets and shortcomings to herself. "Alice, do you care for him?"

"I don't know. I admire him. He can't care for me, that's certain. He was only amusing himself. I know that. Why else would he …?"

"How can you be so sure? After your appearance in that gown last night, I know he sees you differently."

"I don't want to be seen like that."

"Like what?"

"Like … like some fragile porcelain shepherdess in a pretty gown, who needs to be protected and escorted and wrapped in cotton wool when she's put away at night."

"I'm sure he doesn't—"

"I'll tell you for true, he never thought about kissing me before he saw me in that dress."

Put like that, Claire could hardly argue. "He sees you as a woman, perhaps, not as a mechanic in pants and flight goggles. There is nothing wrong with that."

"Shouldn't make any difference. I'm still me, whether I've got grease on my face, or powder."

"You're quite right, it shouldn't." She squeezed Alice's shoulders and made a decision. "Cheer up. We're both in the same boat. Captain Hollys kissed me last night, too, and very thoroughly at that."

Alice sat up straight and gaped at her. "He did? When?"

"At the ball. A moment later I came in from the terrace and found you, and then we met Peony."

"No wonder you were all colored up. I just thought you'd been dancing." She huffed another breath, of discovery this time. "So you and Mr. Malvern …?"

Now it was Claire's turn to lay her cheek on Alice's shoulder. "I don't know. I honestly don't. I don't even understand myself. How can I enjoy another man's kiss when all this time I thought I cared for Andrew?"

"Thought? You mean you don't?"

"Of course I do." Oh, how could she explain her feelings? They were feelings, not theories or maps or anything else that could be understood and put into words. "I admire him enormously, and like him. He is my friend, the person I trust with my very life. But the trouble is, I can say all those things of you, too."

A smile flickered over Alice's lips, then went out.

"I care—I must," Claire said, half to herself, "or I would not have felt such jealousy a moment ago, when you told me he'd kissed you."

"Claire, please say I haven't hurt you. I couldn't bear it. It was so sudden, and—and it was my first time, and—"

"I know what you mean. Andrew was my first kiss, too."

"We'll have to form a club."

That startled her into a laugh. Rosie, who had settled onto the nightstand in sphinx-like repose, looked alarmed until Claire passed a soothing hand over her feathers. "You have not hurt me. If anything, you've made me see something about myself that I hadn't before."

"And what's that? We both have excellent taste in men?"

Another smile. "That … and the fact that we can admire the same man and still be friends." How was that possible? If the flickers were any authority to go by, they should hate each other. "That's rather remarkable, don't you think?"

Alice nodded. Her hands, which had been clasped tightly in her lap, relaxed. "You don't hate me? Because

I've seen some pretty ugly things at the Resolute Rose, when two of the girls both wanted the same man."

"I admit, I have been feeling a little jealous since we left Reno, which is ridiculous. I am not proud of it. You and I have seen some dreadful things together. I should think—Alice, I hope—that this would strengthen our regard, not cause us to hate one another."

Alice hugged her. "You're a peach."

"And so are you."

"But meanwhile, here I am with five hundred miles of sky to deal with."

"I imagine Andrew is every bit as agitated about this as you are. Perhaps it will be a relief to know that I would rather act as your engineer than sit on the *Lady Lucy* staring out the window wondering how the girls are doing. We might even send a message to the count suggesting that he give Andrew a working tour of the *Margrethe*. After all, we do not know if he will get another opportunity."

"I knew you would help me."

"Didn't you tell me once that we women must stick together?"

"I meant it."

"And so do I." Claire got up and extended a hand to pull Alice to her feet. "Come. Rosie and I will help you pack. I do not think all of your new clothes are going to fit into your locker on the *Lass*, so we will have to ask Davina if you may borrow a trunk."

The Mopsies were delighted that they were to have the Lady practically to themselves for the flight to the diamond fields ... though by the fourth hour, when it appeared they would not be called upon to defend the ship, they began to get restless.

"How much further?" Lizzie whined, gazing down at the endless stretch of land far below, covered in thin pines and punctuated occasionally by a lake or a river. "There ent a thing down there but trees."

"And reindeer," Maggie put in, pointing. "There's another 'erd."

"They call them *caribou* in these parts," Alice said. "That's a big herd. Must be thousands of them."

"I do hope Davina does not want to put down and shoot one." Claire came to join her at the window as they sailed over the enormous running flow of animals, which swerved under the airships' three shadows and galloped in the opposite direction.

But the *Lady Lucy* did not alter her elevation, merely kept a steady speed and an unchanging heading of north by west.

Lizzie wandered back toward the engine, and a moment later popped back into the gondola. "Alice— we gots a pigeon coming."

"A pigeon," Alice repeated blankly. "Where on earth from? There is nothing here for miles."

"It dropped out of the *Land*-whatsit's belly, behind us. Maybe the count will fly over and visit."

"Lizzie, the count is hardly likely to strap on a rocket rucksack at his age," Claire said, smiling at the picture. "It is probably a message between captains."

But it was not.

When the pigeon tucked itself into its landing bay, Alice pulled the pouch out of its belly and read the piece of paper within. Then, her lips thinning, she handed it to Claire and stalked forward to relieve a protesting Jake at the tiller.

Dear Alice,

In the absence of a single moment alone with you, and in the face of Claire's sudden change of mind, I have contrived to communicate in this rather unusual manner. The count is a gracious host, and his pigeons being otherwise unoccupied, he has allowed me the use of one.

I wish to apologize for my behavior of last night. It was unpardonable and you have every right not to speak to me.

However, I hope that in time you will find it in your heart to forgive me. I should not like to see you take to the skies knowing that you had not.

Sincerely,
Andrew Malvern

Claire folded the letter under Lizzie's inquisitive gaze. "I beg yer pardon, wot's 'at?"

"It is a letter to Alice, and none of our business."

"But she gave it to you to read."

Drat Lizzie's logical mind. "She did. It is from Mr. Malvern, on the *Margrethe*."

Lizzie's jaw dropped a little. "Mr. Malvern is sendin' our Alice letters in the middle of the sky? Is 'e in love wiv 'er, now, and not you?"

Good heavens. "Lizzie, for pity's sake, where on earth do you get your ideas?"

"Tisn't an idea, is it, Mags?" She appealed to her sister, who was sitting at the map station cutting up a slab of chocolate with Jake's knife. "Mr. Malvern's sweet on t'Lady, innit?"

Alice's back became ramrod straight as she tipped the wheel a degree to port, following the course of the *Lady Lucy* ahead of them.

"Aye." Maggie handed Jake a piece, then Lizzie and Claire. "Want some chocolate, Alice? It's ever so fine."

To Claire's relief, Alice released the wheel long enough to take some. "If you nosy Nellies are done discussing my letter, you might clear out and let Jake see his charts. I want this route plotted before we moor, in case I ever need to come back."

Maggie cleared away the chocolate—after carving off several healthy chunks—and Claire saw that Jake had been plotting their route all along. Careful notes had been made in his laborious capital letters, following the land forms.

"Well done, Jake," she said with honest admiration.

His cheeks reddened. "I done it for Alice," he mumbled as he drew a careful line to the side of a curving river. "I remember wot the charts and the land look like, but she don't."

"His memory is prodigious," Claire told Alice. "It is almost as though his brain takes a photograph, with all its detail. If he can see something, he remembers it."

"Wish I had that talent," Alice said. "Would've come in handy in the schoolroom back when."

"Ent never been to school," Jake said, "'cept lately, when the Lady made us—er," he corrected himself with a hasty look at her, "—helped us learn our letters and numbers."

"You can be glad she did, then," Alice told him. "Navigation means reading a lot of letters and numbers, not just clouds and land forms. It means filling out forms at the port authority and sending messages on pigeons to other captains." She paused. "If a man intends to be legal, anyway. Ned Mose never held much truck with letters and forms. Quickest way to get permission, in his mind, was to wave a pistol."

"I ent plannin' to be like Ned Mose."

"Glad to hear it. Me neither. Stand watch, please. It can't be long now."

"Aye, Captain." Jake finished a last notation and resumed his duty with the solemnity of a career military man commanding a bridge the size of the *Margrethe*'s.

"Lady, look." Maggie pointed out the window off the bow. "Izzat smoke?"

Claire helped herself to a second piece of chocolate and joined her at the window. As she did, the *Lady Lucy* dipped in the air and suddenly they were looking down upon the top of her great golden fuselage.

"The Dunsmuirs have begun their descent," Alice said.

"I see them." Jake reached over and made a note on the chart while Alice flipped a series of switches. "Seven and Eight, stand by. Claire, I'll need you at the engine to decrease power from your cell."

"Aye, Captain."

"But Lady, the smoke—"

"Maggie, I'm sure it is safe." Claire cast an anxious look over her shoulder at the thick plume, which must be huge, considering how far away from it they were. "Come with me. Lady Dunsmuir would never put Willie in jeopardy," she said as they walked back to the engine. "You must remember we are going to a mine, where there are engines working and digging in the earth." She had only the vaguest knowledge of what went on at a mine, but surely she could safely say this much. "It is likely a plume of dust, or smoke from those engines."

Maggie looked doubtful, but when Claire required her assistance at the switches, she seemed much more interested in ordering Seven about than in asking any more questions.

After all, nothing was managed better than a Dunsmuir holding, was that not what Captain Hollys had said?

The only thing they had to fear this far north was catching a chill.

13

The Firstwater Mine had its own landing field, of course, for the cargo ships and the *Lady Lucy*, a short distance from what appeared to be a town and the vast open pit that was the mine itself. As the *Lass* was moored to its mast by the ground crew, Alice saw that a dun-colored ship with no name, merely a string of letters and numbers on its fuselage, was already moored some distance away.

"No, you may not go to the edge and look down," her ladyship informed Willie as they disembarked. "It is far too dangerous. That is why it is surrounded by a palisade."

"Chin up, son." The earl tossed the boy in the chilly air and then set him on his shoulders, where he clutched his father's ears and giggled. "We shall tour the mine tomorrow, and you may come along. One day you will be running this empire. We must waste no time in making you familiar with it."

A party of men approached in a vehicle that rumbled and hissed and emitted great clouds of steam.

"Same traveling mechanism as my locomotive tower," Alice said in a low tone to Claire. "The continuous track is more stable than wheels when the river keeps washing out the road."

"Let us hope they do not have that problem here. My goodness, it is cold. If this is what it is like in October, I shudder to think of January."

The men disembarked and introductions were made all around. The driver of the enormous vehicle turned out to be Reginald Penhaven, the managing director of the mine, and his eyes were anxious as he turned his fur cap in both hands.

"You'll have seen the smoke, then, your lordship?"

"I have," Lord Dunsmuir said gravely. "It's visible for fifty miles. What happened?"

"One of the diggers was sabotaged. It took three engines with hoses to put out the fire, and the digger is beyond repair. That leaves us with four, sir."

"Four? We have—had—six, did we not?"

"We did, sir. You'll recall we had the same kind of trouble a month ago, sir."

"And you have apprehended the culprits?"

Penhaven's hands tightened so much on his cap that it bent between them. "Despite best efforts at investigating, sir, and a doubled watch on the vehicle yard, we have not, sir. Though we have our suspicions."

His lordship bent a long, thoughtful gaze upon him. To the man's credit, he didn't quail or look aside, but swallowed and kept his chin up and his return gaze level.

John Dunsmuir shook himself and seemed to come to a decision. "We will meet in the office in an hour."

Count von Zeppelin stepped forward, and Alice realized that the other occupants of the vehicle had been nudging each other and murmuring among themselves since the great inventor had been introduced. "Once you have concluded your business, I should like to propose dinner on the *Margrethe* this evening," he said. "I would be pleased if *Herr* Penhaven and his officers could join us, as well as your family, Dunsmuir, and the crew of the *Stalwart Lass*. Shall we say eight o'clock?"

"I would not hear of it, Count," Lady Dunsmuir said. "The mess hall here is not ornate, but it will accommodate all of us and more. There is no need to put your crew to any trouble on our account."

"It is no trouble, good lady, it is an honor," he said gallantly. "I insist. I would like to join you on your tour tomorrow, and then the day following, I must lift and make my way back over the sea. I have been away from my home these four months, and the Baroness will be growing anxious. So you see, I must seize my opportunity to issue an invitation while I can."

"You are very gracious," she said. "We would be delighted to join you."

Oh, no. Alice leaned over enough to murmur, "Claire, does that mean...?"

"Yes, I'm afraid so. Full evening dress. Isn't it fortunate we packed your blue gown so carefully? It will not have had time to become crushed."

Alice groaned. She'd had enough of formal occasions this week to last her for the rest of her life. "I'll just go to the mess hall with the men. No one will miss me, and I need to find out if anyone's seen my pa."

"Indeed you shall not." Claire gripped the sleeve of her flight jacket as if she thought Alice planned to cut and run that very moment. "Don't you remember what the count said? He wishes to discuss your automatons more at dinner. I should think he, at least, would miss you. As would I."

"Miss you?" Alice's stomach dipped and steadied at Andrew's voice behind them. "Are you going somewhere, Alice?"

"I was going to try," she said with some asperity. "Th—thank you for your letter, Mr. Malvern. I accept your apology, though none was needed."

Lizzie tugged on the skirt of the canvas coat he had bought in Edmonton to replace the one lost in the Texican Territory. "Are you in love with our Alice?"

"Lizzie!" Claire pulled her away. "That is none of your business."

"But we just—"

"Never mind, Lizzie," Alice said, and extended a hand. "I wonder if you'd come along with me to the cargo ship? Jake, too. I want a word with the watch, and it seems like this is my only chance."

"I'll escort you," Andrew said promptly.

"No, thank you, Mr. Malvern," she said as steadily as she could. Her heart was jumping in her chest like a fish on a line, but the fact that the very word *escort* set her teeth on edge went a long way to settling that down. "My navigator will come with me. I don't want too large a party. Makes it hard to ask questions."

"I'm good at ferreting out things," Lizzie said happily. "Maggie's coming too, ent she?"

Alice couldn't imagine the two of them being separated for any reason. "If she likes."

Lady Dunsmuir looked over her shoulder. "Claire, are you coming with us?"

"I shall catch you up, Davina, in just a moment." She leaned over and whispered something to Mr. Malvern that made him straighten and put a cautioning hand on her arm. With a shake of the head, she said, "Maggie, would you come with me, please?"

Maggie hesitated between Claire and Alice, clearly torn. "But Lizzie's going wiv Alice."

"Because Alice needs her. And I need you." She raised her eyebrows in a way that caused understanding to dawn on Maggie's face.

Some wordless communication passed between the twins, and before you could say *Jack Robinson*, Maggie was tripping off with Claire and Andrew, meek as a lamb. Lizzie looked positively gleeful as she trotted alongside Alice and Jake.

"What just happened there, young lady?" Alice asked her, only half joking. "Do you have some kind of mental telegraph that lets you talk without words?"

"No, 'course not. Wot's a telegraph?"

"It's a device for messages," Jake informed her. Then he said to Alice, "The Lady wants Maggie for some scoutin', same as I expect you do for Liz."

"I do not," Alice protested. "I just thought she could come along as some—some cover, you might say. Men tend not to suspect women and children, and I figured they might be freer with their conversation, that's all."

"So why am I going?"

They were nearly to the cargo ship, and the watch appeared to have figured out they were about to have company.

"Because you are my crew," she said simply. "And I need a good hand on the ground as well as in the air."

Jake could not have looked more pleased if she had told him he was going to get his own ship.

"Hallo, the ship!" she called, taking Lizzie's hand in a sisterly fashion. "Captain Alice Chalmers of the *Stalwart Lass*, and navigator, at your service."

"Bob Grundage, botswain of cargo ship one-oh-seven, at yours," the man guarding the gangway responded. "This here's my friend Joe Stanton, and that there is his brother Alan. And who's this, might I ask?"

Lizzie gave him a sunny smile. "I'm Lizzie."

"Well, Lizzie, you and your captain are a darned sight politer—not to mention prettier—than some folks I could name. What's your business here?"

"We came with the Dunsmuirs' party," Alice said, releasing Lizzie's hand. The little girl drifted away, looking up at the cargo ship's plain canvas fuselage with something akin to awe, as if she'd never seen such a magnificent one. "But my purpose here is a little more personal. You boys been flying the cargo ships long?"

"Long enough," Bob said, lighting a cigarillo. Its acrid smoke smelled familiar. Ned Mose had smoked the same kind during his rare moments of leisure. "If you're looking for a job for your young man there, you're out of luck. Ships are crewed out of Edmonton."

"Good to know," Alice said easily. "Matter of fact, I'm looking for a man and wondered if you might have seen him. About your age, with one blind eye. Was a mechanic—a pretty talented one, if my information is right. Ring a bell?"

Bob glanced at Joe, then released a cloud of smoke and shook his head. "Nope."

"Might not be recent. Maybe a year ago or more?"

Again the glance and the shake of the head. "Nope. Sorry."

Alice saw Jake frown and crane his neck, looking for Lizzie, who had managed to drift out of sight.

Alan hawked and spat on the gravel. "We're expecting a convoy any day now, to start taking the miners' families out before the snow flies. You might have better luck then if you're still around."

Joe waved the smoke away as it drifted in front of his face. "What's your business with him?"

"He's my pa, I think." Alice gave the same story she'd given Mike, which might or might not be true, depending on how events played out. "If you hear of him, maybe you could let them know at the mine, and they'll get word to me."

"Chummy with the Dunsmuirs, are you?" Bob asked. "Ain't many can say that."

"I'm chummy with friends of theirs," Alice said cautiously. "Can't have too many friends up in these parts, I'd think."

"You're right there." Bob tossed his cigarillo to the gravel and ground it out with the heel of his boot. "Well, it's back to work for us."

Alice could take a hint as well as the next person. "Nice talking to you."

She moved off, and Jake followed her, his hands in his pants pockets, cool as you please. "Where is she?" Alice murmured out of the side of her mouth.

"Behind a bunch of crates near the gangway. Any minute now ..."

They got halfway across the field between the cargo ship and *Lady Lucy* when they heard a shout. Turning, they saw Alan leading Lizzie by the hand as if she were four years old and they were learning to cross the street.

"Captain Chalmers, looks like you forgot something," he called.

"Sorry, Alice," Lizzie said in a breathless voice about five years younger than her normal one. "That ship is just so big I couldn't resist seeing if it were as grand inside."

"Lizzie, you rascal." Alice shot an apologetic look at Alan. "I appreciate this, sir. She loves the airships. I can't keep her out of them."

He laughed and handed Lizzie over. "She reminds me of my granddaughters back home. Their mother can't take 'em into the big houses with the laundry, without them running upstairs to see how the rich folks live."

Alice laughed, as if she could see it. "You sound like a Texican man. What part? I'm from down Resolution way, myself."

"Santa Fe is where I hang my—" He was cut off by a yell from his companions. "Nice talkin' to you. Goodbye, Lizzie. Stay out of trouble, you hear?" He jogged back the way he had come.

"Alice, they—"

"Not yet, Lizzie. Wait until we're back on the *Lass*, if you please."

She hustled them aboard and made sure the gondola hatch was good and shut.

"What's the matter, Alice?" Lizzie wanted to know. "You're awf'ly pale."

Alice chewed the inside of her cheek. "Maybe I'm making a river out of a raindrop. Maybe it's nothing that don't happen all the time up here. But I'd sure like to know what Texican men are doing aboard a ship this far north in the Canadas."

"I'll tell you wot they're doin'," Lizzie said. "They're tellin' you fibs."

Alice nodded at her to go on.

"Soon's you were out o' earshot the fat one said to that Bob, 'Better send word someone's askin' about 'im' and Bob says 'Maybe she's kin, maybe she's not' and then the one 'oo brought me over, 'e says, 'We don't owe them dadburned toffs nothing but a distraction' and then they saw me sneaking up the gangway an' that were that. Wot's *dadburned?"*

Alice felt her stomach go cold, and goosebumps broke out on her arms.

"Something you don't need to say," Jake informed her. "Sounds to me like they're talking about someone 'oo's actually 'ere. They know a man wi' one blind eye."

"It does, don't it?" Alice said slowly. "But send word to who? Him or someone else? Why make such a secret of telling me where he is? And what kind of distraction?"

"And 'ere's something," Lizzie said, digging in her pocket and removing a small piece of brass. "Look wot I found behind them crates, dadburn it."

Jake cuffed her, but there was no energy in it. He took the object and frowned. "This 'ere's a bullet casing. Not a bitsy engine casing like wot got shot at the count, but look." He held the object up to the light from the gondola's viewing windows. *"M.A.M.W."*

"It must be an arms manufacturer, like Colt or Sharps," Alice said. "But it doesn't prove anything. Those bullets could be sold all over the territory."

"Perhaps." Jake pocketed the casing. "The Lady ought to know anyhow."

Alice nodded slowly. "And I'd give a lot to know what the toffs are going to talk about in that meeting."

"Just wait," Jake told her. "Our Maggie won't let us down."

14

It did not take long to learn the lie of the land, but that did not ease Claire's frustration in the least. On closer inspection, what she had thought to be a town turned out to be a series of long sheds set into the ground, so that one had to descend a staircase in order to enter each one. The mess hall hunkered in the center, and arrayed in neat rows around it were housing for the miners, supply sheds, the mine offices, and management quarters, as well as what she was informed were wash houses, equipment sheds, and storage.

"There's no shortage of water here, of course," said the young engineer who had been seconded by Lady Dunsmuir to show Claire and Andrew around. "Those larger buildings there contain great steam engines that produce heat and electricks for housing and offices."

"But why is everything set into the ground?" Andrew asked.

"Because of the storms and the cold, of course," the young man said, as if this should have been obvious. "The ground may freeze as hard as iron, but at least it's some protection from the gales from the north. If we didn't build this way, homes and offices would be torn from their foundations during the winter, and we'd arrive in the spring to nothing but debris. The Firstwater Mine is like an iceberg, you see—ninety percent underground—and that includes the settlement as well."

Claire nibbled on the inside of her lip to stop herself from telling the young man he was boring her to tears, and could they return to the office where the meeting was, please?

"Lady." Maggie tugged on her skirt. "Lady, I've got to—to—" She rounded her eyes in a wordless plea.

"Sir, thank you for a most informative tour," Claire said at once. "But I am very much afraid my ward and I must find a powder room posthaste."

He blushed scarlet, and pointed. "Lady Dunsmuir's powder room is in that row there, third stair from the end. I'll take y—"

"I wonder if I might prevail upon you to tell me more of the engineering side of mining?" Andrew put in smoothly, taking his arm and walking on.

The young man looked over his shoulder in some distress, but Claire took care that he should see nothing but a lady hustling a child to the nearest facilities. "Well done, Maggie."

"I weren't fibbing. I'm fit to burst."

They located the indicated door without difficulty, and found the tastefully appointed powder room empty. And what luck—somewhere in the neighborhood was where the meeting was to be held, if the gentlemen milling about in the square outside were any indication.

When she and Maggie had completed their ablutions, Claire whispered, "We must find a way to hear what they're saying. See if we might get into the ceiling."

But they could not. On one side, the single window was at ground level, the ceiling not much higher. Other than the door, there was no other exit.

Behind her, Maggie opened the other lavatory stall, and drew in such a sharp breath that Claire turned. "Lady, look. This ent a loo at all."

Expecting to see a sink or cleaning supplies, Claire was intrigued to see an empty cubicle, neatly paneled in wood. "I cannot imagine her ladyship ordering this for mere entertainment. Do you suppose it is something like the hidden closet you found at home?"

A few taps upon the panels revealed its dimensions, and it was only the work of a moment to spring the latch. A set of steps descended even deeper into the ground. "Maggie, you are a treasure. Where do you suppose these go?"

"Dunno. Let's find out."

Cold air breathed up from the depths, and Claire was glad once more that they had both worn coats. The steps were clean and well kept, which meant this passage was not secret, and was even regularly used. A thin line of electricks glowed along the ceiling.

"Lady! A signpost." Maggie squinted at it in the dimness and spelled out the words slowly. "Managing Director that way. Owner's soo—syu—"

"Suite." Claire turned to gaze down a second passage, equally gently lit.

"Supplies. Mess Hall."

"Good heavens," Claire said. "These are underground streets. That young man was not exaggerating. It is like the Tube in London, Maggie, so that people—or perhaps only the Dunsmuirs—do not need to venture aboveground in the cold."

"I thought everyone left when it got cold."

"But if a storm should strike early or late in the season, one must still come and go."

"Which way, Lady?"

"The Managing Director's office. I wonder where we shall come out?"

A short distance down the corridor, they found another set of stone steps. "Quietly, now." At the top, she pressed the latch slowly, and pushed the door open a scant half inch. The two of them pressed one eye to the gap, one above and the other below.

In the time it had taken them to find the door, the men had gathered around a heavy mahogany table—the Dunsmuirs, Count von Zeppelin, Captain Hollys, and the mine officers. And what she heard during the next half hour made her wish that her corset had not been secured so tightly, because she felt a distinct need to gasp for air.

Maggie sat on the steps after about ten minutes, and when that proved to be too cold, she got up and went exploring down the tunnel. Claire took this in at some level, but like the iceberg, ninety percent of her mind was taken up with understanding what was going on around that table.

For the Dunsmuirs were not merely a wealthy couple who dabbled in natural resources in various locations about the world. No, they intended to change it—and for the better, too, as far as Claire could see.

"Why should all the commerce from Europe be funneled through New York?" the earl asked, indicating a huge map of the continent on one wall. "Any market needs competition to be viable, and since Charlottetown and the Maritime Territory have so recently declared for the Canadas, it makes sense to locate the airfield, port, and seat of government there."

"And Zeppelin ships shall be the first to enter the new port," the count said with satisfaction. "It will be profitable for all concerned when I do not have to pay the tariffs that New York extorts from me."

"But we must be cautious," his first officer warned. "It seems the Texicans may have infiltrated as far into the Canadas as Edmonton. It is my belief that they are responsible for the events of last night, when *der Landgraf* was attacked."

The count nodded. "They are foolish, then, if they believe a single bullet can derail the development of a country's economy. Whether I had fallen or not, these plans will proceed."

"We shall return to London immediately following our tour, then," Lady Dunsmuir said. "I will meet with Her Majesty to inform her of these developments."

"Do you fear reprisals, your ladyship?" the mine director asked.

"I fear they have already occurred," she said bluntly. "With the sabotage here and the attempt on Count von Zeppelin's life, we would be fools if we did not believe them related. The only thing we do not know is who is behind it."

"We shall find out," the count said grimly.

"I'll tell you who's behind the sabotage," the mine director said, his brows lowering in a frown. "If it isn't Frederick Chalmers and his Esquimaux, I'll eat my hat. Who else knows this mine like the back of his hand? And—begging your pardon, your ladyship—who parks his boots under the bed of a woman of the Esquimaux, the whole kit and caboodle of whom are in Isobel Churchill's pocket?"

Frederick Chalmers! Claire gripped the door-frame hard so she would not fall headfirst through it. She must find Alice immediately. Could her father really be so close? It had to be he they meant. How many men named Chalmers would have intimate knowledge of a mine's workings if he were not an engineer?

And then what the man had said sank in. They suspected Frederick Chalmers of the sabotage. Oh, dear. Which would be worse—never to know your father, or to know him for a saboteur and a criminal?

When Claire joined Andrew and their guide topside once more, she was hard put to keep from spilling her news. But of course one must not blab indiscriminately what one had learned by eavesdropping—though this was not a rule of etiquette her mother, Lady St. Ives, would ever espouse.

They joined the others in the office, conveniently too late to have been included in the discussions. The meeting had broken up and everyone was enjoying thimbles of port and brandy. Claire and Maggie had just accepted cups of piping hot tea when a messenger came in.

"Beg pardon, sir," he said to the earl, "but a pigeon's just arrived." He handed his lordship an envelope bearing a most flamboyant script.

The earl tore it open and read the contents. "Good heavens," he said blankly, and handed the letter to the countess. "We are to be inundated with guests, it seems. The news of your visit, Count, seems to have traveled far and wide. And is about to travel farther."

Davina's brows rose and she handed the letter to Count von Zeppelin. Then she turned to Reginald Penhaven. "It seems the end-of-season convoy is arriving a week early, in the company of Julius Meriwether-Astor and his family, plus a rather large contingent of reporters from the Texican, Colonial, and Edmonton newspapers. Do you know of Mr. Meriwether-Astor?"

"Is he the railroad baron out of New York?"

"He is indeed," Count von Zeppelin said. "We have met on one occasion, but I am afraid it was not a happy one. He is expanding his interests from railroads to airships, you see, and did not look upon my newest designs with a friendly eye."

"His ships fly with the older Crockett steam engines, do they not?" Claire asked. And when surprised faces turned her way, she fought the tendency to blush under their scrutiny. "I went to school with his daughter Gloria. And when I was looking for a company with which to invest, naturally I first investigated a concern that was familiar to me." She smiled at the count. "Their ships do not hold a candle to the Zeppelins, though, I am happy to say."

The count smiled back and waved the letter. "It seems he has been making a world tour in his newest model, seeking to drum up publicity."

"This seems a strange stop to make, then," Mr. Penhaven observed. "A bit out of the way, wouldn't you say?"

"Not if you bring reporters with you," Davina countered. "The world comes with them. Count, I am afraid our dinner *en famille* is about to be augmented by several orders of magnitude. May I offer our mess hall once again, and recommend we move dinner to tomorrow evening?"

He bowed gracefully. "If your chef will agree to working with mine, we will put on an event that will give these reporters something much more interesting to write about than Meriwether-Astor's creaky old ships."

The door opened and another messenger came in. "A pigeon for you, your ladyship."

Davina tore open the envelope, scanned the letter, and raised her eyes to the heavens. "We may as well invite the governor of the territory and be done with it. This is from Isobel Churchill. She is on her way from Edmonton with what she says is an order from Prime Minister Darwin himself that we suspend production of our diamonds pending a hearing of the Esquimaux's case before the Bar."

"Poppycock!" the earl exploded, taking the letter as if its contents would wither to nothing under his furious glare. "The prime minister has no such authority— particularly since the diamonds for Her Majesty's thirty-fifth anniversary tiara are being cut and finished as we speak. I'm sure she would have a thing or two to say about a suspension, particularly since she chose the stones herself."

"Not to mention the fact that our mine is not under Esquimaux control," Davina said more mildly. "It seems I may have to reveal my parentage to the dear lady after all this time, and settle the matter."

"That is your choice, my dear." The earl touched her cheek, his temper fading as he regarded his wife with fondness. "You have the family and Her Majesty behind you, whatever you decide."

"I am not ashamed to let it be publicly known to Isobel Churchill ... and twenty foreign reporters." Davina raised her chin and looked positively wicked. "Perhaps I might even upstage Mr. Meriwether-Astor's world tour."

15

Claire found Alice shortly thereafter, pacing to and fro in the gondola of the *Stalwart Lass*. She lost no time in telling her about Frederick Chalmers—and about Mr. Penhaven's suspicions concerning his activities.

"I ain't going to judge him one way or the other," Alice said after a short silence, during which Claire wondered if she were revising the appearance of the dream figure she had called *Pa* for most of her life. Adding shadows and angles. Taking away a certain amount of the glow.

Or perhaps she was merely wondering about the presence of a woman in his life who was not her mother.

"I ain't interested in his politics. I'm just interested in whether he's my pa or not, and if he is, why he went away and left me and my ma."

"The question is, how do we find him without raising the ire of the mining people? It would not do to be seen consorting with one whom they consider a saboteur."

Alice's gaze was uncompromising. "Are you afraid, Claire?"

Alice's inability to prevaricate could sometimes produce most uncomfortable results. "Not afraid, no. But our situation is rather delicate, both of us being guests of the Dunsmuirs."

"I'm not really a guest. I'm here under my own steam."

"But you've eaten at their table—and will again, if the ball tomorrow night goes off as planned."

"I don't have to go to that. Would rather not. But we're getting off track. How are we going to find my pa?"

"That nice boy who was guiding us might know," Maggie said suddenly. "You could say you wanted to take Lizzie an' me to see some real Esquimaux."

Claire gazed at her in admiration. "What an excellent mind you have, Maggie. The very thing. How difficult can it be to locate a Texican man in an Esquimaux village? Let us ask the ground crew to unload my landau at once. We shall be back for dinner before anyone notices we are gone."

Within half an hour, the thing was done. While Tigg, who was given land-leave by Mr. Yau to accompany them, supervised the unloading of the landau, Claire and the Mopsies changed into raiding rig.

"Not that I expect any danger, of course," she assured them, buckling her leather corselet. "But it would be foolish to set off into a wilderness populated by bears and caribou without some means of protecting ourselves. And the lightning rifle cannot be holstered in a sash."

The young man had innocently provided them with a map and an offer of assistance, one of which was accepted with gratitude and the other declined with the same. And before long, they set off along a track of packed and already frozen gravel, which seemed to receive frequent use.

"How far is it, Lady?" Tigg asked, leaning over the bolster between the compartments. "Will we see a bear?"

"Mr. Eliot said about five miles as the pigeon flies, but that does not take into account the turns and— ouch! My apologies, that was a big one—the potholes."

"We're lucky there's a road at all," Alice observed, hanging on to the seat with both hands. "Oh, kids, look—a bear, to be sure!"

An enormous brown heap of fur back in the trees lifted its head to observe their chugging passage. They probably looked as strange and exotic to it as it did to them … but nevertheless, Claire increased the steam as they passed just in case it took exception to their presence.

She had never been so glad to see the end of a road—if eight miles of unrelenting torture could be called a road. They crested a rise in the ground to see a river valley spread out below them, and clustered along it, a series of gleaming humps in the ground, in front of which smoke rose gently in the afternoon sun.

"They bury their 'ouses, too," Tigg said. "Bet they gave the miners the idea."

Claire rolled slowly to the outskirts of the village and before she could even begin to shut down the boiler, they had been surrounded by children of all shapes and sizes, in colorful dresses and thick jackets, their awed, bright-eyed faces rimmed in fur hoods.

"Now, now, don't be touchin' this landau, you lot," Tigg warned, trying to push the wing open wide enough to get out. "That bonnet'll be 'ot."

Smiling, Claire and Alice descended, and lifted the Mopsies down. Two little girls who couldn't be more than Willie's age immediately reached out to touch Lizzie's golden hair where it streamed over the breast of her coat, their velvety eyes huge. "Chama," one of them said. Then her gaze moved to Alice's head of blond curls, which she'd drawn up carelessly in a bunch and tied, unfettered by either pins or hat. "Chama."

"Chalmers." Alice pointed to her chest. Then she swept a hand out to indicate the village. "Chalmers?"

The children shrieked and ran like a pair of rabbits, bouncing and dodging between two of the mounds and disappearing.

Alice's shoulders sagged. "So much for trying to talk. Maybe Chama means *Shove off or I'll shoot* in Esquimaux."

The chattering crowd of children seemed to be pushing them willy-nilly toward the village. "Tigg, stay with the landau," Claire called over her shoulder, rather unnecessarily. For Tigg had planted himself bodily between the bonnet and two older boys who were trying to see where the tendrils of steam were coming from. She had no doubt that by the time they returned, Tigg would have given them a lesson in basic physics and they would be using a wrench for the first time.

As they approached the strange silvery mound where they had last seen the little girls, a door opened in its basal structure and a woman stepped out.

Claire's first thought was that this was Alaia—the Navapai woman who had cared for her and her friends in her dwelling on the mesa outside Santa Fe. Her face held the same calm confidence edged in joy. But there the resemblance ended. Where Alaia had been slender and graceful, this woman was stocky and solid—at least, she appeared to be under her red dress and fur-trimmed coat. Clinging to each hand was one of the little girls.

Ah. This must be their mother.

The deep brown gaze passed over Claire and Maggie, lingered a moment on Lizzie, and proceeded to Alice, where it missed no detail of Alice's appearance. Then she lifted her chin.

Alice found her voice. "Um. Chalmers?" she said, no doubt feeling as foolish as she sounded.

The woman planted her feet, as if she were expecting a blow. Claire received the distinct impression of a ship's captain, giving the command to fire all cannon even though he knew the battle was lost.

"Chalmers," the woman said, in a voice as mysterious and deep as an owl's call, and just as musical. "Alice?"

"What do you mean, the Esquimaux village?" Andrew Malvern couldn't decide whether he most wanted to ream out his own ear, or to box those of his companion.

"Just what I say, sir," said the young man who had been their guide that afternoon. "The young ladies went off in a landau to the village, about eight miles from here. I offered to go with them, but they refused."

"And you let them?" Andrew's eyes were practically bugging out of his head, and he reined in his temper with difficulty. "You let two young ladies go off into the wilderness without protection of any kind?"

"They were better protected than I, sir," he protested. "Have you seen that mucky great gun Lady Claire carries? Can she really shoot it?"

"Yes, she can, and—" He stopped himself with a physical effort. "That is not the point! The point is, they do not know their way, nor do they know the extent of the dangers in this country. How could you have been so foolish?"

The young man wilted. "It wasn't just the two young ladies. The girls and that young blackamoor went as well."

This time Andrew was bereft of speech entirely. When he could speak again, he managed to get out, "That young *blackamoor*, as you call him, is my laboratory assistant and a midshipman on your employer's personal vessel." He breathed heavily. "You will refer to him as *Mr. Terwilliger.*"

"Yes, sir." By now the boy was close to tears. "What can I do, sir?"

"Despite the fact that I would put the Mopsies up against anything except a bear, I see no option but to pursue them. But I swear, sir, that if any harm has come to so much as one hair upon their heads, you will pay for it with your hide."

"Yes, sir," the young man whispered miserably. Then his gaze shifted upward, past Andrew's shoulder. "Oh, no."

Andrew turned. A ship had emerged from the clouds over the forested tops of the hills—a ship with an ornate brass gondola and a bronze keel that ran the length of the fuselage. They could feel the sound of its engines as a vibration in the stomach—rather the way dread felt.

"Whose is it?"

"That would be the *Skylark*, Mrs. Churchill's ship," the young man said on a sigh. "We're in for it now."

"Why? Is she so terrifying?" Andrew followed his guide, who broke into a jog as he headed in the direction of the airfield. "I've read about the lady's political and charitable works, and she seems rather admirable to me. Do you suppose her daughter will be with her?"

"I imagine so. Don't let your admiration blind you to the facts—she is determined to shut the mines down. The Firstwater is only one of several."

They emerged from between the low-slung buildings as the *Skylark* sailed low over their heads. The ground crew swung into action, and within a few moments, the ship was secured to its mooring mast and settled into position. The gangway folded down and two ladies descended, allowing the crewmaster to hand them to the ground.

Andrew, slightly out of breath, realized one of them was Peony Churchill. The other, then, must be the famous and redoubtable Isobel Churchill—intrepid explorer, fearless speaker, and scourge of Parliament.

She did not look like a scourge. Indeed, her daughter was taller than she by a head, and her figure was trim and set off becomingly by a tobacco-brown tailored suit and a small hat set over one eye that somehow involved netting, silk roses, and pheasant feathers. It managed to add to her height, however. Her hair was russet brown and piled up under the hat in fat curls. She looked, in fact, like one of the smart set so frequently seen in Kensington High Street and the Burlington Arcade.

But upon closer inspection, it was in her eyes that Andrew saw the woman who made members of parliament quail and newspapermen uncap their pens. For those eyes did not suffer fools at all. They saw the world as it could be, and had very little patience with it as it was.

That sharp brown gaze also noted the distinct lack of an official welcome—if you did not count Andrew and his guide.

Andrew swept off the fedora with the driving goggles affixed to the brim that had seen him from New York to Santa Fe to Edmonton, and bowed. "Mrs. Churchill. Miss Churchill. I trust you have had a pleasant flight?"

"Why, Mr. Malvern," Peony said before her mother could speak. "How lovely to see you again. Mama, this is Mr. Andrew Malvern—you remember, the scientist for whom my friend Claire was working in London. We met him last night in Edmonton, at the governor's ball."

Had it only been last night? For Andrew, it seemed a lifetime ago.

Isobel Churchill extended a gloved hand. "How do you do, Mr. Malvern? You are a long way from home."

"As are we all. I am here as a guest of the Dunsmuirs —mostly, I am afraid, because they do not know what else to do with me."

"I am sure that is not the case." She smiled, and Andrew felt the power of her intelligence, not to mention that of the dimples that flirted at the corners of her mouth. He began to see why individuals at the highest levels of government believed her to be one of the most dangerous women in England. And maybe even the world. "Perhaps you can tell me where I might find the Dunsmuirs."

"If you will allow me to escort you, I believe they are in the offices still."

"Are you sure you want to do that?" The dimples twinkled, and he found himself losing track of his concentration. "If you are their guest, being seen with me could put your next meal in jeopardy."

"I am quite sure that not only my next meal, but yours as well, is already being taken into account."

"You are very gallant, but the Dunsmuirs know why I am here. I shall say my say and be back in the sky by sunset. There is weather coming, and I wish to be safely in Edmonton before it does."

"Weather is not the only thing coming," he said. "Apparently we are to have a visit from the Meriwether-Astor family and a flock of reporters. Mr. Meriwether-Astor is on a world tour, we are given to understand, and he and his entourage are expected at any moment."

"Meriwether-Astor?" Peony repeated in tones of amusement. "The family of Gloria Meriwether-Astor? Do not tell me so."

"Claire said nearly the same thing."

Peony laughed. "Mama, if there is to be a grand to-do, we simply must stay. Seeing Gloria here in the wilderness will be worth the price of admission. If she met a bear in the forest she would demand to know who its parents were, and whether it had *expectations*."

"Is she a Buccaneer, then?" Isobel asked, but only with half her attention. They had been spotted, and a small party had set out from the mining office, Lady Dunsmuir's slender figure at the head.

"A most determined one. Rumor has it her dear papa wanted her to bag a duke at the very least, the moment she was out of school. The fact that she is accompanying him at all tells me she did not succeed."

"Barbaric," her mother murmured, and raised a hand in greeting. "Lady Dunsmuir, I trust you received my pigeon?"

"Isobel." Regardless of her politics, Andrew could see that Davina Dunsmuir would not treat a guest with anything less than the utmost courtesy. "Welcome to the Firstwater Mine. Peony, dearest, you are looking very well. The brisk northern air seems to suit you—as does that smashing emerald suit. Do come inside, I have tea waiting for all of us. Mr. Malvern, will you ask Claire to join us?"

"I would if I could, my lady, but she has taken the landau to the Esquimaux village with Alice, the girls, and Tigg."

"I beg your pardon?" Lady Dunsmuir came to a dead stop and stared at him. "She did what?"

"It was my fault, your ladyship," his young guide said. "She said the girls wanted to see the village, so I drew them a map. And then they wouldn't let me go with them," he finished rather miserably.

"I have already pointed out the foolishness of such an excursion to our young friend here," Andrew said, "but—"

Davina had recovered her wits. "You must fetch them back at once. Good heavens, any number of dreadful things could happen. Two girls and the children? What on earth were they thinking?"

"Do you think the Esquimaux will set upon them?" drawled Isobel Churchill. "Like wild animals? Beings of lesser intelligence than you?"

"Certainly not," Davina snapped. "I am afraid that *wild animals* will set upon them. The caribou are migrating down from the north, and if they should be trapped in a river of moving animals, the consequences could be disastrous. Did you not see the herds as you flew?"

Isobel looked the tiniest bit taken aback. "I did. Are they really such a danger?"

"I will not take the chance." She gave rapid orders, and several men separated themselves from the party.

"I'll go, too," Andrew said. This was his fault. He should have kept a closer eye on Claire and not let her go rambling around the camp getting odd ideas.

"And I," Peony said.

"Certainly not," her mother informed her, unconsciously echoing Davina's words and snap. "If there truly is any danger, we do not need more inexperienced people out there. You will stay with me."

"But mama, she is my friend."

"All the more reason to stay out of the way and allow the men here, who know what they are doing, to fetch them back."

Peony got a distinctly mulish look in her eye, but the men were already jogging toward what appeared to be a large equipment shed. Andrew hurried after them, and did not hear her reply.

16

Alice wondered if it were possible to be turned to stone by surprise.

The silence stretched out, punctuated only by the wavering laugh of some water bird on the river. Lizzie gave her a nudge with her elbow. "'Ow does she know your name?"

She would have given up another automaton to know the same thing. Or rather, to have confirmed what must be the truth—that the only reason this woman could know her name on first sight was because she had been told it, and been given a very accurate description.

Which, if Frederick Chalmers was indeed here and had done so, was a good thirteen or fourteen years out of date.

"Alice?" the woman repeated, a little more cautiously now. With either hand, she gently moved the two children behind her, so that a curious eye peeked out from either side of her fur-trimmed jacket.

With another dig from Lizzie's elbow, Alice roused herself, like an automaton given a command. "Yes," she said. "Who ...?"

"I am Malina, wife of Chama. These are my children."

"You speak English?" Alice said, unable to come up with a more intelligent reply.

"Chama taught me. And the children." She extended an arm to encompass the village. Not just her children, but all of them, apparently. Did he teach in a school when he wasn't being a saboteur and who knew what else?

"Where is ... Chama?" Claire asked.

Alice was grateful that someone was asking the right questions. Chama might not be the man they were after. If it wasn't, they could steam right back to the airfield and she'd pull up ropes two minutes after.

Malina glanced at the sun, which just brushed the tops of the trees. "He comes soon. He hunts with the men. Come."

Without waiting for a reply, she ducked into the nearest buried house. The little girls giggled and followed her.

She met Claire's inquiring gaze as her eyes filled with tears. "Do you think he's here? With his little family? Do you think he forgot me?"

"I do not," Claire said stoutly. "That lady knew you immediately, as did the children. How would that be possible if he had not told them about you?"

A little figure popped out of the door. "Come!" she shouted impatiently. "Tea!"

Lizzie and Maggie needed no further prompting. They followed the little girl through the door, while Claire took Alice's elbow firmly and propelled her through it ahead of her. Inside, the warmth gathered them in like a mother's hug. The walls were curved, and what appeared to be ribs of some white stone arched up from below the floor to meet nearly over their heads. Above that, the silvery roof seemed to let in a kind of pearly light that illuminated the entire house. Beds were made up neatly on wide shelves that doubled as benches in compartments between the ribs, and at the far end, about twenty feet from the door, a—great snakes, it was a kind of mechanical oven that bubbled and clanked, simultaneously boiling water, baking biscuits, and ... Alice peered through the gentle light. Washing dishes? Two slender figures worked the gears. Who were they? More possible half-sisters? Above it, steam went straight up through a mechanism that appeared to be part window, part bellows, and part fan.

The interior smelled of herbs and hot metal and baking, and Alice realized she had not eaten anything decent since breakfast in Edmonton. Not that she could manage much. Not until she knew.

Malina waved them onto the benches near the stove, and the little girls offered them cups of tea in curious vessels.

"What are these made of, ma'am?" Maggie asked, indicating her cup, which was as transparent as one of Claire's tortoiseshell hair combs, and colored much the same.

"The goddess has called me Malina, and you must, too. They are teeth of whale. We offer tea in holy vessels as welcome."

Whales had teeth? And sacred ones at that. Maybe that made this the next thing to drinking tea out of the chalice at church of a Sunday. Or was the welcome of a guest a holy act in this village?

"Thank you." Maggie smiled at her, and Malina's eyes crinkled in return. "It's awf'ly good. Like honey and grass. We 'ad something similar a long ways south of 'ere."

"Are you the sister of Alice?" Malina asked her gravely.

"No. Me and Lizzie, we're wiv the Lady."

Claire rose, cup in hand. "I am Claire Trevelyan, and these are my wards, Lizzie and Maggie de Maupassant."

Alice realized with a tiny shock that this was the first time she'd ever heard the Mopsies' surname. And it was quite a mouthful.

Malina frowned in confusion. "So many strange words. What is *ward*?"

"It is used when a child is— When one looks after—" Claire resumed her seat, her brow furrowing as she sought a definition. "They are my young sisters of—of the spirit."

Malina's face cleared and she beamed at the three of them. "I understand. The goddess has given them to you, though you have not birthed them, nor has your mother."

"Quite so," Claire said with some relief.

Lizzie exchanged a look with her twin, then both the green eyes and the blue turned to Claire. "Izzat wot wards are?" Lizzie asked. "Sisters?"

"Technically, no, but I rather like 'sisters of the spirit,' don't you?" Claire smiled down at Maggie, who leaned against her. "It's like *flock*, only closer. Nicer."

They looked so comfortable together that Alice's heart ached just a little, missing something it had never really had.

"I like it," Maggie said. "Now all we 'ave to do is find a dad for Alice."

The words were no sooner out of her mouth than they heard a commotion outside, muffled by the walls of the house. It sounded like a crowd of people were arriving, and Alice heard hoofbeats and shouts, along with the barking of dogs.

But the women of the household did not move, other than the two young women operating the mechanical contraption, who put another kettle of water on to heat.

Alice got halfway to her feet, but Malina leaned over from her bench and put a hand on her knee.

"They must give thanks to the goddess for good hunting, and prepare the kill. Then he will come. Drink tea and I will talk story."

Standing on the tip of Alice's tongue was a refusal—they had to be going, they had come a long way to find Frederick Chalmers—but Malina began to speak in a soothing tone. The hasty words settled like chickens on a roost and instead, pictures formed in Alice's head … of a beautiful woman birthing stars, of whales that came to her hand to feel the joy of her touch, of caribou and wolves bowing to her and offering her children their lives so that all might be sustained through the winter.

And as she concluded and the final image—a man bowing to a strong, brown-skinned woman before she took him as her husband, and offering her food and drink and a home—the door opened and daylight poured in.

Alice sucked steam- and tea-scented air into lungs that didn't seem to be working right. But they had to work. Otherwise, she'd faint in a heap on the floor.

Malina stood while Claire and the Mopsies looked a little dazed, as if they were struggling to come back from the place where legend was still alive, and influenced the hours of every day in this village.

Alice found herself on her feet, watching a tall man push through the door and close it behind him. "Malina, we saw the landau and the watch told me we have guests? It's hard to believe it would be the Dunsmuirs, but—"

He stopped. Alice swayed, taking in his face, trying to match it to the hazy one in her memory. He was fair complected, as she was, his skin reddened from wind and sun. He had frizzy blond hair, as she did, though his was cropped close to his head, she saw as he pulled the fur hat from it. One eye was blue, the other covered by an ocular device held over the socket by a leather strap. It seemed to move in tandem with the gaze of the healthy one.

Both false and real eye locked on her, standing motionless and voiceless next to the fire. "Alice?" he said.

She had dreamed of this day for years and years, had figured out a speech that would make him sorry for leaving them, make him respect her, even if he didn't love her.

But she couldn't remember a word of it. All she could remember was strong hands, and a hard knee that formed a horsie she had loved to ride on as a tiny girl.

Both his gazes seemed to devour her from head to foot. "Is it really you?" He stepped closer, his hands coming up to touch her face, and she stepped back.

"Surprised?" Whose voice was that? And what had it said *that* for? Where was her speech? Where was her brain, for that matter?

But he took her at face value. "Surprised. Overjoyed. Astonished." His voice dropped to a whisper, but his gazes did not leave her face for an instant. "Relieved."

What?

"The last pigeon came back with no photographs of you. I've been living in fear that Ned Mose—that he finally—" Moisture glistened in the corner of his good eye. "Thank the goddess and the Lord and all good spirits everywhere. You're alive and well and standing right here," he whispered. "It's a miracle."

"Photographs?" Lizzie said to no one in particular. "Pigeons?"

"Every solstice, I sent one of my pigeons to your coordinates. Every solstice, it came back," he said. "A little blond girl grew into a young woman, and no matter where I was, I knew what you looked like."

If he had struck her, it could not be worse than this. The color rose hot into Alice's face, and her jaw worked before words came out. "You sent a pigeon to photograph me, but you couldn't send a letter to let us know whether you were dead or alive?" Tears clogged her voice, as bitter as the words tasted in her mouth. "You took the time to invent that kind of device, but you couldn't have told me in fourteen years that you cared? That you were sorry you left? That you were even alive?"

"Alice." He said her name like a blessing, the way Malina had said the name of the goddess. "Ned Mose had a price on my head. If I had contacted you or your mother in any way, he would have found me and put a bullet in my skull."

"I s'pose that was why Ma married him." Sarcasm dripped from every word, as though the poison she'd kept hidden deep inside had finally been lanced.

"She married him to save her life. And yours. A deal went bad—oh, I've made mistakes, sure enough. But one mistake I didn't make. I got myself out of his way and that was the price I paid. Never to see you again. Or rather, never to let him know I saw you. But the birds told me how to make a way."

"The pigeon came back with no plates of you. He thought you had died," Malina said to her gently, going to his side. "He mourned you as if you had."

No wonder the children had looked so overjoyed at the sight of her appearing so suddenly in their midst. For them, she would have come back from the dead.

"I ain't dead." Alice wasn't ready to give in. The urge to punish him as she had felt punished beat behind her breastbone like a frantic, caged thing. "I came across the continent to find you and tell you—tell you—" She struggled to finish, but the tears in her throat got the better of her. Her voice rose to a squeak. "Tell you, darn you, that I hate you! Hate you for leaving us—and for being such a dadburned coward!"

Lizzie's eyes widened. Frederick Chalmers's ruddy face turned pale.

"Do you know what Ma had to do to put food on the table? Huh? She was a *desert flower*, that's what!"

His throat worked, but he didn't speak, so Alice struck again, like a rattler, mindless and terrified—anything to make these feelings go away.

"And now she's a different woman—a hard woman. The kind it's easy to leave. So I did what you did, Pa, and I left her, too. And you know how that makes me feel?"

What could he do but shake his head?

Now the tears were coming in earnest. She had to say the rest of her say quick, before she broke down and did something completely stupid, like throw herself on his chest and bawl.

"I came all this way to look for you, and now that I have, I just want to spit in your eye. But I won't, because there's young 'uns here and I got responsibilities. Instead, I'm going to leave you, too, Pa." She caught her breath, pushed it in and out. "Don't bother sending any of your dadburned pigeons after me, either. I'm a darned fine shot, and if I see one, I'll shoot it out of the sky."

She made it to the door without her knees collapsing. And turned.

"Thank you for your hospitality, Malina," she said with as much dignity as she could muster. "Claire, I'll be with Tigg at the landau."

And then she did exactly what she said she'd do.

She left, and she didn't look back.

If his head didn't fall off or his spine snap, it would be a miracle. Then again, if his head did fall off, at least this cursed journey would be over.

The huge vehicle with the continuous track in place of wheels jounced into a pothole the size of a pond and labored out the other side. "Is this the only road?"

Andrew shouted in the ear of the young man who had been their guide, who possessed the unlikely name of Errol Eliot.

"Don't need any more than this," was the hollered reply. "There's nothing out here but the Esquimaux and a whole lot of nothing."

Andrew doubted that the Esquimaux considered their home nothing, but it was too difficult to talk over the roar of the steam engine powering the vehicle. Andrew could feel the heat from its exhaust stack against his back, and the thing was all the way across the cabin in which they sat on benches bolted to the floor.

But a question had to be asked.

"Do the migrating herds attack?" he shouted.

One of the men in the front, who operated the rate of steam and thus their land speed, glanced at his companion, who turned the great wheel used for steering. "Depends on whether they get spooked. And whether the bulls are feeling frisky. And whether there are a lot of calves in the herd with a lot of protective mamas. But don't worry, sir," he yelled, "they won't bother this vehicle."

It was not this vehicle that concerned him.

Six miles. Seven, if he was lucky.

Errol must have noticed the grip he had on the back of the bench before him. "Nearly there, sir," he shouted. "This hill is the five-mile marker."

Only five? Andrew sagged, then straightened as he jounced sideways and back with neck-snapping suddenness.

They topped the hill and the country spread itself before him. The road wound down in long, looping steps to a river valley far in the distance. To the east were low, beetling mountains that probably had never seen a piton or pick, and to the north were endless ranks of spindly trees that seemed to become even thinner with distance. To the west, the sun had dipped below the tree line, and with it went what little warmth the day had possessed.

Movement caught his eye—not the movement of bird or beast, but a flash of gold.

"Look!" He pointed out the viewing port, which was made of isinglass. "Is that their landau?"

"Sure enough." The man on the lever made some adjustments, and a great billow of steam issued from the stack, like a signal. "That should let them know we've seen them."

The driver hunched over his wheel, peering into the distance. "Hey. That look like a herd to you? Light's going. It could just be one of those big flocks of geese."

Andrew half rose from his seat, peering down the long slope and past the first loop in the road, where the landau was now laboring upward toward them.

"That ain't geese." The lever operator spun a pair of wheels, and the engine groaned back into life. "That's a herd, and that landau is dead in its path."

He kicked a pedal as the wheelman spun his wheel, and the great engine turned down the face of the hill, its continuous track grinding stones and plants and small trees under and spitting them up into the air at the rear.

"What are you doing?" Andrew yelped, grabbing onto the first things that came to hand, namely Errol's shoulder and the back of the bench. "We're off the road!"

"Won't make it in time if we stay on it," shouted the wheelman. "Hang on!"

They plunged down the slope at a precarious angle. All Andrew could see was the earth rushing up at them, as though he were falling out of the sky instead of rolling over the surface.

They crashed onto the last loop in the road for about ten yards, then took the next plunge over. And still the landau made its steady way up the first loop and into the second.

Now Andrew could see them in the distance—a thundering wave of animals, galloping, running, tossing their heads in the headlong joy of the moving herd. A herd that would break against the fragile landau with its precious human cargo, overturn it, and whirl it away in pieces, treading bodies into the earth under their galloping hooves.

No rifle could stop this tide—no man could throw himself in its way and hope to survive. The only thing that could save Claire and Alice and the children was this great lumbering behemoth of a vehicle, if it could wedge itself between animals and humans in time.

"Faster!" he cried.

"We go any faster we'll overset," the steam operator roared. "Sit down and shut up!"

The continuous treads bit into earth that was not quite frozen, and chewed its way down the hill.

SHELLEY ADINA

"We're not going to make it," gasped Errol, his eyes bugging out of his head in horror. "The herd is almost upon them!"

What was wrong with Claire that she didn't see the approaching maelstrom of hooves and antlers and thousands upon thousands of pounds of hurtling flesh? Could they not feel the drumming in the ground? Or see the grinding progress of the mining engine laboring toward them on its elephantine track?

"Claire!" he shouted, though of course she couldn't hear. "Alice!"

The herd burst over the shoulder of the hill and poured onto the loop of the road, a hundred feet from the landau.

And now, when she should have been accelerating, the foolish female brought it to a stop!

"What are you doing?" he screamed.

Fifty feet.

The top folded back and Claire stood, the lightning rifle on her shoulder.

Forty.

Bracing herself against the steering lever, she aimed the rifle straight toward the center of the herd and fired.

A bolt of lightning leaped into the clear air like a pheasant exploding out of cover. It sizzled through the atmosphere, burning oxygen as it went, a foot above the sharp antlers of the lead animals.

The enormous males snorted, bobbed, and in a move that was almost balletic, bounced to either side of the road. The herd parted like the Red Sea, one half washing up the slope between the landau and the mining vehicle, the other half pouring down the lower side. Then everyone stood—children, too—and waved their arms, making themselves a large, strangely colored organism that the caribou had never seen. Smoke puffed from the animals' nostrils as they bounced out of reach of this strange apparition, and the pouring tide passed around them, then past them, and before Andrew could even think to draw his next breath, a thousand animals had regained their joyous momentum and were receding down the valley and into the distance.

The last cream-colored, bouncing caribou behind vanished into the trees and Andrew fell onto the bench as though it were he who had been shot.

"Who is that girl?" The steam tender recovered himself and got the vehicle moving again.

"She's a dadburned fool," the wheelman groused. "Putting eight people in danger, and for what?"

Errol gripped the bench, his eyes still wide. "Did you see that? Did you see her fire over their heads? What kind of rifle does that? And what kind of woman fires it?"

"A lady of resources," Andrew said, feeling as winded as he sounded. "Just don't ever ask her to dance."

17

Claire drove the landau carefully up the loading ramp into *Lady Lucy*'s cargo bay, and began to shut down the boiler as Tigg leaped out to stuff sandbags against the wheels so it would not roll about during flight.

Not a minute later, Andrew came striding up the ramp under a full head of steam. "Claire, you lunatic, what on earth were you thinking?" he shouted.

The landau ticked softly to itself and settled onto its axles with a sigh. She turned, raising an eyebrow at his disheveled appearance and red face. Lunatic? Really. He of all people should know better than to call a woman such a thing, when a woman's invention had just saved their lives.

"Can you be more specific?" she inquired coolly.

"At every point!" he shouted. "What possessed you to go to the village unescorted?"

"I had Alice and Tigg and the girls with me. Any more and we should have had to requisition a second vehicle."

"You put their lives in danger, to say nothing of your own." Andrew took a long breath, as if he were reining in his temper before it ran away with him. He gripped the top of the landau, his fingers tightening in a most alarming way. "I have never been so afraid in my life—not even in the pinnacle cell, or during the crash in the Idaho Territory. Claire, for the sake of my heart, please think before you do such a thing again."

"She was helping me." Alice came to her side and helped her disconnect the boiler, then replace the bonnet. "I went to find my pa, and since Claire is the only one who can pilot a landau, she took me."

"We promised you lessons," Claire remembered. "I must keep my promise."

"Well, you won't have to worry about me going out there again," Alice assured her. "In fact, I'm going to pull up ropes shortly and be in the sky by sunset."

"That's exactly what Isobel Churchill said, and she was disappointed, too," Andrew told them both. His tone still held an edge, but at least he was no longer shouting.

In fact, his gaze as he watched Claire was so intense that it almost looked as if he wanted to pull her into his arms. A sign, a look, the merest softening, and she was certain he would do it.

And then she remembered Alice's face as she had confessed her feelings for him, and the moment passed.

"Cheer up, Mr. Malvern." Maggie came to his side and took his hand. "The Lady wouldn't 'ave let us be run over by them ruddy great creatures. It were touch and go there for a bit, though."

He gazed at her for a moment, then sank to his knees and pulled the little girl into an embrace that was half relief, half …

Well, sometimes a gentleman could relieve his feelings by hugging a child, without other emotions being ascribed to it, could he not?

He released her and stood up, leaving Maggie looking both puzzled and pleased. "Just promise me that the next time you go rabbiting off into the wilderness, you'll let someone know."

"We did," Lizzie said. "That boy wot was our guide, he drew us a map."

"Someone in charge," Andrew said. "Someone in a position of responsibility."

"Oh, they prob'ly would've told us not to go," Lizzie informed him with airy unconcern. "Say, d'you suppose Mr. Andersen 'as food on the sideboard? That grassy tea were nice, but it didn't go far and me stomach is stickin' to me backbone."

They scampered up the ladder to the A deck, dragging Tigg with them.

Alice roused herself out of a brown study. Claire felt rather brown herself. The adrenaline of their near escape, the pell-mell journey back to the airfield with the mining engine practically climbing up into the steampipes, and Andrew's show of temper, had worn off rather suddenly, leaving her nearly exhausted. Claire couldn't blame the Mopsies for wanting to raid the sideboard. She could think of nothing better than to do the same—and seek her quiet cabin and Rosie's soothing company immediately thereafter.

"I'd best be going, then," Alice said.

"Please don't," Claire pleaded. "It's nearly sunset, and you don't want to fly at night."

"Night, day, it's no nevermind to me. I want to put this place to my rudder and get as far from it as I can."

"Alice, what happened?" Andrew asked her, his eyes calming now, and filling with concern. "Did you find your father?"

"I did, and now I'm done."

"But—"

"Andrew," Claire said quietly. "Do not press her. We must instead convince her to stay at least until morning. Better yet, until after Count von Zeppelin's reception."

"Absolutely not." Alice backed away as if they were about to forcibly restrain her. "Fine, I can maybe see the sense in waiting to lift until morning. But I ain't sticking around for that hoedown. You can show him Nine and be done with it, if he wants to talk about automatons."

"It would be most unwise to snub the count, you know."

"Why? I ain't ever going to see him again."

Claire took her arm and shot Andrew a speaking glance as they made their way over to the ladder. "Do you not see what you are doing? You are cutting people dead right and left—people who could mean something to you."

Alice went up the ladder like a monkey, as if she couldn't wait to get away from the sound of Claire's voice. But Claire could climb a wall with or without a rope. A ladder was nothing. She emerged onto A deck at practically the same moment, so that Alice could not escape.

"Please, dear; reflect upon what you are doing. This is a harsh land," she said as they entered the dining saloon. "We all need friends if we are to survive here."

Lizzie turned from the sideboard. "Alice, you said the same to them crewmen on the cargo ship," she said around a mouthful of fruitcake and marzipan. "Oh!"

"What's wrong, Lizzie?" The girl was digging in her pocket. "Did you bite down the wrong way on a nut?"

"No, I forgot about this." She handed over a gleaming cylinder of brass. "It's like them other ones. I meant t' tell you, I found it underneath that cargo ship. There's a lot more ships now, but I mean the first one, that were 'ere when we landed."

M.A.M.W.

Claire handed it to Andrew. And a pair of facts settled into place in her mind, like sparrows landing together on a twig.

"Why didn't I see this before?" she murmured. Then, "Does it not strike you as strange that Mr. Meriwether-Astor and his entourage should journey all the way here as part of his world tour?"

Andrew gazed at her thoughtfully while Alice nabbed a piece of cake for herself. "It does," he said. "But I try not to comment on the vagaries of the wealthy. They are often beyond the understanding of mere mortals."

She held up the casing. "This is the second time one of these has appeared where it does not belong. Do you suppose *M.A.* stands for Meriwether-Astor?"

Andrew blinked at her. "As in Meriwether-Astor Manufacturing Works? But Claire, they do not make bullets or arms. They make parts for steam engines, and rivets for ship hulls and connectors for train carriages. I've ordered one or two parts from them myself, in the course of my experiments."

"What if there's a smaller group?" Alice asked, her mouth as full as Lizzie's had been. "Meriwether Astor Munitions Works, say?"

"Who buys bullets, then?" Claire mused aloud. "There cannot be enough hunters and sportsmen in all the Territories to make such a division profitable."

"Armies," Andrew said. "Countries at war."

"Or about to be," Alice added, and swallowed.

And suddenly Claire understood why Count von Zeppelin had nearly been assassinated.

Gloria Meriwether-Astor's hat defied the laws of gravity. Perched upon her forehead, its rear tilted up nearly to the vertical by virtue of its resting on her piled-up blond curls, it seemed on the verge of sliding down her face and coming to rest upon her petulant lower lip.

Claire smiled and extended her hand. "Gloria. How lovely to see you again. You have not changed one whit since last we met."

Gloria took her hand, her gaze puzzled. "And when was that? Have we been introduced?"

Lizzie snorted like a horse who has unexpectedly met with a groundhog in its path. "O' course you have. At the Crystal Palace, wi' Lord James Selwyn, when me and Maggie was skating."

Gloria stared at Lizzie, her brows raised in affront. "Really. Forgive me. I do not recall."

Claire could not hold back her laughter. "Oh, Gloria, do give over. Your town manners will not win you any points here. But to refresh your memory, we also saw one another at Julia Wellesley's costume party last month." She smoothed the folds of her raiding skirt with affection. "I believe I wore this very rig."

"I'm sure Miss Meriwether-Astor will have no trouble remembering both occasions if she puts her mind to it, won't you, dear?" Lady Dunsmuir slipped an arm around Gloria's waist and the air exploded in a flash of light and the smell of phosphorus as a phalanx of journalists recorded the moment for posterity. She steered Gloria and her father toward the dining hall and the welcoming party followed. "Lady Claire is our honored guest. She has been touring the Americas with us and sharing our adventures."

"Lady Claire, is it?" Mr. Meriwether-Astor puffed along behind the women like a steam train. "Better mind your manners, Gloria. She might have a brother."

"I do, in fact," Claire told him, trying not to show her amusement at the poisonous glare Gloria threw him. "But as Lord Nicholas is not even two, he is more interested in his stuffed giraffe than he is in young ladies."

"Ah well, it never hurts to know these things." The poor man's short legs could barely keep up with Lady Dunsmuir's effortless glide. "Don't want to cut ourselves off from possibilities, do we, girl?"

"Father, please," Gloria said softly, her head up and slightly turned away, as if she could not bear the sight of him and was admiring the view instead.

For the first time, Claire felt a pang of sympathy for the girl. Though the days immediately following her graduation from St. Cecilia's Academy for Young Ladies now seemed as if they had been lived by another person altogether, she distinctly remembered how uncomfortable she had felt, being on display at the few parties she had attended, and dreading her presentation at court.

It was one thing to travel across the ocean as a Buccaneer and set one's cap at a title in exchange for a Fifteen Colonies fortune. It was quite another to be bullied and bossed into it by one's father, whom one might expect to take one's tender feelings more into consideration.

Though, if what she suspected was in fact true, Julius Meriwether-Astor, who appeared to be merely a blustering, insensitive buffoon, was nothing of the kind. Could this man now talking with such animation with Lord Dunsmuir really be the one behind the attempt on Count von Zeppelin's life?

It hardly seemed possible. And yet …

She had sworn her friends to secrecy on the matter. Secrecy, and vigilance. Though how they were to watch out for the count's wellbeing without actually telling him what they suspected was a puzzle she had yet to work out. Because of course they had no proof of anything, only mad speculation hanging by the thinnest of threads. If she accused Gloria's father of such a heinous crime, and was proven wrong, they would all be disgraced, and Claire could not bear the thought of any taint upon the Dunsmuirs—not after they had shown her and the children such kindness and support.

Nor could she risk Tigg's future as a midshipman on the *Lady Lucy* for the sake of mere speculation. So for now, they must keep an eye peeled, as Maggie would say, and be alert for the slightest hint that this visit was not as it seemed.

"Lady Dunsmuir, a photograph opportunity, if you please?" called one of the journalists. "If we get a group shot, we can send the plates by pigeon and get the pictures in the Sunday papers."

"Very well." She turned to Claire and Alice. "While we are doing that, you girls might like to change for dinner. Count von Zeppelin's invitation, you know, aboard the *Margrethe*."

Alice looked as though she was going to be sick. "I thought that was tomorrow. And anyhow—"

"Tomorrow we shall host a dinner for the entire camp, and a ball. But tonight is a smaller, more intimate party."

"No, I can't," Alice said, a little desperately.

"Please, dear." Davina put a hand on her arm. "You and Jake. As a personal favor to me."

Alice let out a long breath in defeat. "Very well. But I'm pulling up ropes in the morning."

"You must do as you think best, of course. But may I say that we women will be far outnumbered by partners tomorrow evening at the ball. The loss of one of us will be a tragedy for a great many men."

"Dancing with me would be a greater one," Alice mumbled.

The journalists began to clamor for Davina's attention. "I must go. Eight o'clock, ladies, with sherry at seven."

Claire took the Mopsies' hands so they would not get lost in the pushing and shoving as the journalists set up their equipment and vied for the best spots in the central courtyard. Alice accompanied them back to the *Lady Lucy*, where she said, "Jake's waiting on me. He won't be too happy about being shanghaied tonight, either."

"If there's a spread, he'll be fine," Maggie told her. "Can't we come?"

"I'm afraid not, darling," Claire said. "You are not yet out in society, and won't be for some time, so I hope you will keep Willie and Tigg company here on the ship."

"Wot's 'out in society'?"

"It means you go on display in your mama's shop window when you're sixteen, waiting for the highest bidder," Alice told her without much grace.

"We ent got a mama," Lizzie said. Then she turned a horrified gaze to Claire. "Lady, you ent goin' t'put us in a window, then, like a pair of plucked geese wiv frilly paper round our feet?"

"Certainly not." She must not laugh, for if her limited experience was anything to go by, the image held more truth than the little girl knew. "Alice is being a poultice, and you must not listen to her. Being out simply means that you may go to balls and parties, and receive calls from gentlemen. When the time comes, you and Maggie will go with me and—" She stopped.

Dear me. She had come within a breath of saying—

"You an' 'oo?" Lizzie prompted her.

"My husband, whomever that gentleman may turn out to be, if I am indeed married five years from now."

"Mr. Malvern," Maggie said with an air of one who knows.

"Captain Hollys," Lizzie shot back with equal certainty.

"The man in the moon, if it were any of your business!"

Honestly, she was going to pack them both back to London for further lessons from Snouts McTavish in keeping their mouths shut, and that was a fact.

18

Alice took a deep breath and felt the determined grip of her corset as it restricted her air intake to ladylike levels. No wonder ladies in novels fainted every time they got scared. They couldn't ruddy well breathe.

Beside her, Jake indicated she should precede him up to the gangway, and she looked at him, surprised. "Where did you learn to do that?"

"Wot?"

"Allow a female to go first."

He flushed, and let out a croak that turned into a squeak. He coughed and tried again. "I watched 'is lordship and Mr. Malvern. Go on, then. D'you want to freeze standing out 'ere?"

"Thank you, Jake," she said as politely as any lady, and picked up her turquoise skirts to manage the gangway. At the top an officer was posted, and he assisted her from the last step.

"Welcome again to the *Landgrafin Margrethe*, Captain Chalmers," he said. "I am the assistant steward. Will you follow me?"

"Good evening," she replied. "This is Jake, my navigator."

Awkwardly, Jake bowed, clearly uncomfortable in the one good suit that Claire had prevailed upon him to get in Edmonton. It was clear he had never worn a jacket and shirt so fine in his life, and it was that which made him uncomfortable more than how the fabric felt.

"Never mind, Jake," she whispered as she rustled down the passage after the assistant steward. "It's only a couple of hours and some good grub, and then we can go."

Their guide motioned them through a set of carved double doors and they entered the flagship's huge salon. Alice's breath caught and Jake whistled, a low sound like a half-empty teakettle taken off the burner.

The room could hold a hundred people, though at present there were only half that number. What appeared to be gambit tables for the planning of battles had been seconded to duty as buffet tables, which were laden with food and phalanxes of crystal glasses and goblets. At the far end, uniformed men formed a small orchestra, at present engaged in a graceful waltz.

"Oh, blast, can they really be planning to dance after dinner? I thought all that palaver wasn't until tomorrow."

"They've room to," Jake observed tersely. "You could 'ide behind them velvet curtains, or pretend to be one of them trees in pots."

"Best shut up, or you'll be the first one I ask to be my partner."

Jake clamped his lips together as if he never meant to speak again. Still, he stuck by her side like a burr as she wended her way across the room to where Claire and Captain Hollys stood, looking picturesque and annoyingly comfortable in all this posh crowd, next to the punchbowl.

"Captain Chalmers. Jake." Hollys knew better than to kiss the back of her gloved hand, so he shook it instead. "You're looking uncommonly well this evening, Alice, considering your brush with near death this afternoon."

"I'd rather face a herd of caribou than this lot," she told him.

"Buck up, old thing," Andrew Malvern joined them just in time to hear her, and she immediately wished she could drop through a hatch in the floor. "Did you stash a pistol in that rig to ward off potential partners?"

"That dress is the latest design from Paris," Claire informed him down her nose. "It is not a weapons holster."

"If it were, it would be the prettiest one ever made," said Captain Hollys gallantly, coming to Alice's rescue. "You wore this to the governor's ball, did you not?"

"She did," Andrew said before she could open her mouth.

He remembered. And Alice had not forgotten her feelings then, either, when it seemed he finally saw her as a woman, not a companion at arms. What was up, then, with his cavalier treatment of her now? Didn't she deserve to be treated like a lady, the way he treated Claire, instead of one of his chums from the honkytonk?

She turned her back on him and laid a hand on Captain Hollys's arm. "I wonder if we might walk over to the windows, sir? I thought I might lift in the morning and would like your opinion of the sky."

Since it was pitch black, all they'd be able to see would be their own reflections, but Captain Hollys was too much of a gentleman to say so. He tucked her hand into the crook of his elbow and led her away, leaving Andrew standing there gaping like a barn owl.

Alice's spine straightened with satisfaction, which had the added effect of making her corset sit more comfortably. Her skirts whispered across the Turkish carpet and Captain Hollys cut a tall, debonair figure next to her in his dress uniform.

Very satisfying indeed.

"Are you really planning to lift tomorrow?" he asked. "We've had reports of weather on the way, but not for a few days yet."

"Who do you get weather reports from? Are there other mines further north than this?"

"No. I mean, there are other mines, but they are scattered to the south and east. We obtain our reports from the Esquimaux."

"But I thought—the miners—"

"You've seen the tension between them."

"I understand some think the Esquimaux are responsible for the sabotage," she said as delicately as she could, considering Isobel Churchill, resplendent in green-and-gold brocade and a train you could make a set of drapes out of, was talking in low tones with one of the journalists not ten feet away.

"That is a mystery her ladyship is determined to solve," he said softly. "The Dunsmuirs have excellent relationships with the Esquimaux in these territories. Did you know the latter have thirty-five different words for snow?"

"I did not. But what that tells me is that they know it intimately."

"Quite so. They know weather just as intimately, and many of the young men have shown an aptitude for mechanics, to the point that they operate a fleet of pigeons themselves. Pigeons, and many other marvelous devices."

"So they do more than hunt and fish?"

"As do we all, my dear. The trappings change, but one must still eat and drink and protect oneself from the weather. The Esquimaux have honed all three skills to a fine art—among many others. Her ladyship encourages as many of the crew as are able to spend a winter with them here. It is a hard winter, mind you, but the ones who survive it have the ability to read skies that cannot be replicated anywhere else. One of my engine masters can practically feel a storm two days before it hits."

Alice was silent a moment, taking this in.

"So the bad blood between the miners and the Esquimaux … is it a fabrication, then?"

"I cannot say for certain. Only that her ladyship is distressed by it and is determined to get to the bottom of it. Such fabrications, as you say, would tear the substance of what we have built here—and I do not mean mines and such." He looked across the room, where Lord Dunsmuir was offering his wife his arm. "Dinner is served, I see. Will you join me at my table?"

For a moment, Alice thought he was joking. "Are all the captains put together?"

"No indeed. But my opportunities to dine with a young lady are few and far between, and if you lift tomorrow, I shall not get another chance."

Alice hardly knew which way to look. And here she'd thought the captain was sweet on Claire! Well, maybe he was, but he was also a gentleman who would not leave a lady in the lurch. Claire had told her in Edmonton that people paired off to eat according to some confusing set of rules of precedence. He was a captain. She was a captain. He was handsome and interesting and she'd be gosh-darned if she let Andrew Malvern see how much his treatment bothered her.

"I would be delighted and honored, sir," she said. "May we include Jake?" She took two steps over behind a potted palm and snagged the boy's arm. "Otherwise the poor git will hide back here all night and not get a single bite."

"Nothing would please me more." Captain Hollys smiled, and for a wonder, Jake grinned back.

"Someone's got to look after our Alice," he said. "Some days it takes two."

"Says you, you rascal," she told him with no small amount of affection, taking the captain's arm and offering the other in a more ladylike fashion to Jake. "Just for that, you can dance the first waltz with me. Then we'll see who's looking after who."

Which shut him up properly until they were well into the second course. By the time dessert was set out—a flaky pastry filled with apples that made Jake's eyes roll back in his head with ecstasy—Alice was feeling much more at ease.

So much so that she didn't even mind when Captain Hollys responded to a glance from Lord Dunsmuir and left her to her coffee with a murmured apology.

"This ent so bad," Jake said, relaxing on a settee next to her as the stewards cleared the tables, pushing the chairs back against the wall for the dancing. "Even Count von Zeppelin's speech. Hard to believe a toff like 'im could be so funny."

"I'm finding folks aren't often what we think," she agreed. "I wonder what—"

"Is this seat taken?" Gloria Meriwether-Astor sank onto the settee next to Alice as though the weight of the world lay on her lace-covered shoulders. "You're the Texican, aren't you?" she said, and when Alice nodded, she sighed so deeply her stays creaked. "What a relief. Talk to me. I long for the accents of home."

Alice couldn't think what to say. This girl had insulted her friend to her face, and now she was sidling up to her? "Have you been gone a long time?"

"A year and a half. It feels like forever. I swear, when we put down in New York I nearly fell to the ground and kissed it. I was highly tempted to simply run away. It's only a day on the train home to Philadelphia."

"Why didn't you?" Jake wanted to know.

Gloria's gaze inspected him for flaws, or so it seemed to Alice. "You're not Texican."

"That's right observant of you."

"Jake," Alice said in warning.

"It's all right." Gloria waved a hand. "Who might you be?"

"I'm navigator aboard the *Stalwart Lass*." Jake nodded at Alice. "This 'ere's 'er captain, Alice Chalmers."

"That's right, I remember now. You were with Claire when we landed." While Alice marveled at the sudden resurrection of her memory, Gloria gazed out across the room to where her father was engaged in a lively conversation with the *Margrethe*'s first officer. "And my father made a fool of himself and me."

"Does he do that a lot?" Maybe that had been rude. But Gloria didn't look offended.

"I'm afraid so. Goodness knows what he's saying now—probably some burble about how much money he has."

"That's the first officer 'e's talkin' to," Jake said. "Might be he's talking sense, like ships and guns and such."

Gloria touched her forehead delicately with the back of her hand in its fine kidskin glove. "Save me from more talk of guns," she sighed. "It's pressure rifle this and steam cannon that until I swear I'm fit to scream."

"Ah, the Meriwether-Astor Munitions Works?" Alice inquired, as if she hadn't made up the term out of thin air not an hour past.

"The very same. Papa's pet project, and one I'd cheerfully blow up myself if I thought it would do any good."

"Wot's a steam cannon?" Jake asked in a tone that almost sounded social.

"Heavens, don't you start. Because of the wretched thing, we could not bring the second landau—the one that *I* should have had use of. If I hear its name again I swear I *shall* scream. On the other hand, maybe that handsome captain would come back to rescue me. Do you think I should try it?" And she straightened so gracefully that it took Alice a second to realize she was craning her neck to find Captain Hollys in the crowd.

"Don't think so," she said through her best smile. "Captain Hollys, if that's who you mean, isn't much for fragile flowers. He seems to prefer the strong and sensible type."

"That will never be me." Gloria subsided, her brief spurt of energy gone.

"Why not?" Alice asked her. "This room is full of strong and sensible types. Why shouldn't you be one of them?"

"Because strong and sensible types don't land titles, you ninny," Gloria snapped, her company manners peeling back abruptly to reveal what might be the real person underneath.

"More to this world than titles," Jake observed.

"Not when you have the father I do."

Jake shrugged. "So leave. Go do something sensible yer own self."

She glared at him. "Mind your manners, you young scamp, or I'll have you put off this ship."

He grinned at her. "I'd like to see you try. You ent no fine lady. I know a few, and you ent one. You're just content to sit and whinge about yer lot. There's a pair of eleven-year-olds 'ere got more spine than you."

"How dare you!" Two spots of color appeared in Gloria's porcelain cheeks, and she looked almost ready to get up. "Do you know who I am?"

"I expect you need the answer to that worse than me," was the laconic reply.

"Well, I never." Gloria stood and turned on her heel so swiftly that Alice felt the breeze from her train. She stalked across the empty space in front of the orchestra, heading for the bluster in the corner where her father seemed to be holding court.

"Nicely done, Jake." Alice toasted him with her china coffee cup. "We're about to get tossed off this boat thanks to you."

But he only shrugged. "I got no time for whingers, whether they've got a fat purse or not. If I can make something of meself, then so can she. You don't 'ear the Lady orderin' people about and moanin' about 'er lot, nor you neither."

Rough-and-tumble though they might be, those few words from her young navigator made Alice feel better than any number of compliments could have.

"Jake, about tomorrow. I don't think it's fair to ask you to leave all your friends to go gosh knows where with me."

She would have to figure out the location of *gosh knows where* pronto. Now that she'd found Pa, she didn't really have a destination in mind once she got herself away from him and his infernal pigeons. It was one thing to ask a young man to help a girl in her quest. It was another thing altogether to drag him around the skies while she figured out what to do with the rest of her life.

Jake dragged his gaze from Gloria, who was now propped against a table while she tried to get her father's attention. "But I'm yer navigator."

"I know, and a fine one, too. But—but I'm not sure you've thought this through. If you go with me, what are the odds you'll see them all again?"

"When I play cowboy poker, I stack the odds in me own favor by rememberin' the cards."

"That's all very nice for clever-boots with memories like cameras. But I'm talking about wind currents and continents and many miles between friends."

"Them wind currents blow east as well as west. And wiv a stout ship that don't leak, one continent is much the same as another. I say we gets to choose our course, Alice Chalmers, not be blown about like this-tledown."

"You sound like Claire."

He snorted.

"So you wouldn't object to the occasional voyage to, say, England—" An idea swooped into her head like a cliff swallow to its nest. "—if we could pick up a proper cargo?"

"I wouldn't. There's a field hard by the cottage. Lewis and Snouts can do some pickin' at the scrap yards and rig up a mooring mast there in jig time."

She needed to speak with Lady Dunsmuir. Surely an empire as big as theirs needed folks with the skills to ferry things around?

She looked over to where the Dunsmuirs were laughing with the count and clinking glasses with him, when the music started up. What was it with these Prussians that everything they played was a waltz? And worse, there was Andrew Malvern heading her way like one of those mining engines under full steam.

"Oh, blast." She put her cup and saucer down and turned to Jake. "Dance with me."

"Wot?" He goggled at her as if she'd given him orders to fling himself off the top of the fuselage.

"I don't want to dance with Mr. Malvern, and he's headed this way. It's an act of charity, Jake. Get a move on."

"I dunno 'ow to dance, Captain!"

"Just *get* me *out* on the *floor*," she said between her teeth.

He grasped her in a fair approximation of a waltz hold, and she realized that he had grown four or five inches while no one was looking. "One two three, one two three. Just move your feet. That's it." Well, this was a blessing. A lifetime of being nimble on his feet in order to survive seemed to be paying off—he picked up the rhythm much more quickly than she had in her few lessons in Edmonton. "Now lengthen your step—I want lots of people between us and him."

Within a few bars of music, he had done what she asked.

"Well, done, Jake. Remind me to cut you hazard pay for this."

"Any pay 'ud be good, Captain ... one two free, one two free."

"Point taken. Now see if you can—"

"Excuse me, may I cut in?"

A large body in a black dinner jacket levered Jake out of the way. She got a glimpse of the boy's astonished face before she thought to look up at the man who had removed him so cavalierly—and so efficiently.

"Evening, Alice," Frederick Chalmers said as he waltzed her smoothly into the whirling stream of dancers circumnavigating the salon. "You sure do clean up nice."

19

Alice was so gobsmacked that even the swear words that might have been appropriate to the situation fled her empty skull. The best she could manage was a lame, "What are you doing here?"

Chalmers—she would not think of him as Pa, she just wouldn't—whirled her into a spin and caught her on the other side of it without missing a step. "I'm trying to find a way to apologize to my daughter without getting shot."

"I didn't mean that. I meant, how did you get past the officers at the gangplank when half the camp thinks you're responsible for the sabotage at the mine?"

For six full bars of music he stared into her face as if he were trying to translate what she'd said from Navapai to Esquimaux. Finally, he said, "You've been here less than a day and you've heard this?"

"Is it true?" If he could butt in on her nice evening with society folks, then she could butt in on his peace of mind. If he had any.

"It is not. And I am sorry you had to ask. But it's my own fault, isn't it, for not providing you with a father you could trust."

Well, that took the gas out of her balloon good and proper. Maybe she should just shut up and hope that Andrew Malvern would come and cut in. Because getting to the end of this waltz seemed about as simple as flying back to Edmonton in the next three minutes.

"Please don't lift tomorrow," he said quietly, his breath disturbing her hair. "I would consider it a gift to spend a few hours with you and find out what kind of woman you've become."

Alice tried to think of a scathing reply, but mostly she just wanted to pull out of his arms and find a pair of drapes behind which she could cry.

"I never stopped loving you, dearling," he said. "I know what they're saying about me and the Esquimaux here, and I know Reggie Penhaven will probably have me arrested as soon as he knows I'm aboard, but it was worth the risk to find you and say my say while I could."

"Is there a price on your head here, too?"

"As soon as they manufacture some proof, I'm sure there will be."

"But why? What have they got against you? The Dunsmuirs seem like decent sorts—they know who I am and they've treated me downright civil."

"So you've told them you're related to me?"

"Well, sure. That's the whole reason I came all the way from Resolution. I tracked you to Santa Fe and then to Edmonton ... and then here."

She felt like a fool for admitting it, but it was the truth. When he didn't reply, she looked up, and was stunned into silence a second time by the expression in his eyes.

His wet eyes, blazing with admiration, with grief, and ... with love. For her.

"You tracked me from one end of the continent to the other?" he breathed at last. "No wonder you were so angry. You went through all that, and I must have seemed like ten kinds of yellow-bellied coward for not being willing to do the same."

Another whirl, and she found herself being danced down a short corridor and into what appeared to be a galley. It was narrow, and cramped, and empty but for racks of dinner plates and cups.

Frederick Chalmers released her, all except for her gloved hand, which he held the way some people held gold, in both hands.

She had not been prepared for honesty. It was one thing for *her* to say her say and call things as she saw them. It was another altogether to have someone be just as honest with her. It left her nowhere to hide, no smart remarks behind which to take offense, no lies and affectations to poke fun at and gain the upper hand.

It left only herself, in her silken finery, feeling lost and naked in the cold.

"Yes," she said at last. "That's exactly how I felt. But that's no reason for you to come here and risk getting tossed in the brig."

"They need proof for that, and since it's all rumor and innuendo and third-hand information, it's not likely they'll find any by the end of the evening."

"But why? That's what I don't get. The Dunsmuirs don't—"

"It isn't the Dunsmuirs. I don't want to say any more in case I'm wrong, and to burden you with knowledge might harm you."

"I know a thing or two, Pa. I know that the Dunsmuirs trust the Esquimaux who work here, and the folks in your village. And I know there's someone out there who doesn't want Count von Zeppelin's ships to land anywhere but New York City. And I know—"

His grip on her hand tightened. "What do you know of that? Alice, keep your voice down. Men can be killed for saying things like that out loud."

"But it's true," she whispered. "Men have already been killed. They nearly got Claire and me—it was only chance that we didn't get shot full of bullets with tiny propeller engines and *M.A.M.W.* stamped on 'em." She tugged her hand out of his. "Ow."

"I'm sorry, dearling. You just—you surprised the stuffing out of me. Please tell me you haven't said any of this to anyone."

"Just to Claire and the kids."

"Kids? Are you serious? Children are being burdened with this knowledge?"

"They're not ordinary kids," she said dryly. "Those twin girls with us—they know everything."

"They can't. You can't. Alice, it's worth your life to speak of this."

She eyed him. "You sound like some kind of spy. What are you really doing up here?"

Now he slid the galley door closed and locked it. His voice dropped to barely above a whisper. "You've got your ma's brains, and that's a fact. So it has happened already? The count knows his life is in danger?"

"Hard to avoid it, when a bullet creases your head and lays you out. But like you say, there's no proof. Someone shot at us, and the bullets' engine casings have those initials on them, but that don't mean anything. Lizzie found something similar under one of the cargo ships, too, but—" She shrugged. Said out loud like that, most sane people would just roll their eyes and sidestep away.

"On the contrary, it means a great deal. Alice, are you acquainted with the count? I mean, outside of being in the vehicle when the attempt was made?"

"It does tend to bring strangers together," she said dryly. "I guess I'm on speaking terms. He wants to talk with me about my automatons."

"I do, too, but it will have to wait for a sunny day and crisp snow." She must have looked confused, for he smiled and said, "It's something Malina says. Alice, I must be quick. You must find a way to convince the count to leave here as soon as possible. By dawn at the latest."

"How d'you expect me to do that?"

"I am sure you can find a way."

"But Pa, I can't just waltz up to one of the greatest men in the world and say, excuse me, sir, but a suspected saboteur says you're to leave pronto. Why would he do anything but laugh and pat me on the head?"

"Because I have reason to think there will be another attempt if he stays much longer. If not tonight, then definitely during the tour of the mine tomorrow. They mean to blame it on poor management by the Dunsmuirs, thus discrediting the family and destroying the enterprise here. It might even—" He clamped his lips shut.

"—start a war?"

He stared at her, his face going so still it might have been turned to stone. "Where did you hear that?" he whispered.

"Nowhere. Claire and Andrew and I were talking of it. Why start a bullet business on a continent where you can't sell enough to keep it going? The only place you could sell them would be to countries who are at war."

He drew in a shallow breath, then seemed to force himself to breathe more deeply. More calmly. Finally he was able to speak. "Governments have fallen for saying such things."

"Lucky it's just you and me and the plates and cups, then." She waited for him to reply, and when he did not, said, "Pa, how do you know all this? What's a man living in the back of beyond with a lot of Esquimaux got to do with anything?"

He seemed to come back to himself with difficulty. "Thirty days from now I will tell you, when it's all over."

"When what's over?"

"Alice, please just trust me. You must whisper in the count's ear and get him to lift by dawn. Can you do that?"

"I can probably whisper in his ear, but I don't fancy he's the type to ask how high when I say jump."

"Just do your best. It is all any of us can do."

Frustration and about a thousand questions roiled in her gut under the constricting corset. She stared at him, her lips compressed so she wouldn't blurt out a bunch of swear words, and his gaze softened.

"My dear brave girl. Have I told you how proud I am of you?"

She shook her head. "You ain't spoken to me in fourteen years, Pa."

"But I have. Every day. Every time I learned something new, I shared it with you in my head. Every time I saw a new landscape, I imagined exploring it with you. And every time the pigeons came back, I saw you growing and changing, and my heart broke a little more."

Now she really had to press her lips together, or she would break down and weep. As it was, the hot prick of tears made her blink. She must not cry. She must not let him see.

"Alice." He said her name like a prayer. "Whatever happens, I will find you when what the Esquimaux call the caribou moon—the full moon following the caribou migration—is at its brightest. Our time here is nearly over, anyway. I just wish—"

She followed his gaze to the ring of delicately carved ivory on the fourth finger of his right hand. "Is that from Malina? Is she your wife?"

"Yes. And yes. I am trying to steel myself to leaving her and the girls. The shadow side of my actions is that I have no funds to keep them with me. It is a simple fact that in doing my duty, I must leave them."

Alice raised her fingers to her hair, and touched what was fixed there. "You need money?"

"Not here, no. But if I were to travel with my family, I would."

She was already undoing the clasp of the diamond watch pin that Claire had given her back in Resolution as thanks for helping her. She had offered to give it back to Davina, but the latter had only laughed and asked if she would like the earrings to match. The latter were in her ears at this moment, as a kind of security deposit against the future. "Take this. If you can get as far as Edmonton, you can exchange it for gold. It ought to get you wherever you're going."

"I can't take this from you. Was it a gift?"

"It was. It used to belong to Lady Dunsmuir, and now I'm giving it to you."

"Alice, this is worth several hundred pounds at least—these three diamonds are a carat apiece, and all these brilliants set around them amount to one more. I can't take the most valuable thing you own."

"The *Lass* is the most valuable thing I own. This is just something to put in my hair." She put the pin in his palm and folded his fingers around it. "If this means you can be with Malina and the girls and me all at once, then it's money well spent."

His other hand covered hers. "Just when I believe there is no hope for human nature, I meet the refutation of that belief in my own daughter."

"That's a lot of twenty-five-cent words, Pa."

"I believe in getting my money's worth."

"Will I see you again, really?"

"Look for me by the caribou moon."

"How? I could be in Victoria by then. Or San Francisco. Or—or London, I guess, if I can find a cargo."

"You forget the pigeons. I will send one with you on the *Lass*. Just release it when you moor somewhere for more than a day, and I'll come."

She could say no. She could drum up some righteous rage, and turn a cold shoulder and march out of this narrow little room doing double duty as a confessional. But what would that get her?

More of the same, that's what. More tears, and more empty skies, and a lifetime of feeling as rootless and vulnerable as she had coming in here.

A caribou moon meant the end of one season ... and the beginning of another. Maybe she should open her eyes ... and her heart.

"Alice?" He bent to look into her face. "Please don't cry, sweetheart."

But it was too late. She threw herself into his arms and bawled like the little girl she had once been.

20

"'Scuse me, can I 'ave this dance?"

To Claire's utter astonishment—and that of the young officer partnering her—Jake cut in and manfully attempted to steer her away from the young man and across the floor.

"One two free, one two free … Lady, we gots to rescue Alice. She an' some gent did 'alf a waltz and then disappeared down that corridor there, behind them frondy things."

"Those are palms. And Jake, there are occasions when a lady may be allowed some privacy."

He made a disgusted sound and tripped. His recovery was quick, though, and her skirts disguised most of it. "It weren't that way. 'E weren't one of us, nor one of the *Margrethe*'s crew neither."

"Describe him."

When he was finished, Claire patted him with the hand that rested on his shoulder. "The ocular device confirms it. That is Frederick Chalmers, her father. They had words in the Esquimaux village. Perhaps he has come to repair their relationship."

"P'raps. And p'raps we should make sure she's all right, him bein' a saboteur and all."

"I am convinced he has been unjustly accused, but to set your mind at ease, we will join them."

In seconds Jake had located which of the paneled doors along the short service corridor was the correct one, and Claire opened it, preparing a smile.

She found Alice in tears in Frederick Chalmers's arms.

"Captain!" Jake sprang into the room. "All right?"

Alice lifted her head and snuffled like a child, whereupon her father twitched a linen napkin off a nearby stack and handed it to her. "Yes," she said, and blew her nose. "What's wrong?"

"I thought—"

"Jake was concerned," Claire said smoothly, when Jake came to an abrupt halt. "Mr. Frederick Chalmers, may I introduce Alice's navigator, Jake Fletcher."

"Beggin' yer pardon, Lady, but it's McTavish," the boy said slowly. "Snouts bade me keep it quiet from the others and use a different 'andle. I'm 'is brother. 'alf brother."

"Jake McTavish," she corrected herself, inclining her head in thanks for the information while wondering why on earth Snouts would require such a thing. "Mr. Chalmers, will you be joining us this evening?"

"No," Alice said. She balled up the napkin and stuffed it down the front of her gown. Claire tried not to wince. "He'll be hightailing it off this boat as quick as he can, before Penhaven finds out he's here."

"Or I can be polite and greet the Dunsmuirs and Count von Zeppelin." He gave his daughter a meaningful glance. "And *then*, while the director is dragging me away, you might get a chance to speak with the count."

Instead of answering, Alice proceeded to brief Claire on the particulars of what she and her father had just been discussing.

"I knew it," Claire breathed.

"You know nothing," Frederick said sharply. "I have asked Alice to do one thing, and one thing only. Her friends are not to be involved."

"Gettin' shot at don't make us involved?" Jake asked. "Seems like we got bigger fish to fry than gettin' the count clear of here. Wot 'appens if they go ahead wiv the sabotage anyways? More folks than just 'im could get 'urt."

"For heaven's sake, I will not discuss such secret matters with children!"

Jake eyed him. "Ent been a child in a long time." Then, upon seeing Claire's pointed gaze, reluctantly added, "Sir."

"Give it up, Pa. We're involved and that's that. You can be secretive about the rest of it, but meantime, it's our friends in danger here."

Chalmers struggled with himself, and while he did, Claire thought aloud. "It's safe to expect that Meriwether-Astor wants the Dunsmuirs to survive to bear the shame. Otherwise, why go to all the trouble of bringing the journalists? If they are killed, they become martyrs and the two-inch headlines will announce a state funeral instead of … whatever he is going to accuse them of."

Chalmers let out a breath with as much exasperated noise as a steam engine. "For the last time, you must not—"

The floor jerked out from under their feet as the great flagship reeled from a sudden blow of massive force. Claire and Alice were flung into one another's arms, while Jake fell into Chalmers's back. The dishes slid up one side of their racks and clattered down into place again, while outside the galley, shrieks of terror and the smash and tinkle of glass told Claire that the buffet had not been so carefully engineered for bad weather.

She had just pushed herself up onto her hands and knees when a second blow struck the ship. It swooped sickeningly, as though all its mooring ropes had failed on one side and it had taken leave of the ground. With a cry, she fell against the cabinet doors. At least she had not far to fall this time.

"Alice? Are you all right? Jake?" Dear heaven, she had to get over to the *Lady Lucy*. "We must make certain the Mopsies are all right, and Tigg and Willie. Jake?"

A groan told her he was conscious, at least. The three of them helped each other struggle to their feet, she and Alice impeded by yards of silk and petticoats that they finally hauled up in their hands so they could find their footing.

"What was that?" Alice groaned. "An earthquake?"

"That was no earthquake." After pulling himself to his feet, Frederick Chalmers tugged his waistcoat into place, looking grim. "That was a pressure wave—or else something happened to the gas bags within the fuselage. There will have been an explosion, and close by, too."

Bruised, sore, they tumbled out of the little galley. When they entered the saloon, Claire realized how much luck had been on their side. For the galley had protected them in a way that the large room full of loose objects had not protected the dancers, musicians, and other guests and crew of the *Margrethe*.

Chalmers gripped his daughter's hand. "Are you really all right?"

"Yes, Pa. I'll have a big bruise on my behind to-morrow. Not like these other poor folks—where are the count's medics?"

But Chalmers was not to be distracted. "You must get von Zeppelin off the ship and out of here. Ten to one this is merely a distraction and he is the real target."

"But Pa—"

"Quick, Alice. There is no time to lose. I'm going out to see what happened."

Claire caught Jake's eye and the boy followed him out without a word, quick as a footpad, weaving in and out of the dazed men and women in formal dress who were making for the gangways, instinctively seeking solid ground. The medics, who were coming through from the crew deck with their bags, began to work on the fallen and injured.

The Dunsmuirs were on their feet, and appeared to be having strong words about her ladyship's leaving. Claire wound her way over, stepping over a swath of smashed desserts and three potted palms stretched out on the carpet, their fronds like fingers beseeching aid.

"Davina, we must see to the children on *Lady Lucy* immediately," she said in a tone that made the earl draw himself up in affront.

"You shall *not*—"

"John, I am responsible for the twins and Tigg," Claire told him firmly. "Davina and I will escort each other. You must see to the safety of your crew and officers here."

"But there may be—"

"Thank you, John. We shall return in half an hour."

Davina grasped her hand and the two of them hauled up their trains and dashed helter-skelter for the gangway, leaping over smashed china and fallen chairs, skirting around the medical men bending over their patients, until they gained the ground.

From there it was only a matter of fifty yards to *Lady Lucy* ... where they could see what had happened. For the force of the blast had pierced the *Margrethe*'s fuselage, and in the light from the airfield they could see its great gas bags slowly collapsing. Already aero-nauts were scrambling in the fixed rigging, closing valves and shouting orders to one another as the ship sagged on the ground.

If Frederick Chalmers had hoped the count would leave the north under his own steam, that hope was now dashed. From what Claire could see, it would take days to repair the damage—and with weather on its way, did they have that time?

"Such a noble ship," Davina said, as though of a friend who had died. "We must do all we can to assist. But first things first."

Three of the middies watched anxiously at the windows of *Lady Lucy*'s gondola, and when Davina waved, their heads disappeared and they appeared moments later, jumping down to hold the gangway steps for her.

"Were any of you injured?" she asked, pausing on the bottom step.

"No, your ladyship," young Colley said. "I can't say the same of the furniture, nor the collation on the sideboard, neither."

"Willie?"

"Safe, your ladyship," Tigg responded. "Bumped 'is elbow falling out of bed, is all."

"Well done, Mr. Terwilliger. Mr. Yau shall have my commendation for your prompt action this very night."

Davina took the steps two at a time, Claire on her heels. She ran back to the family's suite, while Claire dashed down the corridor with Tigg right behind her.

"What was it, Lady?" he asked. "Knocked us all to the deck all of a sudden, it did."

"It was a pressure wave from an explosion." She pushed open the Mopsies' door to find them both on their feet. "Are you all right?"

"Aye," Lizzie said. "Wot's a pressure wave?"

But Claire did not answer. Instead, she gathered the three of them into her arms, much to Tigg's embarrassed pleasure. "I am so glad. There were many people injured on the *Margrethe*—I had terrible visions of what might have happened on a ship so much smaller."

"What exploded?" Tigg wanted to know. When he wriggled out of her grasp, Claire released them and stood.

"I'm sure we shall find out shortly, when Jake comes back. Lizzie appears to have been correct earlier, though … Count von Zeppelin is to be the target of another attack, we suspect by the Meriwether-Astors, and Mr. Chalmers seems to think the explosion is merely a distraction."

"Mr. Chalmers?" Maggie sounded puzzled. "Where'd he come from?"

"He and Alice have made up. Come. Enough talking. Help me out of this ridiculous gown and into my raiding rig. I suspect our night has only begun."

Any faint hope Claire might have cherished that the Mopsies would stay on the ship was dashed so quickly it might not have existed.

Keeping close, they followed her to the family suite, where she opened the door without being invited to do so. "Davina? I'm taking the girls and Tigg to reconnoiter."

Her ladyship and Willie cuddled together on a divan that had slid all the way over to the row of portholes on the hull. "You promised John to return in half an hour. See that you do so. Then bring him here if you can, to begin planning for the *Margrethe*'s repairs. Willie and I are quite all right, and Mr. Andersen and Mr. Yau are aboard should we need assistance."

Or protection. Claire could hear the words in her tone, though she did not say them with children present. If any danger to her son were to present itself, Claire had no doubt who would win.

She nodded and closed the door. "Come along, girls. Tigg, are you armed?"

"No, Lady. We ent issued a pistol till we been crew for six months."

"Then stay close."

They had no difficulty discovering from whence the explosion had come; a thick plume of dust and smoke issued out of the open pit as though a volcano had erupted. A crowd twenty men deep clustered at the gates, held back by the Dunsmuirs' security men who had linked arms across it.

But even from behind the crowd, the pit was so vast that Claire had no trouble seeing into its depths.

"Wot 'appened, Lady?" Maggie struggled to see past a large gentleman's coat. "I can't see."

"It appears that another of those enormous digging engines has been destroyed. That is source of the smoke—there is nothing left of it but a burning shell and some of its continuous track."

But there had been two explosions. What had caused the other? On tiptoe, craning her neck past the shoulder of the large man, she scanned the pit for evidence of another burning engine. Perhaps it was closer to where they stood, and perspective did not allow—

And then she saw it, deep in the pit, where the funnel narrowed and it appeared tunnels might have been dug. But there were no tunnels now. The lowest level had been blown to bits, and even now, entire sections of the sides of the pit were sliding into the hole that was hundreds of feet deep, filling up whatever excavations had once been there.

Claire's knowledge of diamond mining was limited strictly to the brilliants that were its end result, but even she could see that the Firstwater Mine was done for. It would take months of excavation to return it to production. Maybe years.

"Lady!" Lizzie tugged sharply on her sleeve.

"What is it? Did someone step on you?"

"It ent me. It's Alice's dad."

"Where?" How on earth could she see in this crush?

But Lizzie, who apparently had grown tired of trying to see around people and had gone out to the fringes to get a better look, was no longer interested in pits and explosions. She dragged Claire over behind a sentry shack and pointed. "Look. That's 'im, innit?"

If the crowd in front of them was awestruck in the face of tragedy, the one over by the mine offices was fierce and savage. Struggling in its midst was Frederick Chalmers, his dinner jacket torn nearly off, and alongside him two young men wearing the colorful fur-trimmed coats favored by the Esquimaux.

"Oh, dear. Come on."

"Pa!" came a shriek from across the gravel of the airfield, and Alice shot between two of the buildings to plunge into the crowd, her aquamarine skirts bunched up in both hands as she used elbows and shoulders to get to him. "Take your hands off him, you dadburned varmints! Leave him alone!"

"Alice, no!" her father roared.

"Shut up, you!" Reggie Penhaven, his face scarlet in the light of the mining lamps held by nearly half the crowd, threw an elbow that made Chalmers double over, gasping. "We've caught you in the act this time and you're not going to weasel out of it. You and your Esquimaux accomplices!"

Claire unholstered the lightning rifle and plowed into the crowd right behind Alice. The butt glanced off someone's head, then between someone else's shoulder blades, and the way was clear.

"What is the meaning of this?" she demanded in such frigid Belgravia tones that Lady St. Ives herself would have been proud. "Unhand this man at once."

Reggie Penhaven eyed the rifle with more respect that he did Claire herself. "You'd best get back to *Lady Lucy*, yer ladyship," he said. "This is Firstwater business, and none of yours."

"Since Alice was dancing on Count von Zeppelin's ship with Mr. Chalmers not half an hour past, and she is with me in the Dunsmuirs' party, I think it is indeed my business," she snapped, gazing down her nose as though Penhaven were the most disgusting sort of insect. "It is impossible that he should be your saboteur."

"I beg your pardon, but it isn't. These two men are his accomplices. They set the explosives on his orders, and if he was dancing and leaving them to take the blame, then shame on him and her both." Penhaven's eyes blazed. "Now get out of my way, yer ladyship, before you get hurt butting your nose into men's business."

The men holding the struggling Chalmers and the Esquimaux in iron grips surged past her, causing her to stagger back or be trampled.

And as he passed, Frederick Chalmers shouted, "Find Isobel! You must tell her—" One of his captors cuffed him right across his bad eye, and his instructions were cut off in a yelp of pain.

"Where are you going?" she shouted. "Lord Dunsmuir is going to hear of this!"

"Hang 'em! Hang 'em!" the crowd chanted.

"Oh, dear Lord above," she moaned. "Mopsies, Tigg, we must fetch Lord Dunsmuir at once. He will see reason."

"Lady, they'll hang 'im before we get halfway across the airfield." Tigg's voice squeaked and then hit bottom, his brown eyes wide with fear. "And 'oo's Is-

obel? Not that Churchill mort wot makes 'is lordship
so angry?"

Claire couldn't imagine what on earth Isobel Churchill had to do with Frederick Chalmers. To her
knowledge, they'd never even met. The only thing they
might have in common would be a regard for the Esquimaux … which was not going to save his life.

"Lady, I know that man." Lizzie yanked on Claire's
sleeve so hard she nearly lost her grip on the rifle.
"That big one holding onto one of the Esquimaux men.
'Is name's Alan, and 'e's wiv that cargo ship where I
found that brass shell."

Alice fell out of the crowd and clutched Claire like
a drowning person. "We have to do something! Did
you see that? They're going to hang him, Claire!"

"Wait—Alice, no, they're not—Alice, dear one,
stop this at once! You cannot help your father if you
fall to pieces now."

Tears glazed Alice's face and the whites of her eyes
showed her fear for her father's safety. She gasped,
coughed, and did her manful best to control herself.
"Please help," she begged. "I can't bear it to only have
known him for a single day!"

"Alice, listen to me. Did you hear what Lizzie just
said?"

"N-no."

"The man holding one of the Esquimaux lads was
Alan, from the cargo ship. Do you remember seeing
him?"

"Yes. He brought Lizzie back. He's from Santa—"
She stopped. "He told us he's Texican." Alice's breath-

ing calmed as her brain began to turn and pick up steam. "I'll bet you my diamond earrings that those men from the cargo ship—maybe more—set those explosives."

"And were the first to turn and point fingers at the Esquimaux, who have no one to defend them."

Is that why Chalmers wanted Isobel? To defend the Esquimaux men? But what good would that do? She would have about as much power in this situation as Claire herself.

Alice took a few steps in the direction of the mining offices, where they could hear the roar of the crowd bouncing between the low-slung buildings. "They won't hang him, will they?"

"They need the journalists to do a proper job," Claire said, thinking fast. "But what they didn't expect was the damage done by the pressure wave. Half the journalists are probably in sick bay on the *Margrethe*, and the other half are in that crowd, trying to get closer to the pit."

"We have to get him away from them." Alice's voice was rising, her hysteria temporarily slipping its reins. "But how?"

Maggie slipped over to her side and put both arms around her waist in a comforting hug. "Don't fret, our Alice," she said. "Maybe they'll lock 'im in the gents'. Then me and the Lady, we can fetch 'im out." She grinned over her shoulder at Claire. "Can't we, Lady?"

21

Claire wasted no time. "We must divide and conquer. Where is Jake?"

But in the shouting crowd, it was impossible to see more than a heaving mass of angry, fearful and therefore bloodthirsty humanity. One skinny boy doing as she had wordlessly asked—follow and watch—was impossible to make out.

"Maggie, find him and find out where they are holding Mr. Chalmers. Then meet Alice and Lizzie in the countess's powder room, at the bottom of the steps in the secret passage."

Alice gawked at her as though she had gone mad. "Secret passage?"

Lizzie clutched Maggie's hand. "I dunno where the passage is, Lady."

"Maggie will show you. I will go to Lord Dunsmuir and fetch him back here to prevent this disaster. You are the backup plan if I fail. We have broken people out of more impossible prisons than this, have we not?"

"Aye," Maggie said. "Don't be long, Lady. I don't much fancy 'angin' about underground not knowin' wot's goin' on."

"I won't. No matter what, I shall fetch you within the hour. Now, run."

She took her own advice, weaving through the crowd of frantic diamond miners still shouting and pressing at the gates, until she gained the relative freedom of the airfield. She had promised to return to the earl in half an hour. It must be well past that, but perhaps the earl would not notice in the urgent need of all those people for his guidance and leadership.

The damaged ship belonged to the count, of course, but she could not remember seeing him in the melee. Which did not bode well. Anxious butterflies began to flutter in her stomach, but she took a deep breath and leaped up the gangway of the *Margrethe*, trying to ignore them. Perhaps Alice had succeeded in convincing him he was in danger, and he had prudently taken cover.

One thing at a time. At least the count, she devoutly hoped, was not in imminent danger of being hanged.

In the salon, the deck of which was now tilted slightly off the horizontal, some semblance of order had been cobbled together. She dodged between people laid out on the carpet with varying degrees of injury. Medics tended to those who had been hurt the worst, which seemed to have been the dancers, knocked out of their turns and thrown several feet. At least those who had been seated or in the orchestra had been closer to the ground, and had not been plucked out of the air in midstep.

Lord Dunsmuir was nowhere to be seen.

"I do beg your pardon," she said to a man with a red band about his sleeve wrapping a bandage around Gloria's arm with swift, firm movements. "Do you know where I might find Lord Dunsmuir? It is a matter of the greatest urgency."

"*Nein, Fraulein,*" the man said. "As you can see, I am busy here."

"Looking after me," Gloria said. "Claire, what a fright. Do you know what happened?"

"Parties unknown blew up the mine and one of the digging engines," she said with heroic brevity. "Have you seen Lord Dunsmuir?"

"Last I saw, he was over there with my father." Gloria waved a hand in the direction of the corridor that went forward to the bridge. "I'll come with you. Good heavens, Claire, is that a gun?"

"Yes. There is no need. You must conserve your strength."

And without a backward glance, she headed down the corridor, trying doors one after the other. The bridge was in a state of organized chaos as the *Margrethe*'s captain appeared to be taking reports on the state of ship, crew, and guests.

No John.

She could not search the entire ship. There was no time. She must ask for help.

Someone tapped her shoulder and she turned to see Gloria, cradling her arm. "I just had a look out the porthole and saw Lord Dunsmuir heading over to that pretty gold ship with Father and some others."

"Oh, thank you."

She headed for the forward gangway at a run, and only realized several moments later than Gloria was running behind her, awkwardly hugging her arm to her ribs.

"Claire, wait up."

"I can't. A man's life is at stake." She jumped down the stairs two at a time, and ran for the *Lady Lucy* faster than she ever had in her life.

She found John and Davina together in the forward salon, her ladyship still with Willie in her lap, and conferring in low, rapid tones with several men, among them Mr. Meriwether-Astor and the first officer of the *Margrethe.*

Oh, dear. And Reginald Penhaven, who had clearly come straight here while she was fluttering about on the great Zeppelin ship attempting to find them, like a moth beating itself to exhaustion against a windowpane as it tried to get to the lamp within.

"Lord Dunsmuir!" she said breathlessly, crossing the room. "I need your help!"

But he did not seem to hear. It was only when Willie wriggled out of his mother's grasp and ran to hug her around the waist that they took any notice of her at all.

"Claire, return to your cabin at once," his lordship ordered in tones he had never addressed to her before. "It is far too dangerous for you to be wandering about."

"It is far too dangerous for me to stay," she retorted in tones equally peremptory. "John, they are about to hang Frederick Chalmers for causing the explosions, but he is innocent."

"My information indicates you are wrong."

"Your information is biased by the self-interest and criminal intent of your informants."

"Claire!" Davina had gone as pale as her cream silk gown, which, Claire now saw, was streaked with brown stains and what appeared to be half the contents of a punch bowl. "Explain yourself."

Too late, she realized she had let her fear and her temper get the better of her. She had no proof. All she had was the goodwill of her host and hostess, and if she did not step very, very carefully now, she would lose even that.

"Please, my lord, forgive me. I only meant that it is impossible. Frederick Chalmers was dancing with his daughter only moments before the explosion occurred. He could not have done it."

"Are you here again, meddling in matters that don't concern you?" Reginald Penhaven appeared to be on the verge of striking someone. She took a prudent step back. "Your lordship, this girl has already importuned me with the same ridiculous story. We don't have time for this nonsense."

"Claire, I am very sorry, but the evidence suggests that Alice's father is behind this terrible destruction." Davina's voice trembled. "You must be brave—and so must Alice."

"He is not!" Claire said in desperation. "And neither are those poor Esquimaux boys with him. It's all a plot to discredit you!"

"The poor girl is hysterical," Meriwether-Astor said, his face arranged in lines of pity, his eyes measuring, calculating. "Perhaps the medics should administer laudanum?"

"A good suggestion," Penhaven put in.

"At least wait until morning to do … anything … and allow him to tell you himself," she begged the earl, feeling the cold of approaching doom on her skin.

"Claire, if you do not have proof, you must see our position." John Dunsmuir visibly controlled himself in an effort to be civil.

"I do have proof. Perhaps if we speak privately—"

"Dunsmuir, this is a waste of time," Meriwether-Astor snapped. "I have fifty injured men, a damaged convoy, and an injured daughter, and I want to know what you're going to do about it, since it's clear your mismanagement of this operation has been the cause of this disaster."

"Mismanage—!"

"I said *mismanagement*, and I meant it. If any of those men succumb to their injuries and—God forbid—die, I am holding you personally responsible along with that Chalmers madman."

Over by the window, she saw now, two journalists had their notepads out and were scribbling furiously. She and Alice and Lizzie had been right. Meriwether-Astor had timed his moment perfectly, for what better time to strike at the heart of an enemy than when he was staggering from a blow?

Claire felt as though she was caught in the middle of a street with two steambuses bearing down upon her. No matter in which direction she chose to run, one bus or the other would strike her.

But Lord Dunsmuir was an experienced man of the world. If he and Davina could not handle Meriwether-Astor, then no one could.

And they were not in imminent danger of being hanged, either.

For the second time in ten minutes, she made Hobson's choice.

As a towering argument broke out between the Dunsmuirs and Meriwether-Astor, no one but a tearful Willie noticed as she gave the world's most abbreviated curtsey, turned, and hurried from the salon.

At the bottom of *Lady Lucy*'s gangway, Gloria Meriwether-Astor had finally caught up to her. She brushed past the girl. "I'm sorry, Gloria, but I don't have time."

Gloria grabbed her arm in a grip surprisingly strong for such a languid person. "Is my father up there?"

"Yes. He is attempting to ruin my friends. You'll forgive me if I do not have much to say to you at present. I must save a man's life."

"I'll come with you." Breathlessly, Gloria matched Claire's pace.

"Your place is with your father," she told Gloria with the calm of despair. "Go away and keep it."

"I'm not responsible for what he does, you know. You don't have to treat me like I am."

In a sudden spike of rage, Claire swung on her. "I'm not treating you as anything at all. Much the way you treated me at school. Now get out of my way."

In the light from the lamps on the mooring masts, Gloria's eyes glittered with unshed tears. "I suppose I deserve that. But Claire, wait. I want to help."

"You want to help?" She couldn't control her own voice—it was shrill with impatience and fear. "Why should you, when your father has contrived to blow up the Firstwater Mine to discredit the Dunsmuirs, cover up the assassination of Count von Zeppelin, and provoke an international incident?"

Gloria's mouth fell open. "Are you insane?"

"Not in the least. I just can't prove any of it. So go on, take that tale back to your father and he can feel free to assassinate me, too. But while you're about it, I have work to do."

She whirled and began to run.

And to her outraged dismay, her plain speaking still did not dislodge the cocklebur that was her former classmate, who seemed determined to stick to her no matter what unpalatable truths she flung in her face.

"All right, so you're insane," Gloria panted. "But I could almost believe you. Insanity is the only thing that can explain why I'm even here. And maybe it explains some of the things I've heard him say—things that made no sense."

"Everything makes sense if you have the right point of view." Claire dove into the shadow of a building and flattened herself against the wall to catch her breath before the next leg. "Gloria, I mean it. You cannot be here."

"A man's life is at stake, I know. Is Father trying to have him killed?"

"He is using him as a scapegoat. He will take the blame for the explosion and be hanged in short order if we do not prevent it."

"You need help."

"If you are going to insult my mental capacities, you may save your breath to cool your—"

"No, I didn't mean that. I meant, you need reinforcements. Surely you're not taking on that mob by yourself?"

"I tried that, and failed. So now I must resort to stealth. What I need is for Penhaven to have locked him in a room to which I can gain access, like—like his lordship's private dressing room, or Davina's powder room, in the building where the management offices are."

"I can do that."

Claire stared at her with astonished contempt, but in the dark of course she could not see it. Just as well. She moderated her tone so that her utter disregard of this mooring-rope of a girl did not leak through. "Now who is the crazy one?"

"I'm serious. I'll simply tell them I've a message from my father and Penhaven, and tell them to lock him in one of those places. It's not like they have a gaol here. We're not in the Wild West."

"Why should they listen to you? They didn't listen to me."

"You haven't been yawning through all those meetings with the management. Father doesn't think I have a single feather in my brain, and maybe I don't, but he makes me sit with him anyway. Family solidarity or something. But the directors know me. They might believe it—at least, for long enough that you could do … whatever it is you plan to do."

Now it was Claire's turn to grasp Gloria's elbow and drag her into the light from the main square, so she could see her face properly. "Or for long enough for you to tell them to trap me, too, once my back is turned?" A spasm passed across Gloria's pale, elegant features. "Why are you suddenly being so helpful, when it means betraying your own family?"

For a moment Gloria gazed at her, as though she were trying to remember where she'd seen her before. "You aren't really governess to those Cockney children, are you?"

Dear heaven, the girl was unbalanced. "I really don't have time for—"

"How did you meet them?"

Impatiently, she said, "They accosted me the night of the Arabian Bubble riots. I accosted them right back, and we came to an agreement—I would teach them their numbers and letters, and they would teach me how to survive in—in less comfortable circumstances than I had been used to. I am now their guardian—we are family. But what has that to do with Mr. Chalmers?"

"I never thought I'd learn anything from an alley mouse, especially one so rude, but ..." Gloria shook her head. "Never mind. For once in my life I'm going to do what's right instead of what's expected of me."

Perhaps Gloria meant to betray them all. Perhaps she was deluded. But the truth was bleak: Claire had no plan other than to trust to chance that four girls could save a man's life. And for that, chance was not good enough.

Gloria was a gamble of a different sort.

So Claire dealt her the cards.

22

Andrew Malvern had been dancing with Davina when the pressure wave engulfed the *Margrethe*, sending them both sideways and toppling over a potted plant. He had managed to roll so that her ladyship's slender form landed on him rather than the other way round, to be followed immediately afterward by a shower bath from the punch bowl, which circled away under a table after it had deposited its contents upon them both.

His first thought, while picking orange slices off her ladyship, was for Claire, his second for Alice. Since then, both those thoughts had remained uppermost and urgent in his mind as he tried to find them in the chaos.

Then, out of a porthole, he had a glimpse of Claire—no longer in evening dress, and with the lightning rifle out and ready, tearing across the field with the Mopsies—which galvanized him into action. He had left the young officer he was tending to the medic who had finally arrived, and sprinted after Claire, only to lose her in the shouting, panicked crowd at the gates of the mine.

Then, to his horror, he heard a man's name taken up with chants of "Hang him!" and realized who the man in the middle of the crowd must be. Tall, blond, one eye, and with the same wide mouth and firm chin—it could only be Alice's father.

"Get Isobel!" Chalmers shouted into the screaming crowd—and a second later, Andrew tripped over a pair of booted feet and fell to his hands and knees with bone-jarring force.

"All right, sir?" Someone hauled him up by one arm. Someone with a familiar voice.

"Jake?" He got to his feet to see that the crowd had moved on, dragging Chalmers deeper into the circle of buildings. "Jake, what is going on? Is that Alice's father?"

"It is. They're going to blame the explosion on 'im and 'ang 'im for it. I just saw the Lady run off—I 'ope she's gone to fetch 'elp."

"Is she all right? I must find her."

"Ent nowt you can do for her, but you can give me a hand."

"Jake, you don't understand—she will be hurt."

"The Lady?" The boy snorted with derision. "Not likely. She's armed and in a fine uproar of a temper. Don't you worry about 'er—worry about yer own self. She gave me a job and I can't do it and do wot Alice's dad said, too. You gots to 'elp me."

Was he ever to be useful to Claire on this benighted journey? How was she to see him as a man she could trust with her life and future if she kept leaving him behind to go and save people? Andrew reined his emotions in with an act of will and focused on the boy in front of him, whose desperate eyes belied the curl still on his lip.

"All right, then. What can I do?"

"The Lady bid me follow Alice's dad and report back to 'er when I found out where they're goin' wiv 'im. But he needs someone to find that Isobel Churchill, and I reckon that's you."

"I heard him shout. But why—"

"Dunno, and it don't matter. A desperate man shouts for 'er, seems a bloke ought to find 'er."

Privately, Andrew thought that a desperate man might call a woman's name if he were having a love affair with her and wanted to see her one last time before he met his doom, but that was none of his business. "Right. I shall do that, and bring her ... where?"

"You ought'nt to 'ave much trouble 'earing where 'e is, 'specially if they're to 'ang 'im. Folks tend to get loud on such occasions."

"I trust you have not learned this from experience?"

"Mr. Malvern, sir, wiv all due respect, we ent got time."

"Quite right. To the *Skylark*, then, as quick as may be."

Andrew had only had the briefest glimpse of Isobel Churchill this evening on the *Margrethe*. He had wanted to ask her to dance, but by the time he had screwed his courage up to the sticking point, he could no longer see her among the dancers or at the buffet. And after the explosion, he did not remember seeing her at all.

When danger threatened, it seemed logical that a woman would take her only child and flee to safety. He would begin with the *Skylark*.

She did not even have a crewman posted at the base of the steps. "Mrs. Churchill?" he called as he emerged onto the lower deck. "Mrs. Churchill, are you here?"

Peony dropped down the gangway from B deck and landed lightly in front of him. "Mr. Malvern, what a surprise."

"Miss Churchill, this is no social call. They're about to hang Frederick Chalmers for sabotage and he is calling for your mother. Is she here?"

Peony's flushed cheeks drained of all color. "That can't be true."

"I heard it myself. Time is of the essence. Is your mother here?"

"Yes." She turned and climbed the gangway as nimbly as she had come down it, seeing as she was wearing riding breeches. "She's sending a pigeon." He resolutely did not look at the unusual view of a woman in breeches as he leaped up the steps after her. "Mama! Come at once!"

But she did not come. Instead, Peony ran to the stern of the trim little gondola, where they found Isobel Churchill seated on a sandbag, writing furiously, a pigeon with its hold open lying at her feet.

"Mama, they are going to hang Frederick Chalmers for sabotage, and he bids you come at once!"

Isobel signed her name with a flourish, folded the still-wet paper, and stuffed it into the pigeon. A few taps of her fingers embedded the magnetic coordinates of its destination in its small engine. She released it from the nearest porthole with a shove that caused its wings to spring open and catch the night wind as it soared upward.

"I told him to go," she said in a voice like steel. "As soon as I saw him walk into the salon, I told him *Skylark* would escort his daughter and meet him in Edmonton if he would only leave at once, but no. He had to do this himself. Had to reveal himself in front of all our enemies, and now all is lost."

Andrew did not understand, but he did not need to. "He is asking for your help, Mrs. Churchill. He, and the two young Esquimaux men who were taken with him."

Her eyes blazed. "He has dragged them into it, too?" Her laugh cut the air like an axe. "If he survives this and they do not, he will answer to Malina's mother, the priestess. They are her youngest sons."

Why on earth was this woman not—in the Texican parlance—saddling up and moving out? "Will you come to his aid, or no?"

"There are bigger things at stake here than you have any idea of, young man. Frederick Chalmers has been one of the best friends the Esquimaux Nation has ever known, but even he would tell you that the good of the village comes before the good of the individual. He has gone into this recklessly, acting from the heart and not the head, and has put hundreds of people in danger."

She reached for the airman's coat lying on the sandbag, and Andrew realized with something of a shock that she had also divested herself of her green ballgown some time earlier, and was now clothed in breeches, boots, and shirt.

"Come, Peony. I shall tell Captain Aniq we lift in five minutes."

"But Mama—"

"Do not argue. We cannot go charging in there with no weapons and no information and expect to save his life. But we can save the village, if the pigeon gets there and they lift before that mob decides there are more saboteurs where he came from."

Peony turned to Andrew as her mother went forward, presumably to command the engineers to fire up the boiler in preparation for lift. "I am sorry. I would help if I could."

"What did she mean about the village lifting? There were no airships there—I saw the place myself. And what part does Frederick Chalmers play in the lives of the Esquimaux? She made it sound as if they were a government—a country."

"Why, they are." Peony gazed at him in some surprise. "He has been liaison between Her Majesty's government and the Esquimaux Nation these seven years at least. Why do you think the Dunsmuirs have permission to mine here?"

"I understood they own this land."

"Ownership is a foreign concept to the Esquimaux, as is the European fascination with diamonds. It is more of a … partnership with Lady Dunsmuir. Which is, of course, utterly unacceptable to certain business interests on this continent."

"Colonial interests."

She twinkled at him. "My, my, Mr. Malvern. Your quick mind will get you into trouble one of these days."

"I hope it will get Frederick Chalmers out of it. I am going back to do my best to assist him."

She laid a hand on his arm. "Be safe. Tell him I am sorry. And give my regards to Claire. I do not know when we shall see one another again."

For a moment, Alice could not place the tiny, muffled sound. Then she realized it was poor Maggie's teeth chattering.

"Dearling, come close to me." She sat on the stone steps where they gave onto the narrow corridor chipped out of frozen ground and granite. "Lizzie, you too." She lifted the voluminous folds of her turquoise gown and wrapped the fabric around both girls, folding them in close like a mother hen with her chicks. "I should have gone to the *Lass* and changed out of this silly rig."

"You weren't thinkin' of clothes at the time," Maggie said with some sympathy. "Besides, all these petticoats is warm."

"Do you think Claire was able to fetch the earl?" Down here, with only a thin yellow ribbon of electrics for light, she was cut off—buried as surely as any corpse in a grave. And for so long a time, it seemed eternity had passed.

Alice wobbled dangerously close to losing hope. "I'm going to give her another five minutes and then I'm going up there myself."

"Wot would you do?" Lizzie asked from within her turquoise-and-lace cloak. "Come to fisticuffs wiv that lot?"

"No, but I have a set of lock picks and I know how to use them."

"Right, and they'll 'ave left 'em unguarded."

Alice exhaled in lieu of snapping at the child. "How can someone so small know so much about lockups?"

"Did the Lady ever tell you about Dr. Craig, and 'ow we broke 'er out of Bedlam?"

And she made the mistake of saying, "No," and some while later when the two of them wrapped up their tale, Alice realized that the little scamps had actually made her forget what they were all doing there.

"Tell 'er about the time Lewis rescued all our poor 'ens off that barge, Liz," Maggie said. Lizzie opened her mouth to do so when they heard a thump from the ground above them.

"Sssh! Wot were that?" Lizzie hissed instead.

"And which way did it come from?" Alice whispered.

Now they could hear a commotion—boots and angry voices and what sounded like fists landing.

"There!" Maggie pointed down the corridor. "The next set o' steps, I'm sure of it."

The girls scrambled out of the silken embrace of Alice's skirts and all three ran down the corridor. Maggie was right—as they climbed the steps, they could hear snatches of people talking. Or shouting, more like.

"Leave them here," an imperious female voice said quite clearly through the panels of the hidden door at the top of the steps. "My father and Mr. Penhaven will be along shortly to deal with the nasty miscreants. He plans to give them a *fair* trial, right there in the boardroom."

"We'll give 'em fair!"

"Just as fair as they gave our boys on the digger—a long dance on a short rope!"

"But the earl's dressing room, Miss Meriwether-Astor?" said a calmer voice, more worried. "Is that quite proper?"

Meriwether-Astor? Alice's mind felt like an unmanned dirigible being batted around by high winds. Where had the girl come from? And what did it mean that she was doing exactly as Claire had said? How could she? She was their enemy's daughter!

So where were Claire and the earl? Had something gone dreadfully wrong?

Mumbletythump! A body landed against the door, then another a little distance away. And a third beyond that. Someone groaned right next to the panel against which Alice pressed her ear, and it was all she could do not to jerk back and send herself tumbling down the steps.

"Oh, yes. Why should they have the dignity of a drawing room, or even an office? A latrine is good enough for them."

"I'd say so. Nothing but dung, they are!"

"Hey, don't insult good dung!" Raucous laughter greeted this witticism.

"Come along, gentlemen. If you will arrange the boardroom and see that this door is securely locked, with a guard posted outside it *and* outside the window, I will inform my father that his wishes have been carried out."

"Right you are, miss. Careful. Don't step in the blood and spoil your pretty dancing shoes."

"Thank you, Alan. You are the kind of gentleman I despaired of ever meeting in these parts."

The door slammed, and the lock turned over.

Alice took a breath and listened. Nothing moved on the other side.

Oh, please don't let him be dead. Please. I've only had a day with him …

She leaned gently on the lever next to the panel and the door eased open toward her, allowing a crack of light through from the electricks in the dressing room.

The man on the other side sucked in a breath through his nose, no doubt thinking he was suffering from both nausea and vertigo.

Perhaps he was.

Through the crack, she got a glimpse of matted blond hair.

"Pa?" she whispered. "Pa, can you hear me?"

He stirred, and clutched his arm against his ribs. "Alice?" he breathed. "Where are you?"

"There's a movable panel behind you. We've come to get you out. Easy now, not so fast. The steps go straight down."

"But what—I don't understand."

"We're breaking you out of gaol, Pa. But you have to be quiet. Rouse the other boys and come away quick, before they decide to check to see if you're dead."

"I think Alignak might be hurt. Ribs. And Tartok took a pretty bad hit to the head. He's out cold."

"What about you?"

"I'm fine." Gasping, he pulled himself to his feet while Alice swung the panel open.

He was not fine. But it was brave of him not to show it.

She wriggled out of her topmost petticoat. What a lucky thing both she and Claire had lots of them, with multiple flounces of gathered eyelet. At the rate they were going, they'd use every yard for bandages before they got away from this inhospitable country.

"Girls, take this to the bottom of the steps. I want it ripped into strips by the time we get the men down. We'll patch them up as best we can. Then we'll have to hoof it before Penhaven and his bunch come back and find the room empty."

Alignak had heard their whispered exchange and was already on his feet by the time Alice poked her head into the next latrine compartment. He limped out and went immediately to the third one.

"Tartok sleeps," he whispered, his sloe-black eyes worried. "A demon sleep."

"Demons made him that way, that's certain," Alice whispered back. "Pa, can you lift him with just one arm?"

"Yes."

Alice helped him shoulder the young man and bit back a cry when she saw her father lose all color and gasp in pain. But he said not a word. He maneuvered Tartok through the opening and took the steps carefully. Alignak followed right behind, holding his ribs as if trying to keep them in place.

Alice brought up the rear and closed and fastened the door. If only there were a way to block it! But there was nothing in the stone corridors that would help them.

Only cold silence, and the yellow ribbon of electrick light fading into the distance.

A click sounded above them, at the top of the steps leading to her ladyship's dressing room. Alice fell to her knees as her father put Tartok down, and began binding up wounds as fast as Lizzie could hand her the torn strips of eyelet. Maggie went up to investigate.

"Lady!" Alice heard her whisper. "Come quick!"

"Do you have them?" came Claire's quiet voice.

"Aye. That Meriwether-whatsis mort 'ad 'em put right where you said."

"Are they hurt?"

"Aye. Come away down, Lady. We gots to get out of 'ere."

23

Claire wasted no time in assisting Alice, fabricating a sling out of a length of white voile for Chalmers's arm, and binding up Alignak's ribs with half a second petticoat.

"What luck you're still in evening dress," she whispered to Alice. "This rig doesn't allow for petticoats—though I'm tempted to add a number of layers of ruffles. They seem to come in handy rather regularly."

"It's this place," Alice whispered back. "Once we're clear of assassins, our clothes ought to be fine."

"Speaking of assassins, were you able to speak to the count?"

In the dim light, Alice looked stricken. "I forgot all about him," she said in horror.

Frederick Chalmers looked up from tightening the knots on his sling. "You what? You mean you didn't warn him to lift?"

"No, Pa, I was too busy trying to save *your* hide."

"But this is terrible! We must—"

"We must do nothing but get you out of here before you're recaptured and hanged," Claire said briskly. "We're not likely to get a second chance to spirit you out of a locked room. I will see to Count von Zeppelin."

"And I will get you all in the air without delay." Alice's gaze was as stony as the one her father leveled upon her. There was no doubt in the world that the two of them were related. Claire wondered who would win this contest of wills.

"But—"

"Chama," Alignak interrupted, "we must get Tartok to Malina or his spirit will leave him. And we must warn the village so the goddess whales may sail."

Frederick Chalmers gazed from the young man to his daughter, clearly torn between two equally important choices. But to Claire, there was only one.

"You leave the count to me," she repeated. "I will have him in the sky within the hour, I promise you."

"Do you know where he is?" Alice asked.

"No, but it cannot be difficult to find out."

"Just look for an assassin," Maggie put in helpfully.

Tartok stirred, but then his eyes rolled up in his head and he slumped into unconsciousness again. "We must go," Alignak said, his voice hoarse with anxiety.

Alice helped heft Tartok onto her father's back, his wrists tied together with a bit of lace to form a loop under Frederick's chin. Then they set off down the corridor. Claire visualized the route in her mind's eye as they traveled under the mine offices, under the parade ground, and paused at a cross-corridor with another tiny sign.

DINING was indicated to the left.

SUPPLIES lay to the right.

"The supply warehouse is not a hundred yards from end of the airfield where the *Stalwart Lass* is moored," Claire said, keeping her voice low. "That way, as fast as we can."

It couldn't have been more than a quarter of a mile, but to Claire it seemed endless. At any moment a door could open at the top of any of these flights of stone steps, and a horde of angry men pour through clamoring for the immediate deaths of Frederick Chalmers and the Esquimaux men—to say nothing of the girls attempting to save them. Alice reached the final stair first and darted up it, opening the hidden panel with caution as she tried not to gasp for breath.

It opened in a small storage room directly across from an exterior door. The warehouse was pitch black except for a small electrick lamp glowing over the door.

"Come on—" Alice began, when Maggie and Lizzie slipped past her. "Girls, wait—"

Claire touched her arm. "Let them do what they do better than any of us." Then she turned to Frederick, who emerged slowly from the staircase with Tartok's head lolling on his shoulder. "Mr. Chalmers, are you all right?"

"Fine. Alignak?"

"I am able."

Maggie materialized out of the dark. "All clear, Lady, but we'd best be quick. We can 'ear voices behind this building, as if someone's coming to get something."

They ran through alleys of pallets and crates filled with supplies—food, flour, spare parts. They gained the door and Claire had enough time for a frantic glance across the airfield. "Alice, do you hear that?"

An engine.

Even as they ran, peering past the light cast by the lamps on the mooring masts, the *Skylark* lifted, sailing straight up into the night sky and blotting out the stars.

Frederick gasped. "Isobel!"

Alignak let out a low cry of despair.

What…? But there was no time to ask questions, for someone was running across the field toward them. Two someones—one tall, one lanky and shorter.

Claire pulled the lightning rifle out of its holster and took aim.

"No, Lady, don't!" Maggie cried. "It's our Jake and Mr. Malvern!"

But they could still hear an engine, even though *Skylark* had passed out of sight and out of all hope of assistance.

"Someone's fired up the *Lass*'s boiler," Alice said. "Jake, you get double pay for this."

"Here, sir, let us take him," Andrew said to Frederick, and in a trice he and Jake had the unconscious Tartok between them, jogging across the field to the battered old airship. Alice and the men followed, tumbling up the gangway into the gondola.

Claire grabbed the Mopsies by the hand. "We must untie the ropes. I shall attend to the mooring mast. Run, fast as you can."

"Claire!" Alice leaned out of a porthole. "I never got a proper engine in here to replace Dr. Craig's power cell!"

"Take it!" she called, scrambling up the ladder to the rope looped through the *Lass*'s nose ring. "I can make another one."

"I need to make some room and ditch some ballast on the double quick—I'm sending out Seven and Eight. Take care of 'em, will you?"

Must she? Ugh. "Fine!"

"And what about Jake?"

"I'm goin' and that's that!" came a stubborn shout from somewhere within.

"Feed him and teach him, and turn him into a capable man," Claire called, "and I shall be satisfied." She untied the rope. "Free to lift when ready, Alice. Fair winds!"

She heard a clanking crash and the scrape of gravel—the automatons, no doubt, being unceremoniously unloaded in a heap.

"To you, too! Up ship!"

The Mopsies and Andrew ran clear of the gondola as Claire climbed to the ground. The *Lass* fell up into the night sky, her engine running as smoothly as a sewing machine as Dr. Craig's cell gave it more power than it had ever had before this stage of its life. And as the craft turned its bow to the south, Claire saw movement in the sky behind it.

Andrew drew in a long breath.

"Lady, what are they?" Maggie asked in awe.

A cluster of silver craft floated purposefully after the *Stalwart Lass*, their silver fuselages rippling with the speed of their going, for all the world like elongated bubbles swimming through the cold air. The gondolas clinging to the undersides were sleek and shallow, each one ribbed like the skeleton of a long-dead creature.

Ribbed like the interiors of the Esquimaux long-houses.

Like the interiors of great, long-dead creatures.

The goddess whales.

"They live in their ships," Claire breathed on a note of discovery. "That's what Alignak meant by the village lifting. He meant it quite literally. The entire village has pulled up ropes and gone with Alice and Frederick."

"And, I assume, Isobel Churchill," Andrew said. "She sent a pigeon not half an hour ago to warn them."

"So they will all be safe?" Maggie asked, her forehead creased in concern even as she watched the majestic sight of the Esquimaux craft sailing through the stars.

"They will all be safe," Claire echoed. "I do not know where they are going, but with Malina and Alice in charge, they will find a quiet harbor somewhere."

"But our Jake," Lizzie wailed. "They've took our Jake!"

"He has his duty as navigator, Lizzie," Andrew told her gently. "He chose his course like a gentleman, and he will keep to it until his captain releases him from duty."

"Besides, someone's got to look after our Alice," Maggie said, taking her twin's hand. "Wiv Tigg on *Lady Lucy*, we'll be the Lady's seconds in 'is place, won't we, till we gets 'ome to Snouts?"

"I wouldn't have anyone else." Claire laid a gentle hand on each of their shoulders, feeling both girls lean into her skirts as if unconsciously seeking the comfort of someone who would not leave them.

The Esquimaux fleet glimmered one last time, as if in farewell, and passed out of sight over the black shapes of the hills to the south.

Claire took a fortifying breath. "Now, then. I think it is time we located Count von Zeppelin and made sure of his safety, as Mr. Chalmers wished. Even though we have no proof whatsoever that he is in danger, except the evidence of our own eyes."

"Isobel told me that he has been Her Majesty's liaison with the Esquimaux nation for some seven years," Andrew told her. "If he believes the count is in danger, I think you may take that as proof."

They crossed to the small heap of bronze limbs and torsos, and assisted the automatons to their feet.

"Has he?" The mystery of Chalmers's life here began to make a glimmer of sense. "No wonder the Colonials wanted him to take the blame. They would not only discredit the Dunsmuirs, but throw a spanner into Her Majesty's works as well."

"So what is our plan?" Andrew asked her, quite seriously.

She had no idea. But it would never do to say so in front of the children. She straightened her shoulders, and the automatons turned their blank faces toward her as if waiting for instructions. "I think Maggie had the right of it. This whole affair began with a gun that makes no sound. Do you not agree that if we can find that, we might find a clue that will lead us to the count?"

It was fortunate indeed that, while someone had unloaded an enormous number of trunks and cases from the Meriwether-Astors' ship, it appeared no one knew exactly what to do with them afterward. So they sat upon the gravel some distance from the ship, in the inky shadow of the fuselage, providing enough cover for two small figures and two larger ones, with a view of both that ship and the motley group of cargo ships moored around it.

Claire had told Seven and Eight to wait by *Lady Lucy*. The thought of a pair of clanking shadows following them about when a man's life might be at stake made her shiver with revulsion.

"Mopsies, what do you make of our situation?" she whispered.

"This Astor bloke, 'e'd want to keep 'is treasures close, yeah?" Lizzie said in a low tone. "Lightning Luke kept 'is treasure box where 'e slept, innit?"

"So your guess is that the count would be upon Mr. Meriwether-Astor's ship?"

"Aye."

"Which is guarded," Andrew put in. "They've posted a watch."

That was true. A man sat upon the gangway smoking a Texican cigarillo, the noxious fumes of which they could smell from here.

"Ent much of a watch," Lizzie said with some disdain. "Pity we just lost Jake. 'E were a dab hand at dealing wiv such."

"We might shimmy up a mooring rope," Maggie suggested.

"Too dangerous, and we risk being spotted before we reached the top," Claire said. It was one thing for the girls to slide down a rope to escape for purposes of saving a life. It was quite another to labor to the top, exposing themselves to discovery—or gunfire.

"Wot about a diversion?" Maggie asked. "You could zap one of them cargo ships wiv the lightning rifle, and when everyone come out to put out the fire, we could go in."

"You forget that our time here is limited to a few more days," Andrew told her gently. "With the *Margrethe* disabled, the loss of one cargo ship could be devastating to the Dunsmuirs, the count's crew, and the people who work here, once the snow flies."

"Don't care about the Dunsmuirs no more," Lizzie grumbled. "They didn't believe the Lady, and let those blokes 'urt our Alice's dad."

"We have no proof, Lizzie," Claire said gently. "Without that, the Dunsmuirs cannot act except to delay and pray that calm heads will prevail. I wonder if anyone has checked the dressing room yet?"

"Let us hope not," Andrew said. "It will not take a brilliant mind to conclude that you are behind their escape. I wonder where they'd put *you*?"

Somewhere without tunnels, that was certain. Or windows. A memory of a locked room in Resolution assailed her, and she set her teeth. She would not allow anyone to make her a prisoner again.

Lizzie touched her arm, her fingers cold. Claire was seized in the sudden grip of guilt. What was she thinking, bringing the girls along on such an errand? They should be tucked up in bed aboard the *Lady Lucy*, safe and warm, with Tigg and the other middies to look after them, not in danger of being made prisoners themselves.

She was a terrible guardian, Claire thought on a wave of despair.

But Lizzie did not seem to be much inclined to seek either safety or warmth. "Lady," she whispered, "there's that Alan again. See? By that wreck of a ship we visited wiv Alice. Where I found that other brass casing."

"Those other two, they're Bob an' Joe. Alan is Joe's brother," Maggie explained.

Goodness. What a memory she had. Almost as good as Jake's.

Huddled behind the sort of trunk that turned on one end to open into a traveling closet, they watched Bob and Joe pace in front of the nearly derelict cargo ship, from one end to the other, as if doing an inspection while they waited for Alan to come out of it.

"Does it not seem strange to you that that ship is the only one of the convoy that appears to have a proper guard?" Andrew asked. "Aside from our smoking friend behind us, of course."

"I had not noticed before, but you are quite right."

Alan rejoined his friends, and a brief conversation took place before they began to pace again, two heading down to the stern vanes, one to the bow, then reversing and crossing at the gangway in the middle of the gondola.

"And do you see how very large the doors are to the rear of the gondola? One could wheel a landau out of them if one had a ramp."

"What I see is an engine so large and powerful it warrants its own gondola, there at the stern." Andrew paused for a moment for them to see the truth of it. "Jake mentioned something Gloria Meriwether-Astor said to him and Alice, just before the explosion," he went on. "Something about a steam cannon."

"We are not looking for a cannon, Andrew. Those propelled bullets may have been large, but they were certainly not large enough to fill a cannon barrel."

"Still ... if a man transported a cannon secretly, disguised in an old trap of an airship that would be an unlikely target for sky pirates or tariff men, he might be just as likely to transport silent rifles and who knows what else along with it."

"But that does not mean he would conceal a prisoner with them."

"Why waste guards?" Maggie put in. "If yer guardin' yer guns, might as well put the prisoner there. That lot've been there all day. So it would make no nevermind to someone lookin' on whether there was guns or trussed-up gentlemen inside."

"You sound like Alice," Lizzie said.

"And you make a sound point," Andrew told her. "I say it's worth a look."

"I say we are outnumbered," Claire reminded them softly. "Though I would put Lizzie up against a miscreant any day, I should not like to take the chance that she might be hurt."

"Diversion," Maggie sing-songed softly, as if to remind them she had suggested this before.

"But what?" Claire's legs were beginning to cramp. She longed to stand up, to shout and wave her arms and demand to be allowed aboard that ship.

Which would net her absolutely nothing except the relief of movement and the inevitability of imprisonment. It was maddening to be trapped here in the shadows with so little time and so urgent a task. She might as well be one of Alice's automatons, standing uselessly at the bottom of *Lady Lucy*'s gangway.

Wait.

"The automatons," she said.

24

Lizzie and Maggie could not have been more delighted to be in charge of the diversion. Claire was not so sure this was the right course—though it seemed to be their only one. Since the three guarding the airship knew the twins, they would at least allow them to get closer than they might allow Andrew or Claire herself, who were strangers.

And the one called Alan had seen Claire's failed attempt to come to the rescue of Frederick Chalmers.

So there they went, the two little girls in striped stockings and ruffled skirts, dancing and gamboling as they led Seven, Eight, and Nine across the airfield toward the cargo ship. It looked like two kittens leading a trio of tall, awkward storks.

"I hope you know what you're doing," Andrew said in a low tone next to her, behind the closet trunk.

"So do I. They did assure us they have acted as a diversion before."

"Were there guns involved?"

"I do not know. And now is not the time to think of such things. I am quite anxious enough."

"Hey!" Alan called, leaving off marching. He approached the girls, carelessly balancing his rifle over his shoulder like a vagrant's pole. "What are you two doing out so late?"

"We didn't want to go to bed," Lizzie told him with a giggle. "We stole the automatons and we're taking them for a walk. See?"

"You rascals," he said with a chuckle. "Who do those belong to?"

"We dunno," they said together. "Aren't they fine?" Maggie added.

By this time Bob and Joe had joined them, and by their relaxed posture, considered the girls no threat. In fact, Bob put his hands on his hips and laughed outright. "Don't you two beat all. What are you going to do with them?"

Maggie looked at Lizzie, who shrugged, grinning. "Perhaps we can ride them pick-a-back."

"They're too tall, Liz."

"Too tall?" Alan snorted. "I s'pose everything looks tall to little mites like you. Look, they're not as tall as Bob and me."

"Are so." Lizzie crossed her arms. "Garn. Stand next to 'em so we can see."

Bob and Alan straightened up next to two of the gleaming bronze figures, one in front of each. "Come on, Joe, you're the shortest of us all and I bet even you are taller than that thing."

Joe rolled his eyes and sloped over. "Are you two so bored? Got nothing better to do?"

"Humor the little ladies, you old cross-patch. Now, girls, who wants to bet—"

"Seven, Eight, Nine, hold the man," Lizzie commanded.

Simultaneously, the automatons turned, passed their upper appendages—for, since they possessed all manner of parts built into them, they could not properly be called arms—about the men, imprisoning them against their metal bodies.

Bob roared and kicked his legs, then bucked like a horse that has never felt the saddle. All to no avail. Nine stood as if rooted to the spot, clutching him about the torso so that he could neither quite touch the ground nor elbow the automaton away.

"Go!" Andrew said.

Claire staggered a little as blood flowed back into her cramped legs, and sprinted behind the automatons as Maggie and Lizzie led them up the gangway and into the ship.

The men made a terrible ruckus until Andrew took up a rifle and used the butt of it to render them temporarily unconscious. They slumped in the automatons' hold, while the grip of the latter only tightened further.

"Maggie, Lizzie, well done," Claire told them.

"Stay with them," Andrew said. "We will search the ship and return as fast as we can."

"What if they wake up?" Maggie asked.

"Cosh 'em again." He tossed the rifle to her, and she caught it by reflex, then staggered under its unexpected weight.

"I do wish you would not incite the children to violence," Claire told him as they made quick work of searching the navigation gondola. "It is bad enough that *I* must resort to it from time to time in this dangerous country."

"There will be time enough for fine manners and grace when we get ourselves out of this," Andrew said, his jaw flexing as if he were holding back a much stronger opinion. "Though I must say, I will have a whole new appreciation of the resourcefulness of ladies after this."

Was he thinking of Alice? Was he already regretting that he had not leaped aboard the *Stalwart Lass* when he had the chance? Alice would have welcomed him. And if she did not, an educated and trained engineer would not go amiss in any crew in the skies.

But Claire did not have the courage to ask him, and now was not the time in any case. She must not allow her mind to wander to matters of the heart—if he were indeed here, the count's life would depend on quick action and clear thinking.

In fact, perhaps she ought not to think about matters of the heart at all. Because it was a stark and simple fact that she could not make up her mind where men were concerned. She had kissed three—once on purpose, twice not—and the only conclusion she could come to was that, on a purely sensory level, kissing was a most pleasurable occupation. But what it *meant* was an impenetrable jungle of feeling and emotion that she simply was not ready to explore. It was too strange, too frightening ... and too permanent.

She had proven herself capable when it came to helping her friends out of tight spots—and getting out of them herself. But she was as clumsy and inexperienced as a fawn when it came to the connection of committed affection, and she had no idea if it got easier as time went on.

Andrew assisted her up the ladder and onto the coaxial catwalk that ran the length of the ship. "The cargo area will be through those doors," he said. "You might power up that rifle, in case there are guards there, too. They may have heard our friends shouting and be ready with an ambush."

Right. This was not the time to be mooning over men. She must collect herself and be ready to face whatever lay behind that door. But first—

She unholstered the rifle and laid her free hand on Andrew's arm. "Thank you for being with me," she said softly. "I should find this very hard to face without your company."

He turned to her, surprise in his brown eyes. "That is the last thing I should ever have expected you to say."

"What, thank you?"

"No. You are the most fearless, capable woman I know, along with Alice and Lady Dunsmuir and Isobel Churchill."

Alice. First in his thoughts, first in his heart.

"Fearless?" She huffed a laugh. "Hardly. There may not be much time for terror, but believe me when I say I feel it."

He grinned at her. "Don't destroy my illusions. Come. Let us storm the door. Together."

He pushed the door open, and together they stepped into a large cargo space, illuminated by a strip of electricks that ran from strut to strut of the iron gridwork supporting the fuselage. Claire's hands tensed on the rifle, but the two of them were not accosted. In fact, the space was silent except for the excited scrabble of rats, off to one side, down one of the alleys formed of boxes and crates.

Andrew inhaled and his shoulders lost some of their tension. "I do not believe there is a guard. Hush. Was that a cat?"

A mewling sound issued from the darkness. "A cat … or a person who has been gagged?" Claire whispered.

Slowly, cautiously, fully expecting a guard to leap, firing, out of the shadows, they made their way down the corridor, dirt crunching under their soles. An odd smell hung in the air, like smoke and kerosene and something sour.

The mewling sound came again. Claire flicked the lever on the lightning rifle, and it hummed to life. The globe on its underside began to glow as the lightning woke, flickering and exploring its rounded prison. She held the rifle upright so that the globe became a lamp.

"Mmmph!" someone said in response to the light.

"That is not a cat, nor is it a rodent," she said, and stepped out of the darkness of the corridor into a wider area formed by crates piled high.

On a pallet on the floor lay a man with his hands and feet tied behind him, his knees bent nearly double so that his ankles and wrists could be tied together. A calico sack did duty as a hood, concealing his face. But no sack could conceal the fact that he was in evening dress, his white shirt front gray with grime and dried blood, his tie gone altogether, and his trousers torn.

"Count von Zeppelin?" Claire said softly, rushing to his side. "It is I, Claire, with Mr. Malvern. We shall have you free in a moment."

From the pocket of his duster, which he had had replaced in Edmonton, Andrew pulled a knife, its lethal blade advertising to everyone that it had been made by Mr. Bowie in the Texican Territory. The ropes parted as if they had been made of pie pastry, and when Claire whisked off the hood, the count gasped and curled up, his knees to his chest, as if to give relief to muscles that had been strained in the other direction to the point of torture.

"Count, are you hurt?" Claire said quickly. "Bones broken, wounds?"

"*Nein*," he gasped. "Blood is returning. I shall be … all right in a moment."

She and Andrew massaged his lower limbs until the blood flowed unobstructed and he was able to stand.

"Thank the merciful God you found me. Is there any water?"

Andrew surveyed the barren prison. "Not here, I'm afraid. We shall search the galley once we reach the gondola."

Half carrying the older man, Andrew helped him down the corridor while Claire went ahead with the rifle-turned-lamp. It took ages to get him down the ladder from the catwalk, but she could tell that with every step, his strength was returning.

They emerged, breathing heavily with exertion, into the navigation gondola.

Three automatons stood there at attention, as if waiting for a command.

Their prisoners were gone.

And so were the Mopsies.

25

"Nine, where are the girls?" Claire snapped.

But the automaton remained maddeningly blank and silent, and she resisted the urge to clap a hand to her forehead in chagrin. Of course Alice had designed them to follow orders only. They had no ability to give information. They didn't even have mouths.

"And where are our prisoners?" Andrew said aloud. "The girls would not have moved them elsewhere, would they?"

"How? And where? We passed through the crew quarters on the way."

"The engine gondola at the stern?" Then he shook his head. "Never mind. That would be nonsensical."

"The only logical conclusion is that your prisoners have made off with your little friends," the count said, heroically resisting the urge to examine the automatons. Instead, he contented himself with, "Are these the work of *Fraulein* Alice? And they can give no information?"

"No." Fear had formed a hard ball in her stomach, and Claire was very much afraid she was going to be sick. "We must find the girls at once."

"And I must return to the *Margrethe*." He tugged on one of the sleeves of his dinner jacket, and it came away in his hand. "The crew will be on the point of despair—or worse."

"Your disappearance and eventual death are meant to provoke an international incident," Claire told him. "Meriwether-Astor is behind it."

"*Ja*, of such I am well aware. The hood they put over my head did not impair my hearing in the slightest."

"So we have our proof after all," Andrew said. "The count himself will corroborate what you have to say when you tell the Dunsmuirs, and the crew of the *Margrethe* can take Meriwether-Astor into custody and return him to Edmonton."

"Andrew, they cannot. Remember? The *Margrethe* is grounded."

"*Was sagen Sie*?" Von Zeppelin made for the gangway with only the slightest hitch in his stride. Then, when he saw the mighty fuselage of his flagship wilted and flapping, he let out a cry. "I must return— Lady Claire, who is this who comes?"

She crowded behind him on the gangway and leaped to the ground. The night wind caught at her skirts and sent them belling out to the side, the air frigid on her stockinged legs.

Snow's comin', whispered the voice of Polgarth the poultryman in the back of her memory.

The Mopsies were running full tilt across the airfield, Tigg right behind them, loaded down with—good heavens, he carried her valise in one hand and the twins' in the other. Lizzie carried a hatbox by its cord, swinging in the wind of her going, and containing something somewhat heavier than a hat, by the look of it.

"Lady!" Tigg shouted. "You gots to get out o' here quick!"

"What has happened?"

"I'll be keelhauled if they catch me." He dropped the valises and flung himself upon Claire with such force she staggered. His arms went around her in a ferocious hug. "I don't want to leave you, Lady. Wot'll I do?"

Good heavens. Why should he be forced to leave her? But there was only one answer to the question that was obviously uppermost in his mind. "Your duty lies aboard *Lady Lucy*, my dear one. That is—if the Dunsmuirs still consider us friends?"

"That's the trouble, Lady. That Meriwether bloke 'as 'em over a barrel good and proper." He looked up. "Izzat the count?"

"Indeed," said that gentleman.

"Cor," Tigg said on a breath of disbelief. "You ent dead?"

Claire put her hands upon his shoulders and gave them a gentle shake to return the boy's attention to her. "Tigg, tell me what has happened."

"The Dunsmuirs are under 'ouse arrest and can't leave *Lady Lucy.* The Mopsies and me snuck out through the ceilings and down into the cargo bay, an' out through the loading doors. That Meriwether-Astor cove 'as took over. These cargo ships, they were full of 'is Texicans and Colonials, not proper crews at all. And sir—" He looked up at the count. "—if you ent dead now, you will be shortly. You gots to get out. I can commandeer one o' them mining engines an' we can go to the Esquimaux village. They can 'ide you."

"Can't," Maggie said. "The village flew away."

Panting from his lengthy speech, Tigg stared at her. "Are you off yer 'ead, Mags?"

"Their 'ouses was ships," Lizzie said. "Lifted not 'alf an hour past. We saw 'em."

Claire straightened and passed an arm about Tigg's shoulders. He was trembling, and not from the cold. From fear, she had no doubt—fear for the people he loved.

"What of Captain Hollys and the crew?"

"Outnumbered an' confined to quarters. Lady, I know it's me duty, but must I go back?"

She hugged him close, then looked into his eyes. "What are your own feelings?"

"I dunno wot to do. I want to 'elp. But I also want to come wiv you an' leave this place be'ind for good. I 'ate it 'ere."

He was not the only one. "A year from now, what will you wish you had done?"

Her hand slipped away as he turned slightly to gaze at *Lady Lucy*'s fuselage, barely visible beyond the sadly listing *Margrethe*.

"I s'pose I'd wish I'd've 'elped, 'specially if some 'arm comes to our Willie. I'm the only crewman got free."

"I suppose the marauders relieved the crews of all their weapons?"

Tigg nodded. "First thing."

"And the air rifles in the ceiling cabinets were confiscated by Ned Mose back in Resolution. I imagine Captain Hollys would be glad of a few weapons smuggled in to them, would he not?"

"Claire, are you mad?" Andrew demanded. "You would send a child back into danger, loaded down with guns?"

"I ent a child," Tigg retorted with spirit. "I'm nearly fourteen, and I got a duty to 'elp."

Her gaze met Tigg's, and in his brown eyes she saw the hardening of resolve. She nodded briskly. "We shall conceal as many upon your person as we can, and once we are clear, you must board and assist your captain in retaking the *Lady Lucy* for our friends."

"Clear?" Andrew repeated. "What do you propose?"

She lifted her chin. "I have stolen a coach and a scientist. It cannot be any more difficult to steal an airship."

"You cannot mean to steal Meriwether-Astor's ship." Andrew's eyes practically stood out on stalks.

"Of course not. After Tigg has what he needs, I mean to steal the one with all the guns on it." She looked up at the fuselage above their heads, which only looked ragged and poorly maintained. But under the torn exterior they had observed a sleek substructure that meant business. "I mean to steal this one."

But time, it seemed, had run out.

In the distance, a large group of men issued from between the mining offices and the outlying buildings, shouting the alarm and streaming past the now deserted mine gates.

"Oh dear," Claire said. "It appears someone has noticed the prisoners are missing. Tigg, inside, quickly. We must get you armed before we are seen."

"We do not have time to open crates," Count von Zeppelin said. "And it is imperative that I return to my ship immediately."

"Sir, you can't!" Tigg told him. "They'll shoot you on sight."

"Better an honorable death trying to reach my crew than a dishonorable one hiding with women and children."

"I doubt the Baroness would see it that way," Claire said with some asperity.

"Lady, we got Alan and Bob and Joe's guns over 'ere. And that cove wot were smokin' earlier—we got 'is, too."

Claire had barely made sense of these astonishing facts when the Mopsies dashed over to the pile of luggage sitting under Meriwether-Astor's ship. They flung some clothes aside and pulled five pistols and a smaller, more portable version of Mr. Gatling's repeating cannon out of a trunk.

"Maggie, pray tell, what did you do with our prisoners?" She saw now that the pile of luggage was in somewhat more disarray than it had been.

"We locked 'em in these big trunks, Lady. The automatons stuffed 'em in, and we sat on 'em and shut the lids."

Andrew let out a startled exclamation that might have been a laugh. Then he turned to the count. "I should not complain about being left with the women and children, if I were you, sir. You might find yourself set upon by mechanicals and locked in a lady's trunk for your pains."

The count had lost his spectacles at some point during the course of the evening, but his manner of looking at the Mopsies as they armed Tigg with speedy efficiency reminded Claire of someone looking over his lenses, as if unable to believe the evidence of the naked eye.

Then he raised his gaze to the *Margrethe* and the muscles flexed in his jaw, forcibly holding back either action or words. "If I knew how to reverse our situation, I would," he growled at last.

A contingent of men poured down the *Lady Lucy*'s gangway. The two groups conferred for a moment, and then split off into several smaller groups.

"They are going to search," Andrew said. "Tigg, now is your chance, while there are fewer men aboard."

"Goodbye, Lady," Tigg said, turning to her. His voice cracked.

"We shall meet again, my brave darling," she told him with a fierce hug that drove the lumps of the arms concealed on his person into her chest. "At the very least, you shall have a pigeon from me each week, and—and I expect good penmanship in the replies you return." The lump in her throat choked off the last word.

"Goodbye, old man." Andrew shook his hand. "Thank you for all your assistance in the past."

By now Tigg was too close to tears to speak. He gave each of the Mopsies a rough hug, saluted the count, and vanished into the shadows with the suddenness of a boy who cannot take any more, and must flee—or break down.

It felt as though he had taken a piece of Claire's heart with him. She had suffered the loss of her father, of her home, and of all she had held dear … and none of it felt as though a vital organ had been torn from her chest, leaving the ache of emptiness behind.

"I cannot bear it," she whispered, and attempted to take a fortifying breath.

She must bear it. She must get the Mopsies and the count through the next hour in one piece.

The hour after that, she could collapse in a heap and cry her heart out.

"Come quickly," she said. "We must lift now, while they are distracted by the search."

She and the Mopsies ran up the gangway into the navigation gondola, where the automatons were standing exactly as they had left them. Let them stay there. They had done their part, and done it surprisingly well. They all owed Alice's genius a debt. But as soon as she could, she would find somewhere to leave them so that she would no longer have to look upon those blank, soulless faces.

She turned to find Andrew and the count bent together over the tiller and the panels of gauges. "How long until we are ready to lift?"

Out of the gondola window, shadows moved and darted and lamps danced in the middle distance as the search grew more intense the more frustrated the searchers became. They did not have much time. At some point the men would turn their attention to the luggage pile, and then the fat would well and truly be in the fire.

Andrew conferred with the count in a low voice, and Claire felt a needle of impatience at being thus ignored. "Well?"

"Claire, we have a problem. We cannot fly this ship."

"What do you mean? An engine is an engine, and you flew the *Stalwart Lass* on our journey to Edmonton."

"Yes, but the *Lass* is a much smaller ship. And its engine was a part of the navigation gondola."

"So?" She did not like this. Not one bit. And not the least of it was the dawning dismay in Andrew's face.

"This ship must be crewed by at least a dozen men. The engine gondola is so far astern that the two cannot communicate except by mechanical means."

"And there does not seem to be a means of communication," the count put in. "The controls are here, but they do not respond. Surely they did not send messengers astern every time they needed more steam or a change of course?"

Of course they did not.

"What is that?" She pointed above their heads, at what appeared to be tubing wrapped in copper wire. The two ends of it hung down, shredded as if they had been cut with a sharp knife or a pair of pliers.

"Um. Lady?"

She turned. "Lizzie, if you must find the powder room, it will be in the crew's quarters. I do not have time to take you."

"It ent that, Lady. It's about that 'ose there."

"And that one." Maggie pointed to a similar hose that snaked along the ceiling, heading in the direction of the stern. "And that one across there, too."

All of them had been cut.

"Girls, what is it?" Had Alan and his friends sabotaged their own ship?

"I'm—I'm afraid we done it." Lizzie took Maggie's hand and they huddled close, as if they expected someone to toss them down the gangway and they were determined to go together.

"You did—what?" Andrew said, so shocked his voice had hardly any sound. "You cut the lines that carry the signals from this gondola to that of the engine?"

"We thought we was 'elpin'," Lizzie wailed, on the point of tears.

"We didn't know the Lady were planning to nick *this* ship," Maggie said, her voice thick with horror. "After we stashed them blokes, we came back 'ere and did a nip and tuck before we went and found Tigg."

"Didn't know what them cables were, only that it might slow 'em down should they try to chase us."

The count let out a cry of frustration and even Andrew clutched his head as if it were about to explode. The tears overflowed Lizzie's eyes and streaked her dirty face.

"We're awful sorry, Lady. We thought we was doin' right."

The count turned away with a string of Prussian epithets that had no business in the hearing of young ladies. "I shall have to return to my ship," he got out at last, in English. "Perhaps there is room for negotiation."

"Certainly—negotiations will net you the choice of a pistol, or a long fall from an airship in flight," Claire snapped. She pulled the twins into her arms, and Lizzie sobbed against her heart. "It is all right, darlings. So we cannot communicate from one end of the ship to the other. We shall simply have to come up with an alternative, even if it means using you two as messengers, as the count suggested."

"Impossible," Andrew said.

What business did he have making the girls feel worse than they already did? Claire lost her temper.

"I am aboard a disabled ship in the company of two of the finest engineers the world has ever seen," she said with barely concealed impatience. "Do not stand there telling me it is impossible. Do something!"

26

The men wasted a good two minutes running through alternative plans, one of which included smuggling members of the *Margrethe*'s crew out of that vessel to take over crewing the cargo ship. Another involved flying blind and hoping for the best—a plan that was shot down as quickly as they would have been had they tried it.

Finally they addressed themselves to the problem of recreating the mechanical system that transmitted orders from the bow to the stern. They found an extensive officers' toolbox where logic dictated it should be, and while they put their heads together to find a solution, Claire and the Mopsies stood at the window, anxiously keeping an eye on the progress of the search.

"Wot'll we do when they get to us, Lady?" Maggie asked, gripping the brass trim of the viewing glass with fingers whose knuckles had whitened.

"We must be gone by then. Look, two of the groups are returning to *Lady Lucy*, perhaps to receive new orders."

"They think that Astor cove's ship is safe?"

"They think both are under guard, and the darkness is concealing us," she replied. Half of her brain watched the search. The other half worried at the problem of the communication system. It was a simple one—various levers were employed to convey commands such as full steam and reverse, and direction: port, starboard, and all points of the compass in between. Wires conveyed pressure and produced a corresponding command in the engine gondola and in the tiny room on the uppermost deck where a crewman controlled the vanes.

They would have to go around it all somehow. But how?

The ship lay silent and unresponsive despite the frantic beating of her heart and the increasingly frustrated attempts of Andrew and the count to make repairs. As silent as the automatons standing in the loading area, waiting for a command to make them come alive.

A command.

A *spoken* command.

Claire's heart nearly stopped as her mind seized this thought and ran away with it. They had used the torso of the unfortunate Four to create an engine housing after the crash. Could they not do something similar now? She had three automatons here, all of whom were useless unless activated by spoken commands.

The principles of mechanics were the same whether one referred to automatons or transport. If one could command an automaton to activity inside a bronze casing, why could not one command it to activity if its casing were ... an airship?

She hardly dared to breathe as her mind expanded with the idea. She saw it all, the way she had seen the layout of the tunnels superimposed upon the land-scape—the way she saw the hands of cards in cowboy poker, laid out among the various players. A glowing network of wires and switches and possibility, rerouted and commanded to perform new tasks that they had not performed before.

Just because something had *never been* done did not mean that it *could not* be done.

"Maggie. Lizzie," she whispered. "Tell the automatons to come here. And then fetch three screwdrivers. We must take them apart immediately."

She had the automatons in pieces before Andrew and the count realized what had happened. "Claire, what on earth ...?" Andrew clearly believed her mind had given way under the strain of losing Tigg, and their impending capture.

Quickly, she explained, her words tumbling over one another in her haste to make them understand. Andrew's eyes widened, and the count gave an oath that made Maggie jump and fumble for Lizzie's hand. "By Jove, young lady, you are either quite mad or a marvel," he said.

"Well, she ent mad," Lizzie told him, being of a very literal turn of mind.

"Then she is a marvel," Andrew said softly.

The admiration in his eyes caused Claire's cheeks to burn. In a moment she would blotch, and that must not happen. They did not have time for missish behavior. "We must hurry," she said, rather breathlessly. "Meriwether-Astor's men will be upon us at any moment."

Working at top speed, the three of them removed the engines in the automatons' chests that controlled their response to command. Nine, being the most sophisticated, should be installed in the navigation gondola, Seven could control the vanes, and Eight was designated for the engine gondola. They no longer needed the cables controlling the levers, so they rerouted them into the ship's infrastructure, in effect turning the ship into an enormous, obedient mind with three nerve centers.

Claire put down the screwdriver and wiped her hands on her skirt. "Count, if you and Andrew would begin the ignition sequence, we will lift."

"Aren't you going to test it?" Andrew asked with a final turn of his wrench.

"How? We can ask Nine to move the rudder, but we cannot see a result until we have air flow with which to change direction."

"Claire, we can't just lift and hope to heaven that this works. We'll be shot out of the sky as soon as they see us hovering here like a big brown cloud."

"We have no choice. And we have only one chance," she told him tersely. "If we cannot trust our own abilities, then we deserve to be shot out of the sky."

"She is right," the count said. "Come, Mr. Malvern. Let us put some fire in the ship's belly and hope she listens."

"*She* is the cat's grandmother," Maggie said to no one in particular as the men ran down the coaxial catwalk to the stern. "Can't just call 'er 'cargo ship' all the time, poor old thing."

"An excellent point," Claire said. Across the airfield, a second contingent of men poured out of *Lady Lucy* and began to run, lamps bobbing, toward Meriwether-Astor's ship not thirty feet away. "Athena was the goddess of mathematics, and if it were not for adding together Seven, Eight, and Nine, we would not have our chance to escape."

She hoped desperately they *would* have a chance to escape.

"*Athena.*" Lizzie tried out the syllables on her tongue. "I like it. Could she fly?"

"Of course she could, silly," Maggie told her. "She were a goddess."

"Even the goddess whales could fly, if you remember the story Malina told you," Claire reminded them. "And so can we." She tilted her head as she felt the thrumming of the engine through the soles of her boots. "Seven, Eight, Nine, prepare for lift. Seven, vanes full vertical. Nine, stand by for course. Eight, engine full ahead."

But nothing happened.

Or rather, the stern rose obediently, pressing up against their feet and causing their knees to bend to compensate, but the bow remained stubbornly attached—

"Lady, the mooring mast!" Lizzie shouted. "We're still tied down!"

And now the teeming mass of men had seen the ship do its odd bobble in the air, and had swerved in their direction.

"Seven, lift!" Claire shouted, and plunged down the gangway.

She leaped for the ladder of the mooring mast, scrabbling up the rungs like a frantic spider. The seething crowd of men, angry at being denied their quarry, set up a roar as they caught sight of her. Her fingers had turned to rubber as she worked the knot. Finally she bit it with her teeth and gave a mighty pull, and the rope loosened. She felt the strain on her arms as the airship lifted ten feet off the ground.

I won't get aboard—they won't wait—the count must be saved—

The first of their pursuers leaped for the mooring mast and it shook with the fury of his ascent.

Not a prisoner! No, never again—

Claire flung herself off the mast, clinging like a monkey to the mooring rope, just as the man screamed in fury and lunged for her.

He grabbed, and caught only empty air as *Athena* fell straight up into the stars.

Cold.

The wind howled and snatched with icy fury, blowing her skirts up around her waist and her hair into her face, while freezing her hands to the rope. Claire had managed to twist a foot in it to give her arms a tiny bit of relief, but there was no way she would manage to hang on for more than a few minutes.

Had anyone seen her? Did Andrew and the girls even know she was out here, freezing to death and likely to plunge a thousand feet through the air at any moment?

A sound like the cry of a bird needled through the howl of the wind, and she managed to turn her head enough to see that she was nearly on a level with the navigation gondola, swinging like a pendulum about ten feet in front of it.

Three people crowded the gangway port. One of them—Andrew—held something long and gleaming.

"—end—rope!"

What?

"Claire, slide to the end of the rope!" the count's much louder voice boomed upon the wind.

Oh, no, she didn't dare do that. What if she slipped right off the end of it and fell to earth like Icarus, doomed to death because she chose to fly?

"Claire, you must give us some slack in the rope! Slide to the end!"

Something tugged at the holster on her back in which the lightning rifle was secured.

Suddenly terrified, Claire threw a glance over her shoulder. Her hands were freezing. Had some giant creature landed? She could not use her hands—

Tug. *Tug.*

The rifle. The rifle was being drawn backward, back toward the gondola, as if under a magnetic compulsion.

Something bronze flashed in the running lamps.

Nine's leg, with its magnetic foot.

With a gasp, Claire loosened her death grip on the rope by the smallest margin and clutched it between her legs, inching like a caterpillar toward the end. With every foot, the rifle on her back was drawn closer to the gondola by the power of Nine's feet, both of which were now being employed to bring her in.

Thank God she had not removed the rifle. Thank God she had not left the automatons behind.

Thank you, God, for watching over us. Oh, please, protect Tigg and Willie and Alice and all of us who love them—

"I've got you!" Andrew grabbed her, and while the count used Nine's legs to draw her further into the port, the Mopsies pulled on the tails of his dinner jacket to make sure he did not lose his footing.

Andrew rolled her into the loading area, Lizzie and Maggie sprang to close the port, and Claire curled herself into Andrew's warm, blessed arms and burst into tears.

27

Cargo ship she might be, but *Athena* was exceedingly well stocked with provisions as well as more munitions than any of them—with the possible exception of the count—had ever seen in one place. Much to Claire's surprise, the count informed them that he enjoyed turning his hand to cooking now and again, tied an apron about the remains of his evening clothes, and fell to work. As *Athena* flew steadily south, they decided against eating in the crew's quarters away at the stern, opting instead to clear the charts from the navigation table and remain where Nine could hear them.

"I'm very glad you ent dead again, Lady," Maggie observed, spooning stew into her mouth at a terrific rate. Both the girls had not left her side since her rescue, as if they feared the wind would blow her out of the gondola and they would not be able to fetch her back, with or without the assistance of Nine's magnetic feet.

"I am very glad I am not, as well. When do you suppose we shall land in Edmonton?"

"I do not think we should go to Edmonton." The count put down his spoon and indulged himself in a stiff tot of what appeared to be very fine brandy. He offered one to Andrew, who accepted with alacrity. "I suggest that we make straight for Charlottetown and inform the authorities in the new government at once."

"Charlottetown! But that is at the other end of the continent!" Claire objected.

Thousands of miles from Tigg, and Willie, and the Dunsmuirs, and everything she cared about on this side of the wide world.

"What do you suppose are the odds that a pigeon was launched long before we lifted?" the count asked. "Whether to report my death or the supposed perfidy of Frederick Chalmers, I think it very likely that any ship coming from points north that is not *Lady Lucy* or Meriwether-Astor's ship will be treated as suspect. The Canadas have only the very beginnings of a fleet of law enforcement, but from what I have seen of the Royal Canadian Airborne Police, they will not suffer us merely to take on fuel and be on our way."

"And it is not likely that a pigeon or a telegraph message will be heading for Charlottetown," Andrew added. "We are the only ones who can help the

Dunsmuirs now. The sooner orders come from the Viceroy to the Airborne Police, the better."

Their logic was sound, and in light of the greater good, Claire swallowed her distress at being separated by so many miles of land and air from the ones she loved.

By the third day in the air, they had not only covered a great many of those miles, but they had fine tuned the operation of what Maggie had taken to calling "our *Athena*'s brains." Claire had explained to her the properties of the engines that Alice had created— that they were capable of obedience only, not thought—but Maggie airily dismissed such details. Claire suspected that she regarded the airship as something of a pet, like a spaniel. She could only hope that the girls did not try to make poor *Athena* do tricks.

By the fourth day, they could see a wide blue vastness on the farthest curve of the horizon. Claire stood at the viewing window, Rosie the chicken in her arms, stroking the bird's feathers. Count von Zeppelin had never quite accustomed himself to Rosie's release from the hatbox, nor to her being a member of their company, and looked askance at her each time she shared a meal with them.

He joined Claire at the viewing window, slightly out of range of Rosie's beak. "The Atlantic," he said. "Our journey is nearly over."

"I confess I shall be glad to step on the ground again. Have you been to the new capital?"

"*Nein.* To be on the safe side, I have dispatched a pigeon to the Viceroy's house announcing our arrival and including my letters of passage from His Majesty the Kaiser of Prussia."

"Let us hope the Viceroy appreciates engineers as well as representatives of foreign governments."

The count smiled under his handlebar moustache, whose jaunty curl had now been restored. "I have heard a rumor that it is so. Lady Claire, may I ask you something?"

"Of course." She turned to him, curious.

"Please forgive me if I am too personal, but I was a soldier and am a man of blunt speech. What are your plans for the future?"

Rosie protested as the familiar arms about her feathery body tightened, and Claire forced herself to relax. "I am not certain. Return to London, I suppose, and take up my life where I left it."

"Which was what? Do you plan to marry young Malvern?"

Claire nearly dropped poor Rosie on the gondola's polished deck. "Gracious! No indeed. I mean ... that is to say ..." She controlled her babbling mouth with difficulty, settled Rosie once again, and wondered where Andrew was at this moment. She devoutly hoped he was nowhere within hearing. "I had planned to begin at the university in September, but I suppose that opportunity is now lost until next year. I—my plans are unsettled at the moment."

Going home seemed monumental enough that she could not see past it. And in some ways, she did not want to.

"I wonder ... Lady Claire, forgive me, but a mind such as yours comes along so rarely that I must speak. I admired you before, but only in a general sense. Now my admiration is tinged with ambition. For myself, and for the Zeppelin Airship Works."

Puzzled, she gazed at him. "Sir?"

"Would you consider attending the university in Munich, and upon your graduation, coming to work for me?"

This time she did drop poor Rosie. The bird landed on the deck in a flutter of wings and claws, and stalked off toward the dining salon, where the Mopsies could be counted upon to have a treat at hand and make a much more reliable cushion.

Claire, bereft of speech, could only stare open-mouthed at the count.

"I realize that this is wholly unexpected, and you must not give me an answer this moment. All I ask is that you consider it. The University of Bavaria, as you know, is second only to the University of Edinburgh for scientific achievement."

"I—yes, I did know," Claire managed.

She felt as if the floor had opened under her feet and left her suspended in air. Her stomach dipped and plunged while her mind flew ahead, across the Atlantic, to the little cottage by the river and the children who lived there.

"I have responsibilities—the children—"

"*Ja*, I realize this is so, and I admire you for considering their welfare before your own. I also admire these young ladies. Not every little girl in ruffled pantaloons can sabotage an airship quite so effectively."

With a trembling smile, Claire nodded in agreement. "They are my wards, count. I cannot leave them, even in the face of an offer as attractive as yours."

"And I should not expect you to. They ought to go to school as well. There are many fine *lycées* in Munich, some not a stone's throw from the gates of Schloss Schwanenburg."

"Is that an hotel?"

He laughed. "*Nein*, my dear young lady. The *schloss* is my family estate in Munich. You might call it a castle or a palace, but it has become much more than that. It is—permit me to say—the center of advanced thinking in Europe, much as the salons of London were a hundred years ago. You and the girls might live there as my guests, until your career is launched and you are able to provide a home for them on your own."

Again Claire lost her breath. "But, sir … How is it possible? What have I done to deserve such generosity at your hands?"

The count rocked back on his heels, his hands clasped behind his back, keeping a keen eye on the slowly approaching horizon. "It is not what you have done, though saving my life is a not inconsiderable part of it. It is what you are capable of doing, my dear. I have faith in you. Perhaps it is time for you to have faith in yourself."

"But—there are other children—at the cottage. In London. Not Munich."

"How are they being supported?"

"They earn their living gambling at the moment. And I have certain investments. The cottage is paid for, and Granny Protheroe sees to their immediate needs."

"Then you must certainly visit during holidays. It is not far, you know. A Zeppelin airship makes the journey from Munich to London in—"

"—three hours. Yes, I know. I should like to see a Meriwether-Astor ship attempt such a feat." She must deflect this conversation, even for a moment, to more prosaic subjects so that her staggering mind could recover.

"After our interview with the Viceroy, I very much doubt you will see a Meriwether-Astor ship at all in English skies. He will be marooned on his own continent and will have to content himself with ferrying groceries and livestock up and down the eastern seaboard." The count looked exceedingly pleased at this prospect.

Then he gave her a little bow.

"As I have said, I do not require an answer immediately. We have work to do first. But when you have consulted with your wards and with your friends, and you know your own mind, I hope you will inform me of it."

"I will, sir. And … thank you. You do not know what this means to me." Her voice trembled as she struggled with tears.

He smiled, his gaze fixed on the distant horizon as if it were the future. "You would be surprised."

And then he walked off in the direction of the galley, humming a jaunty tune that Claire recognized as one of the polkas the orchestra had played on the *Margrethe*.

She turned to the viewing window, hardly able to believe that the mighty Count von Zeppelin, one of the finest engineers of the modern age, considered her so valuable that he was willing to give her and the girls a home for the next four years, in hopes that Claire would add her mind to the storehouse of intellect his firm already possessed.

Ahead, the horizon widened, encompassing the vast oceans of water and air through which *Athena* steamed steadily, doing brilliantly what she had been designed to do.

It was an amazing offer—one prompted by affection as well as appreciation and faith.

Faith, the substance of things hoped for.

Claire could not remember anyone—save perhaps Polgarth the poultryman—ever having faith in her. And now look. She was rich in people who possessed it. The Mopsies. Andrew. The count. Alice. Perhaps even the Dunsmuirs, whom she hoped would regain their faith in her once the Meriwether-Astor affair was settled for good.

She had been through some perilous times, it was true. She had learned and grown and was no longer that shy, unsure, untried girl she had been when

Snouts had pulled her from her landau outside Aldgate station.

She was a woman now. A lady of resources, of intellect—and of faith in herself and the ones she loved.

Maggie and Lizzie crept into the navigation gondola and joined her at the window, passing their arms about her waist and snuggling against her, one on either side. Rosie perched on Maggie's other shoulder, settling there as comfortably as if she were in her own garden.

"All right, then, Lady?" Lizzie asked, peering ahead into the vast sky that enfolded them and beckoned, even as they sailed majestically on.

"Yes, Lizzie." She hugged them both close. "It's more than all right. In fact ... I think it's going to be wonderful."

Epilogue

Palace of the Viceroy
Charlottetown

My dear Claire,

I hope you will allow me to apologize for slipping this missive under your door in this clandestine fashion, but it seems to be my last resort. Amid the joy of Tigg's arrival with the Dunsmuirs here in Charlottetown and the latter's subsequent rapprochement with you, then the meeting with the Viceroy for your testimony in the case—to say nothing of the pigeon from Her Majesty herself!—it has been a mad several days in which I have found it utterly impossible to contrive a moment alone to speak. Hence, a letter.

I must confess that I share both your excitement and your apprehension over this new stage in your life. But I know also that you will manage famously, and so will the girls. Count von Zeppelin has offered you a marvelous opportunity and you must let nothing stand in the way of making it everything it can be. Have no fear as to the welfare of the children remaining in London. I shall visit often and make sure that they want for nothing.

When the time comes, I shall see you off at the airfield, waving farewell with a full heart. (Note: If you are going to keep Athena, Tigg suggests that we see about Snouts & co. building a mooring mast in the field next to the cottage.) Then I shall address myself to my long-neglected dissertation, rebuilding the Malvern-Terwilliger *Kinetick Carbonator and filing all the patents appertaining thereto, including yours. Four years will pass quickly—four years in which we will both achieve a measure of our dreams, and prepare ourselves for what may come after.*

Claire, I shall say only a word of my feelings here. I do not hesitate to be honest, for you deserve nothing less, but neither do I wish to burden you at the moment you have the chance to fly. You are a special woman with special gifts, and I do not mean to stand in your way. So I shall say only this:

When you return to England in triumph, your diploma in hand, for your last summer in London before beginning your career, you will find me waiting, my heart as true as my intentions are honorable. I cherish the hope that some day, you will accept them both.

I remain yours always,
Andrew

THE END

A NOTE FROM SHELLEY

Dear reader,

I hope you enjoy reading the adventures of Lady Claire and the gang in the Magnificent Devices world as much as I enjoy writing them. It is your support and enthusiasm that is like the steam in an airship's boiler, keeping the entire enterprise afloat and ready for the next adventure.

You might leave a review on your favorite retailer's site to tell others about the books. And you can find the print editions of the entire series online.

Do visit me on my website at www.shelleyadina.com, which includes Claire's personal correspondence in the "Letters from the Lady" series on my blog. I invite you to sign up for my newsletter there, too.

And now, for an excerpt from the next book in the series, I invite you to turn the page …

Excerpt

A Lady of Resources
By Shelley Adina
© 2013

A LADY OF RESOURCES

1

Munich, the Prussian Empire
June 1894

"Of all the infernal instruments man ever made, the corset is the worst." Lizzie de Maupassant struggled with the hooks on the front of the glossy brocade undergarment, which one had to wear in order to make everything that went on top of it hang properly. "Look at this, Maggie. It bends where it oughtn't and pokes everywhere else." She smashed the placket together, which only made the hooks she'd managed already pop apart. "Argh!"

Lizzie flung the wretched thing across the Lady's room, where it landed on the windowsill like an exhausted accordion.

"Fits of temper won't solve anything." Her twin's tone held no criticism, only reason. "Come on. Let me have a go."

Maggie rescued the poor corset, bought new for the grand occasion of the graduation of Lady Claire Trevelyan, the girls' guardian, from the University of Bavaria, and passed it about Lizzie's chemise- and petticoat-clad form.

"I don't miss the old lace-ups," Lizzie said, feeling calmer as Maggie's clever fingers made short work of the row of hooks, "but I'll say this for them—they were more forgiving of a mort's curves than these new ones. Even if it were made specially for me."

"Don't say *mort*."

"Ent nobody here but us. We don't have to be so careful about our *diction and deportment*—" She mimicked the squeaky tones of Mademoiselle Dupree, the mistress of their class by that name. "—when we're on our own."

"The Lady says that's the test of a true lady—that she does the right thing even when nobody's looking."

"Aye, more's the pity," Lizzie sighed. "We might pass our exams, but we'll never remember everything she probably knew by the time she was ten."

The door opened and the Lady herself breezed in. "All who knew? Goodness, Lizzie, we're to be in the ballroom in two hours and you're not even dressed, to say nothing of your hair."

A LADY OF RESOURCES

Maggie patted the corset and released her. "Won't be a tick, Lady." The corset now lay obediently where it ought, hugging Lizzie's waist into a satisfyingly narrow width, and flaring out over hips and bust, which possessed dimensions not quite so satisfying. The Lady said to give it time, that she herself had been eighteen before resigning herself to a sylph-like silhouette rather than the majestic curves fashion now favored. But if one didn't have an idea of one's silhouette by now, then the odds weren't very good, were they?

"Darlings, now that you're sixteen, you really must call me by my given name."

The twins, having only the vaguest idea of their birth date, had chosen the first day of spring when they had to make it official, such details being necessary when they had arrived in Munich and begun their formal educations at the Lycee des Jeunes Filles. By this reckoning, they had turned sixteen three months ago, and upon their own graduation from the fifth form at the end of June, would be considered young ladies, permitted to call an unmarried woman by her first name.

Young ladies now ... out in society two years from now. A whole other problem. Lizzie shoved it from her mind and gave the Lady a hug, marveling once again that she was nearly as tall as the young woman to whom she and Maggie owed their very lives.

"But you know why we call you that in private," she said. "And it's got nothing to do with age, innit?"

The Lady hugged her back. "Not one bit. I suppose that if you were to stop altogether, I'd quite go to pieces and fear you didn't love me anymore."

Maggie laughed at this impossibility. "If it hadn't been for you, we wouldn't be here. Wouldn't have lived in the cottage and learned our letters and numbers."

"Wouldn't have gone to the Texican Territories or the Canadas," Lizzie added. "Or come here."

"Or been shot at, blown up, or starved nearly to death," the Lady said ruefully. "I'm afraid my skills as a guardian have been tested rather sorely."

"Nothing wrong with guarding our own selves," Lizzie said stoutly. "And you, even, sometimes."

Claire laughed at the reminder. "Too true. There has been many a time when I've been thankful we were all fighting on the same side. The affair of the Kaiser's nephew, for instance."

Maggie crinkled up her nose. "Frog-face, you mean."

"Precisely. I don't think his dignity has recovered from that fish-pond yet."

"If he wouldn't propose to ladies who can't stand him, such things wouldn't happen," Lizzie said.

"Ever my practical girl." Warm fingers touched her cheek, and Lizzie felt a surge of love mixed with exasperation—a familiar feeling, and one she had struggled with since the very inauspicious moment of their first meeting.

She adored the Lady, and had for most of the six years they had known each other, but tangled in with the love was the uncomfortable knowledge that she could never be like her guardian—so calm, so competent, so sure of what to say and do in any circumstance, from breaking a mad scientist out of Bedlam to curtseying to the Empress.

Oh, dear. The wretched bloody curtsey.

"Lady, do I really have to go?" came out of her mouth before she could stop it—something that seemed to happen with distressing regularity these days.

But instead of a crisp "Of course," which was all such a babyish whinge deserved, the Lady took Lizzie's gown from the wardrobe. It was her first real, grownup gown, the palest shade of moss-green silk, with glorious puffed sleeves and a neckline trimmed with lace as fine as a spider web that dipped just low enough to show her collarbones and no lower. Considering there wasn't much below that to show off, it was just as well.

The cool silk slid over her head, and when she emerged and the Lady began to fasten the hooks behind, Lizzie thought perhaps she had decided not to dignify her whining with a reply.

But no. "Of course you do not need to go, if you don't wish it," Claire said quietly. "You are sixteen, and able to make up your own mind about such things. But I should like you and Maggie to be there. I should like to know that you are proud of me, and that when you write to Tigg and Jake and Willie, you will be able to give a good account."

What a selfish wretch she was! Lizzie turned into the Lady's arms as her cheeks heated with shame. "Of course I'll come, Lady," she said into her neck. "I wouldn't miss it for anything. I'm just afraid I'll do something stupid, is all, and embarrass you."

"Nothing you could do is any worse than I could do—or have done—myself," Claire said on a sigh. "Just ask Julia Wellesley—I beg her pardon, Lady Mount-Batting. Come. Let's practice the curtsey one more time so it's fresh in your mind, and then Lady Dunsmuir has lent us her maid to do our hair. We must give her time to produce perfection."

Lord and Lady Dunsmuir had arrived the night before and were the honored guests of the Landgraf von Zeppelin, as the engineer of the Zeppelin airship and the director of the worldwide "empire of the air" was known throughout the Kingdom of Prussia. But to Maggie and Lizzie, he had become Uncle Ferdinand, the man who smelled of pipe tobacco and bay rum, who kept peppermints in the pockets of even his business suits, and who had changed all of their lives so astonishingly five years before.

MacMillan came in as quickly as if she'd been listening at the door, and proceeded to brush, braid, coil, and generally subdue Lizzie's dark-honey mane so thoroughly that she hardly recognized herself in the cheval glass afterward. The French braid in a coronet about her head was awfully pretty, though. And beneath her wispy fringe, her green eyes sparkled with nerves and anticipation.

"The same for you, miss?" MacMillan asked Maggie.

A LADY OF RESOURCES

They'd never dressed or done their hair alike—because before they'd met the Lady, they'd never had anything better than what they could filch from the ragpicker's pile, where finding a matched set of anything was impossible. But MacMillan's fingers were skilled, and Maggie's gaze so admiring, that Lizzie said, "Do, Mags. You'll look lovely, to be sure. We shall be as pretty as the princesses themselves."

And she was. When MacMillan was done, Maggie turned back and forth before the glass, her nut-brown hair far more used to order than Lizzie's was, her hazel eyes set off by the pale amber—"the color of a fine muscatel," Uncle Ferdinand had said—of her gown. It was fortunate that the Prussians didn't believe that young girls should wear white until they were engaged, like they did in England. Lizzie appreciated a bit of color, and while the Lady tended to go about in navy skirts and blouses with sleeves she could roll up, her eye for color and what lines suited a figure best was keen.

"And for you, milady?" MacMillan asked as Claire took her place at the dressing-table. "I've seen a new look many of the ladies are wearing since that Fragonard gentleman had his exhibition."

"Oh?" Claire's eyebrow rose. "Have you seen the exhibition yourself?"

"I have, milady. That one called *Anticipation* caused quite a stir, with that young lady lazing about with hardly a silk curtain to cover herself."

Claire smothered a smile. "But her hair, MacMillan. I thought it particularly striking at the time, and wondered if you had seen it."

"Seen it and marked it for her ladyship. But I wouldn't mind trying it out on you, if you don't mind."

"Have at it," Claire said, settling back in the chair. "I just hope it doesn't fall down when I curtsey to the Empress. If she finds time to attend."

"No coiffure of mine will fall down under any circumstances, milady, empress or no." MacMillan took down Claire's simple chignon and brushed out her thick auburn waves. "It will look as though you had tossed it up and wrapped it about with a bandeau, but under it will be as much engineering as young Miss Elizabeth's corset."

"MacMillan, you are a treasure."

"Thank you, milady. Her ladyship thinks so."

Motionless under MacMillan's authority, Claire caught Lizzie's eye in the glass. "Does it feel strange to think that our time here is coming to an end? It does to me."

"But it isn't at an end for you, Lady," Maggie put in. It was clear she was trying not to move very much, for fear of mussing herself up. Lizzie was tempted to reach over and give her braid a tug, but discarded that idea almost immediately. The wrath of MacMillan over her damaged handiwork was not worth the risk. Maggie went on, "You're to join Uncle Ferdinand's firm. Or have you changed your mind again?"

Claire rolled her eyes at herself. "I change my mind as often as my shoes—and with less success. But we were not talking about me. You girls have some decisions to make once the term ends in two weeks."

"It's not fair that you graduate so soon and we have all our exams yet to go," Lizzie moaned. "It should all be the same."

"You may certainly take it up with the Regents on the State education board."

Lizzie felt rather proud that her five years in the *lycée* had enabled her to control the urge to stick out her tongue at the Lady. But she came close, all the same.

"How are we supposed to decide something as serious as this?" Maggie asked from the upholstered chair, where she had gingerly seated herself, back straight, feet flat on the floor, hands folded in her lap.

"Too many choices," Lizzie agreed. Heedless of wrinkles, she folded herself onto the end of the bed and leaned on one of the turned posts with the pineapple on top. She ticked them off on her fingers. "Finishing school in Geneva ... two more years of sixth form here ... or sign the exit papers, graduate, and go back to London."

"We're going back to London for the summer, anyway, same as always," Maggie pointed out.

"Well, yes, but in September? What happens then?"

"I should think it would be quite straightforward, miss," MacMillan said. "What do you want to make of yourself?"

"That is the question," Lizzie sighed. "I suppose I want to be a fine lady, but that doesn't mean I'll get to be."

Claire straightened, then winced as MacMillan inadvertently ran a hairpin into her scalp. "I do beg your pardon, milady."

"It's quite all right, MacMillan. I should not have moved so suddenly. Lizzie, what do you mean? Why should you not be a lady and move in the finest Wit circles in any country, as you do here?"

How could she explain this without either offending everyone in the room or sounding like a fool? "Lady, you know as well as I do that it's different here. Here, everyone's accepted, as long as you've got a brain. I suppose that's why you've decided to stay, innit?"

Claire's expression softened. "I must admit it's rather refreshing, considering the way I grew up."

"But that's just it. You grew up a lady, with a posh family, no matter what you chose later." Lizzie swung her legs over the foot of the bed and wrapped an arm around the post, as if anchoring herself in a stormy sea. "Can you really believe that a mort who started out an alley mouse—who still is, never mind all the elocution lessons and walking about wi' books on me 'ead—" She let her accent deteriorate on purpose. "—is going to be accepted in the drawing rooms of London?"

"Every drawing room that accepts me will accept you, Lizzie."

And that was the part that she found so hard to believe. The part that was so frustrating. "Lady, I think you'll find that isn't as true as you think it is."

Now it was MacMillan's turn to catch her eye in the mirror while she carefully threaded a pearl-studded bandeau through the coils and waves of the Lady's hair. "I think you'll find that with Lady Dunsmuir as your sponsor for your come-out, there will be no trouble with any drawing room in Mayfair, should you want to set foot in them."

"What?" Claire straightened again and twisted around to look at MacMillan directly. "What did you say?"

"Milady, you must sit still while I secure this comb. You don't want to come unraveled in front of the nobility."

"I rather feel I have come unraveled now. What did you mean, MacMillan?"

Ooh, look at the Lady's face. Lizzie couldn't tell if she was astonished or angry. But she couldn't be angry. Not at this. Lady Dunsmuir was forever springing surprises of a most delightful nature on them, but they usually came in the mail or in an unexpected visit, not by way of her lady's maid.

"I'll say no more now, but you'll want to know that her ladyship is going to find a way to speak to you about it. At least this way you'll be able to give it some thought."

"Sponsoring a come-out." Claire wilted back into the chair, right way round again. "This *will* require some thought—especially since it never entered my head."

Lizzie thought back to the time the Lady had explained what *coming out* was. She'd been educated on the subject quite a lot since then, but her original ideas had not been so far off the mark. "She really does intend to put us in a window with fancy paper round our feet?"

Claire smiled. "At least you will have the correct posture, and your feet will be together in a ladylike manner. Lizzie, I do not know how you manage to slouch like that when I saw Maggie hook your corset myself."

"It's a gift."

"I don't know if I want a come-out," Maggie said, her voice quiet in that way it had when she needed to speak but didn't want to give offense. "It doesn't seem real for the likes of me and Liz."

"You and Liz are as worthy of society's attention as any girls in London or Europe," the Lady informed her crisply. It was not the first time she had said so, and not the first time Lizzie had not believed her. "In any case, it is still two years off. The more pressing decision is what you will choose to do with yourselves in the interval."

This was why the Lady was so good in the laboratory. She refused to be distracted by nonessentials.

"What about finishing school?" Lizzie surprised even herself at the words that came out of her mouth. The Lady and Maggie looked dumbfounded as they both spoke at once.

"In Switzerland?"

"Aren't you coming back to London with me?"

"Of course I am." How could she make Maggie understand what she could hardly put in words herself? "For the summer, to see Lewis and everyone at Carrick House, and to go up to Scotland with the Dunsmuirs for shooting season. But in September ... Mags, if her ladyship is to see us presented, oughtn't we to do what we can to—to give her a good bargain? With finishing school, we'd be a little closer to being ladies, at least."

"But—but I thought we'd go home," Maggie said, her eyes huge, her voice a disconsolate whisper. "Or at the very least, stay here and do the sixth-form classes so we can stay with the Lady. You can't go to finishing school, Liz. Why, we were laughing at the idea only the other night."

So they had been. Claire seemed to be having difficulty marshaling her words together, so Lizzie took advantage of it. "But that was before we knew what Lady Dunsmuir was up to. This changes everything, Mags."

"It does not." The Lady had finally gotten her tongue under control. It was a lucky thing MacMillan had finished her work, because Claire leaped to her feet. "Lizzie, I am utterly astonished at you. Finishing school? You?"

She wasn't slouching now. "What's wrong with me going to finishing school? See, Lady, this is exactly what I mean. You don't think I'm good enough to be finished, never mind presented, do you? *Do you?*"

Two spots of color appeared in the Lady's cheeks, and too late, Lizzie wondered if perhaps she ought to have kept her real opinion to herself.

"I cannot believe you just said those words to me, Elizabeth," the Lady whispered. "Not to *me*." Her cheeks blotched even more, and to Lizzie's horror, tears welled in her eyes and fell, dripping past her chin and into the lace that edged her *décolletage*.

"I—I—" She looked to Maggie for help, and found none. She had hurt the Lady horribly—the one person in the world to whom she owed everything, the one person who had never shown her anything but respect and consideration and love.

Oh, drat her uncontrollable mouth, that let words fly like birds out of a cage so that she could never call them back!

"Lady, I didn't mean it," she mumbled miserably, unable to look into those gray eyes any more. Outside the window, a pair of swans beat the air, on their way to the lake that was the main feature of the enormous park in front of the Landgraf's palace.

Lizzie heard the door close quietly, and when she dragged her damp gaze back into the room, the Lady was gone.

ABOUT THE AUTHOR

The official version

RITA Award® winning author and Christy finalist Shelley Adina wrote her first novel when she was 13. It was rejected by the literary publisher to whom she sent it, but he did say she knew how to tell a story. That was enough to keep her going through the rest of her adolescence, a career, a move to another country, a B.A. in Literature, an M.F.A. in Writing Popular Fiction, and countless manuscript pages.

Shelley is a world traveler who loves to imagine what might have been. Between books, she loves playing the piano and Celtic harp, making period costumes, and spoiling her flock of rescued chickens.

The unofficial version

I like Edwardian cutwork blouses and velvet and old quilts. I like bustle drapery and waltzes and new sheet music and the OED. I like steam billowing out from the wheels of a locomotive and autumn colors and chickens. I like flower crowns and little beaded purses and jeweled hatpins. Small birds delight me and Roman ruins awe me. I like old books and comic books and new technology ... and new books and shelves and old technology. I'm feminine and literary and practical, but if there's a beach, I'm going to comb it. I listen to shells and talk to hens and ignore the phone. I believe in thank-you notes and kindness, in commas and friendship, and in dreaming big dreams. You write your own life. Go on. Pick up a pen.

AVAILABLE NOW

The Magnificent Devices series:
Lady of Devices
Her Own Devices
Magnificent Devices
Brilliant Devices
A Lady of Resources

Caught You Looking (contemporary romance, Moon-shell Bay #1)
Immortal Faith (paranormal YA)
Peep, the Hundred-Decibel Hummer (early reader)
The All About Us series of six books
(contemporary YA, 2008–2010)

To learn about my Amish women's fiction written as
Adina Senft, visit www.adinasenft.com.
The Wounded Heart
The Hidden Life
The Tempted Soul
And in 2014, the Healing Grace series beginning with
Herb of Grace

Coming soon

A Lady of Spirit, Magnificent Devices #6
A Lady of Integrity, Magnificent Devices #7
A Gentleman of Means, Magnificent Devices #8
Emily, the Easter Chick (early reader)
Caught You Listening, Moonshell Bay #2
Caught You Hiding, Moonshell Bay #3

Made in the USA
San Bernardino, CA
28 October 2013